M
IN
MIAMI
HOTELS

Also by Charlie Smith

MEN IN MIAMI HOTELS

A NOVEL

CHARLIE SMITH

HARPER ● PERENNIAL

NEW YORK ● LONDON ● TORONTO ● SYDNEY ● NEW DELHI ● AUCKLAND

HARPER ● PERENNIAL

MEN IN MIAMI HOTELS. Copyright © 2013 by Charlie Smith. All rights reserved. Printed in the United States of America. No part of this book may be used or reproduced in any manner whatsoever without written permission except in the case of brief quotations embodied in critical articles and reviews. For information address HarperCollins Publishers, 10 East 53rd Street, New York, NY 10022.

HarperCollins books may be purchased for educational, business, or sales promotional use. For information please e-mail the Special Markets Department at SPsales@harpercollins.com.

FIRST EDITION

Designed by William Ruoto

Library of Congress Cataloging-in-Publication Data is available upon request.

ISBN 978-0-06-224727-8

13 14 15 16 17 OV/RRD 10 9 8 7 6 5 4 3 2 1

"But keep watch
that you may hear
your brothers beyond the border . . ."

Johannes Bobrowski

"Jakub Bart in Ralbitz"

Translated by Ruth and Matthew Mead

MEN
IN
MIAMI
HOTELS

Prologue

The years in Cuba are behind me now.
Little spotted dogs, like tiny archangels
followed me around. I smelled of salt
and palm oil. Given the nature

of belief, the effectiveness of the divine will,
unforgettable and strictly
for the birds, I could be said
to be out of touch. I read Aeschylus—

the diaries—Othello on the Beach,
and Peter Gunn. I gave my change
to private charities, something personal
I devised. Her lipstick

smelled like a clown's face. We practiced
tricks the Ringling brothers taught her.
I supported small retainers,
converts and muralists struggling with

the dialect. We waked,
often at dawn, and lay
in the sheets cursing quietly. I will
particularize and dissuade, *she said,*

but it made no difference. I wore hats
of coconut frond and drove a Russian car.
My retreat from life
fit like a glove. Some nights

strange memories, passing for dreams,
of mud-caked shoes, cats
on the table eating scraps, and young men
caressing the faces of their superannuated lovers.

I shivered sometimes. I was on a long run
of quirky asides. Take the monkey, *she said,* and go.

1

Cot Sims got off the early morning bus in the Key West airport parking lot and took a cab over to his mother's place. The morning was coming up fair and blue. The winter down here had been the coldest on record. Up and down the Keys fish washed up dead in the mangroves and onto the beaches. Big trees keeled over and yellowed palm fronds rattled like skeletons dancing on the roof. Salt spray dried white as snow on the sea grapes out at the beach. And upstream, up-ocean in mainland river mouths manatees floated like bloated fat men, belly up. But this day was sweet, rampant, and cordial, soft around the edges. His mother lived on Regent Street in the house Cot was raised in. Marcella's secretary had called to say his mother had taken up residence under her own house. Something about hurricane damage; the house had shifted on its pilings and the town had declared it unsafe for habitation. It didn't surprise Cot that his mother would be living under the house, but he decided he ought to go down anyway and see what he could do. It would give him a chance to go by Marcella's and check if she was still not talking to him. Give him a chance on other things too, get the sense of decay out of his soul—*soul*, that was the way he put it to Sonny Goldberg, his old partner, the two of them at Snooky's sitting with their feet propped on the porch rail out back. *Decay*—he put it that way too. "I don't know what the hell you're talking about," Sonny said.

His mother's not home. But Jackie Bivins, a local itinerant who's sitting on the front steps and says he's guarding her stuff, tells him she'll probably be back in an hour.

"She took a cab over to the clinic."

"What for?"

"Said she wanted some pills for her arthritis."

Jackie's a big wall-eyed man with an unsettling look on his face but no harm in him. He sails around the neighborhood doing odd jobs and arguing with the Bangladeshi clerks over at the Blue Sun market. He's somebody else Cot has known all his life. "I ain't seen Marcella," Jackie offers.

"She's not on the island?"

"I didn't say that."

The house, a solid-looking structure with a wide front porch and a squashed second story peeping out of little square dormers, seems as solid as ever, but when you look close you can see it's slightly askew on its cypress-wood pilings. The house itself is cypress-wood too, unpainted because there's no need (cypress won't rot). It looks habitable enough to Cot. He takes another cab over to the

Authority and asks what the problem is and they tell him it's the law that houses knocked off their pins can't be lived in until they are set back straight and inspected.

"Who was the one inspected it in the first place?" says Cot.

"That was Pollack."

"Wilkins Pollack?"

"He spent half a day over there arguing with your mother."

"And then he put her out on the street."

"Yeah. That's too bad."

Cot goes around to see Pollack, but he's out in the backcountry fishing. Pollack likes to motor out to the remains of the old Hemingway fishing hut, way out in the sparkling wilderness of the flats, and fish there among the leftover pilings. He likes to imagine himself a famous man like Hemingway and a great fisherman. Cot goes around to see Marcella in her law office, but her secretary says she's in court so he goes back looking for her at the courthouse. In the hall he sees people he knows, it's like old times come alive. They nod, some stop to talk, everybody has something to recollect. The place smells boiled and suntanny. Mrs. Coldwell invites him over for a slice of her butterfly cake and he thanks her but says he won't be in town long. It's what he always says. Time passes, and he's still standing in the hall when Marcella comes out. She's talking to Ordell Bakewell, her husband—the county prosecutor—and when she sees Cot she breaks off from him like he was a squashed sandwich and comes right up to Cot. This pleases Cot immensely but the look on her face wipes that away.

"What are you doing here?" she says, pushing her thick black hair up off her forehead, just that little gesture making her look like she's ready for a fight.

"Looking for you."

"Here I am. Just back in town." ·

From where? he wonders, but he says, "D'jou hear about Mama?"

"You know I did. These fools down here."

"I was speculating."

"I'm already working on it."

"You mean you're sweet-talking Ordell."

"Something like that—among other things."

She smiles at him, a smile that throws windows open on sunlight.

"D'you know where she is?"

"Over at the garden I expect."

"I should have thought of that."

"How's the gangster business?"

She always asks this, as if they haven't spoken in years.

"I get more surly every day."

"I'll bet."

The mayor, a short, fleshy-faced man, trots up and after a perfunctory hello to Cot begins to talk to her about the new waterfront. The city these days is always coming up with new ideas about how to squeeze more money out of its properties. "Don't think that'll work, Smushy," Marcella says. She has a risive look in her eye. The mayor looks disappointed. He's wearing a blue safari jacket and Mexican sandals. Just then a man Cot doesn't know runs up and before Cot can stop him he swings at Marcella. His blow is loose and sweeping, fat arm fully extended, and it catches her along the side of the head. She staggers, makes a tight little circle and drops to her knees. The man comes up on her and raises his fist again but before he can hit her Cot steps around the side and catches him under the chin with a quick short uppercut. *Missed again*, he thinks as he swings, thinking of himself—*missed the moment*. It's funny. The man goes down to his knees and Cot kicks him in the ribs, sending him sprawling on the star-speckled, sand-colored marble floor. "Jesus Christ," Cot says. All this in barely three seconds. Time enough for the mayor to've skipped out of range.

"Who the hell is that?" Cot says.

"That's Jimmy Perkins," somebody says. A lobster poacher from Big Pine.

A small fleet of cops rushes out of some hidy-hole, scoops the man up, and begins to drag him away. A couple of the cops have their pistols in their hands. A detective, Arthur Smalls, comes over to Cot. "You'd better come with us, Cot," he says.

Cot is leaning over Marcella who's had the sense knocked out of her. "In a minute, Art. Just breathe slowly, honey," he says.

The look on her face is priceless, the look of a child surprised by some trick she's unable to understand. He loves to see her when she's out of her depth, knows she loves the same for him. He wants to take her home and coddle her, panic her with kindness. Her husband's yelling at somebody, as usual rummaging for links in a chain of circumstance.

"When he was little he used to call it his little monkey," his mother was saying an hour later to some passing stranger as Cot settled into a seat in one of the blue banquettes at the Torella Lodge Restaurant over near Dog Beach, "I used to say stop playing with your little monkey, but he'd go right on—oh, hi, dear."

"Spreading my secrets out to dry, Mama?" Cot said trying not to grimace but failing. She was cutting up celery stalks as she spoke, something she was liable to do— cut things up—when she was piqued, a giveaway, one of many. If he had time and the inclination he could make a catalog, an encyclopedia.

His mother looked pseudofondly at him. The look— given her present situation—made him squirm, the falseness, the displacement, the smile like a line of seaweed left at low tide. It was low tide, he expected, for all of them assembled. Marcella tapped nimbly into her phone. Her husband, pressed into a corner of the booth, talked rapidly and steadily into his device, whisper-shouting into it in his eviscerated and barely audible way, his voice grainy and carrying an accent he never used in everyday life. Our bodies are always a size too small for what's going on inside, somebody had said once. At *least*, he'd thrown in.

"This ought to be a simple matter," he said.

"Things are never simple," Ordell, who had been listening despite his continuous verbiage, put in and dived back into his phone.

"Of course they are," Cot's mother, Ella her name was, said. "We just get uneasy with how simple they really are. Religion and the government have done that to us," she said and went on jabbering, converting mind to roughage. It was like listening to an elephant describe squatting. Why'd I come here? Cot thought. He never could stand it. "What about the birds, Mama?" he said just to throw a plank into the whirling paddles of her mind.

"What's that? Birds? Yesterday I saw a Cuban warbler pecking at a Milky Way wrapper—come all this way to do it—and a kingbird, lounging, I think. And Jackie says he saw a black-whiskered vireo, courting his sweetie in a guava tree."

He turned back to Marcella as if his mother hadn't spoken.

"It wasn't my fault," Marcella was saying into her phone—"oh, wait. You've made me—oh." There was a thin streak of yellow and purple bruise along her cheekbone like a child's war paint, but she was smiling. "How you doing?" Cot said.

"Like you I was born for life," she said.

She looked out the front window at Dover Sole who was kicking a large Harley-Davidson motorcycle. The bike began to fall, and Dover tried to right it but couldn't. They all paused to watch the machine, size of a buffalo, topple slowly onto its side. "I guess it's lucky he doesn't have a car." This last from Connie Jackson, Cot's oldest friend, called CJ, a cross-dressing singer/dancer who was still wearing the costume he worked in nights over at the Velvet Pussycat. His wig, like an orange egret nest, sat puffed and glistening on the table beside his plate. "I'm going out of my mind," he said. CJ and Dover had been keeping company for years but, so Marcella told Cot, had recently fallen out. "I didn't see much of a domestic arrangement there under the house," Cot said.

His mother smiled at him, antically, mockingly, in the sideways way she had. Behind the antic he caught a smidge, or no, the faint hyperkeratosis, of desperation. But he always caught that these days. Everybody was slipping, the masks were, revealing sores and blemishes of dread. People drifted by the table, locals in ordinary clothing, students from his mother's teaching days at the college, lifelong friends, enemies on recon pretending to be friends, stooges, penitents, the raddled and uncomfortable, the shame-faced—a few who wanted mostly to bask in the glow of her latest trouble—nomads, the congenitally misguided, old men with enlarged hernias, ladies in clothes that'd gone out of style before the last war, stragglers, and those who rode tiny bicycles, others carrying their humiliation before them like a scrofula. *How come you got into this?* somebody was always asking him—meaning this outlaw business—and Cot said, *I never wanted to be the one laying down the law*, but this was just what he couldn't stop doing. That was clear to him.

"I still have to talk to somebody directly about this living arrangement," Cot said.

His phone buzzed. It was Spane checking on him. "Comp wants you to drop by to take a look at those beach properties," Spane said.

"I'll have to rent a truck."

"Maybe you can get Eustace to carry you. Tell him to put it on the tab."

"Comp's got a tab with Eustace?"

"Come on, B-boy."

You couldn't tell but they were dead in earnest, playful maybe but also hard and careful, all the names changed and everything in code even though they were talking on unregistered phones. Most names.

Spane always choked up on everything so he could get a better grip, swing faster. His voice like something with most of the juice squeezed out of it. Albertson's second, he was the one went around checking to make sure instructions were carried out, went around figuring as he moved, catching the details on the fly. He had flat hairy wrists and wore a mustache that he regularly shaved off. The first day without the stache his creased face looked an extra size larger, not a reassuring thing.

"I got you," he said, and Cot wondered what he meant but didn't say anything. "You there?" Spane said.

"Sure."

Spane was sorry for Cot, but he didn't say this. There were developments Cot hadn't foreseen—Spane hadn't foreseen some of the developments himself, but most of those were in another area—catches and loopholes and asides and unduplicable scenarios that would bust him up if he knew, but he didn't know. But Spane was aware, as Cot was, that no info was safe from detection. This knowledge made his voice come through a little rougher than necessary. "You got it? he said.

"I do."

"How's your mother?"

"Miz Ella? Bewildered but doesn't know it—or won't admit it."

"Like you and me."

"Don't talk about me as if I wasn't there—here," his mother said looking up from her mango snapper ceviche. This embarrassed Cot, and he said so. Said after hanging up the phone. Spane had told him to go ahead to the island tomorrow. He wanted him to do a count, some idea of Albertson's. Cot didn't know if he would go or not—or no, he knew, he was going; the impulse had clicked over into a plan on the way down. But he had never liked being out on the water, or above it. Odd for a man born and raised on a two-by-four gob of limestone in the middle of the sea. The grit in Spane's voice disturbed him, and he wondered if Spane knew, and if he did, what it was he knew. Across the table Marcella smiled at him. There was a drag in her smile, just a tiny bit left out or trying to break through, and he wondered what it was.

They drove by to look at the house. Ordell carried them in his Range Rover. A high black vehicle square like an old fashioned hearse. "It's not a hearse," Ordell said when Cot pointed this out to him. The coconut palms were still yellowed from the winter's cold. Hung on a board fence outside Connally's Rest House: old wet suits and a towel with a picture of the President stamped on it, among other cracked and dried pieces of paraphernalia. Jell Miller's blind tomcat stared from his front porch into the blank world: *What happened?* his expression said. Mrs. Jamison, an old lady who lived in a house shaped like a fort, raised a gold-painted albatross feather fan as they passed. "She was doing that when I was a boy," Cot said. He was happy to be home, in an offhand, jumpy way.

Jackie was tidying up under the house. The floor was raised four feet off the patinaed white coral ground. An area under the front porch was set up like a small living room, complete with sawed-off table, two cretonne armchairs, a couple of stick lamps, a chest of drawers, a mirror propped against a kitchen chair, and a large rag rug Jackie had laid directly on the coral. There was also a small television and a radio on the table and a hot plate on a separate bench nearby. A small devotion idol squatted next to the hot plate. Cot couldn't believe he hadn't noticed all the gear under there. I must be losing my mind, he thought.

It was a hot day, but a breeze, shifty and cordial-like, blew a coolness over them. "That certainly was a smooth ride, Ordell," his mother said and kissed the prosecutor on the cheek, which was something she only did to those she pitied, which Ordell, grimacing, clearly knew. Quick to move, she was already out of the car and, with Jackie, manhandling her tricycle out of the back.

"I don't think you should be staying here," Cot said.

"I have to show I am maintaining ownership," his mother said.

"I think I can take care of that," Ordell threw in.

"You cannot," Marcella said. She sat in the front seat beside Ordell holding jasmine flowers in a paper cup in her lap.

"I'll talk to Prince Johnson."

"I don't believe that'll do any good," Marcella said. She fingered back her hair that had blown around her face during the trip. Even with air-conditioning she liked to ride with the windows open. Her eyes were as blue as the sky, slightly singed by storms. Getting darker, Cot thought, beginning to lose himself in a reverie. He brought himself back. "What was the name of that guy who issued the order?" He knew but wanted to ask.

"That was Wilkins Pollack," Ordell said.

"I have to find him," Cot said.

He's nervous, skittish, feels as if he doesn't know his way. It's a feeling—or a style—that's come over him recently. He thought KW would snap him out of it but it hasn't, not so far.

He peddles his old bike around to New Town looking for the inspector but he can't locate him. Pollack resides in a handsome wooden bungalow with a wooden incline ramp running from the street to the front porch. He lives with his mother who's crippled by palsy. She's out on the front porch sitting in a big upholstered rocker. Cot gets off his bicycle and walks up to the porch by way of the ramp. Mrs. Pollack eyes him with a rotund, fishy glare. Her big arm waves languidly; of its own volition, Cot knows. Like many crippled people she carries a lot of weight. She won't say where Pollack is. "Would you tell him I'm looking for him?"

She doesn't answer the question.

A few buzzards have gathered out in the street. They're bobbing for a run-over cat. Cot and Mrs. Pollack stare at them.

On the way up to Jimmy's Air Service in her Range Rover—same color as Ordell's—he leans over and kisses Marcella's cheek, sniffing her like a dog, drawing in the fragrance of cinnamon and citrus, the famous old business rising between them with the scent, elaborations, and additions to an alliance still sailing along, the two of them like a country vaudeville act, refreshing to watch, easy to dismiss, the days of their lives adding up still to this, no matter what, as he sees it, no matter family or Ordell or time or hurricanes or men dead in the streets of Miami, Florida, capital of the Caribbean Archipelago.

"I'm breaking down," she says and runs her hand along his thigh, erasing the words as she says them, but this seems now almost an act of carelessness like a carpenter in a failing business slicing his hand with a saw, because he's not even looking at her and she's looking at the road that is white concrete choked with traffic, studying something she'll never speak of. He could say well I'm a dead man and you will soon be dead too, but he doesn't. The sky's streaked with long trailers of white cloud. Over the back end of Cudjoe he can make out the glassy seaward-facing sides of houses in what seems to be a kind of fog but is maybe only pollution not yet blown out to sea. "I'm running on squibs and burps myself," he says.

"Rumors of squibs."

"Fossilized burps."

"Dreams."

"That's something else."

"What isn't?"

At Bastion instead of turning left to Jimmy's they turn right and run along the old county road between high banks of buttonwood scrub out to the point where, parked in the brush near Oscar Bottom Jut, they make love in the car, thrashing like two squirrels in a gunnysack, famished, springing disartfully again and again at each other. After a while they quit and eat the peanut butter and fresh pineapple sandwiches she's brought and then head to the airport. The hollowness he carried down by bus has been momentarily replaced by a coziness he knows is an illusion, the sexual practice that they are only barely game for, the gesture or reflex gone slack and desultory, its progenitor, both of them daydreaming of the silver backs of fishes or some such—this, mentioned as they lay sweating across each other's bodies, a kind of mad circumstance that once would have been a bindery of what they called love but is now only barely acknowledged; it's happened before, many times. "I don't much care," she said and he tapped on the window glass as if to a jailer who's supposed to take him back to his cell after visiting hours. Still, she gasped as she spoke and he himself was breathing hard.

"Weather's coming," she says.

"I see it."

They are sea children, children of the islands, they know weather, know ocean, know sky, you could make a list of what they know and pay only subliminal attention to.

She reaches up and taps the windshield for a yellow butterfly that's lighted there. The butterfly doesn't get the message and then does, wobbles into flight and is caught in a breeze and blown off toward the scrub they've just come out of. "At night," he says, "I stretch out my hand, reaching for you."

"You're lying," she says lightly.

"I got an old cat so I would have something to stroke."

"That too's a lie."

"*You* already got an old cat."

"That's a worse lie."

"Ordell—"

"Don't start lying about him."

"I can't help myself."

"That's a worser lie."

"Devilment is my nature."

"Lie. Freakish and unanchored speculation is your nature."

"I'm a very *practiced* liar."

"I myself lie like a rug."

"Like a sea grass tide. I lie like hot sun on the Gulf Stream."

"I lie like snow on the Andes."

"Like ice on the Ross Ice Shelf."

"I lie like the chemical fogs of Venus."

"I lie like the mists on the fields of Antietam."

"Like rats in the tunnels of Paris."

"Like daisies in Hartz Mountain meadows."

"You get me going one way then you go another."

"I'm cruel like that."

"Merciless."

"Savage."

"Plus kind, sympathetic, and humane."

"Oh, I'm a show all right."

Behind her eyes is a land of shadows and misinformation, slivers of gleaming material withheld, perceptions balanced like birds on a clothesline, reclamations and unalterable facts, the proofs of engagements never spoken of, blueprints from old houses of the heart long since torn down and the lots grown up in *paspalum* grass. The usual, he tells himself. But there's something more he can't put his finger on. He's already told her what he plans to do, about the house, Pollack, the gems, about CJ's part to come. Used to when he called from Miami he'd tell her about his adventures, but she made him stop. You're a defense attorney, he'd said. Not yours. He understood. It made her feel frail, unfit, at a loss. He's the same way. They both go around crackling and clicking, popping off, snapping their fingers, sticking a word in, a sentence, a lifetime of quick talk, just so they won't have to be alone with the cudgeling, clumsy world. You ought to leave CJ out of it, she said. And her saying it already nags him.

They bump over the high crown and speed down the paved road around the wide curve through the tall casuarina trees and on the half mile to Jimmy's Air Service where he gets out, leans back across the wide seat, kisses her as if the kiss is a language of fevers, and, like a schoolboy, whirls and dashes away, thinking I see into the deeps of her but I can't make out what it is I see.

Rattling and clattering, the big red pontoons making a rushing, gurgling, perilous sound, they lifted off the surface of the bay and were airborne. As always when skyward Cot looked back at the island he was born on, the compact chunk, stuffed like a Sunday chicken with its apparatus, its selfdom and clutter. "Where we going?" Jimmy asked. He had filed a flight plan with the Navy for Seminole Town on the tattered edge of the Everglades.

"I'll show you," Cot said and gave him a set of coordinates that would put them up at West Bird Key. His face was wind-burned from lovemaking. In the middle of things she had lifted her head to say, "There you still are, in the exact spot where every night you used to cry yourself to sleep—" meaning his gangster life and all that. "Not the exact bed," he'd said, and they both laughed. But at Jimmy's he had turned away from her as if he didn't know her; she hadn't gotten out of the car, hadn't even looked at him or had already stopped looking at him and turned to jotting something into a little notebook she pinned against the steering wheel as she wrote. She'd already forgotten the real him, he saw that.

"Marcella's my brother's lawyer," Jimmy said. He wore a red baseball cap and shades so dark the lenses looked black. He hunched his narrow shoulders as if flying was an unwelcome surprise.

"That the one went over to the judge's house and tried to dig up his banana trees?"

"That's him. A fool and three quarters."

They flew half an hour north and east until they came in sight of a string of islands like green slathered rocks set in blue and then veered west again and flew another ten until they came in sight of the small uplift of greenery Cot was looking for. He had Jimmy set down along the east side and pull up to the rickety pier. The island was about as wide and maybe three times as long as a football field, mangrove hedged and piled with cassia trees and buttonwood. A few wind-shredded coconut palms stuck up like brooms. Cot told Jimmy to wait and took a path in through the scrub to a clearing by a short—it could have been a runway, or just a raw place. Near a tin shed just past a small clump of redly blossoming hibiscus bushes he uncovered a steel facing set into and covered by the dusty coral sand. He unlocked it with one of the two keys he'd taken off Spane's ring, copied and replaced, lay facedown in the coral dust, reached into the squared rock hole, unlocked the safe, and lifted out the small, square green strongbox, opened it, and took out a hand-sized yellow envelope and emptied the emeralds into his palm. He put everything but the gems back as it was, re-covered the place with the foot of gray sand and sat on the ground looking at the emeralds. Big *trapiche* stones, uncut, they had been flown up from the mines in Muse, in Colombia. This place here—squat, centric Florida Bay island—was Albertson's bank, one of them. He felt the enormous, subsuming weight of what he was doing, but the exhilaration of holding the stones in his hand—or pocket—nearly canceled it out. A heat like a hot thumb pressed between his shoulder blades. The sky, except for a few balled-up clouds low in the west, was clear.

"I'd appreciate if you didn't mention this," he said on the flight back.

"You don't have to say that," Jimmy said jerking his hand at a fly that had gotten into the cabin.

"I know. I'm sorry. Thanks." The exhilaration was being steadily replaced by a slipping, emptying sensation, bits breaking off and sliding into a foggy inscrutability.

They came in low over the fish works off Chicken Leg Key, banked in over the cove and set down just past a headland grown up in casuarina trees. Cot could remember when that piece of ground had been a grassy spot where he and Jimmy and Jimmy's deaf brother Wheeler had thrown a football around as kids, before the weed trees took over. "I'm feeling pretty good," Cot said.

It was true. Suddenly, and despite everything, for a second he was.

Cot bikes over to Connie's and asks him if he knows anyone who wants to buy an emerald, or some. Connie is more liable to know someone—so he tells himself—and more willing to keep his mouth shut, than anyone else. He lives in a big open loft on the second floor of a half-renovated building just behind Duval. From his bedroom he can hear, only slightly diminished, all the caterwauling and dumb shrieking that goes on most nights on Duval as jakes from the states cut loose. But he likes it. It makes him feel, he says, as if his particular detachment of the human race is not about to be overrun.

"I could grope my way to it," he says, speaking of the gems.

"You know somebody?"

"I expect I do. Why don't you leave the merchandise with me?"

"I don't know if that's best."

"You afraid I'll lose 'em?"

"No. I don't want any burn scars on your precious flesh."

"I'm a lover of pirate treasure. That's my whole thing."

"Mine too."

He hands over the Cambo's candy-box tin he'd put the stones in. CJ presses the box to his heart then holds it next to his ear and rattles it gently. The box is bound around the edges with adhesive tape.

"You want to open it?"

"I'd rather picture them."

"How's Dover?"

"Dover's out looking for the . . . bluebird . . . of paradise."

"Me too, man. I been looking for that bird all my life."

"We already know that about you, dear."

Later, in bed at the Constance Hotel where he is given a quarter-priced room by Aldy Tillman, hotel owner and former cheerleader from their high school gridiron days, he sits in bed reading Virginia Woolf's diaries. "All the formulas are now a mere surface for gangsters," she says. He feels queasy, dislocated, a foolish person following wisps and stinks down blank-sided alleys. He gets up, washes his face and drinks water from the tap, gulping it down before he remembers he's in KW where the local water tastes like Milk of Magnesia. Jeez. He wipes his mouth. In the mirror he gets a glimpse of a partially rectified soul whose face retains blips and streaks of a confusion as yet not completely erased. He throws on his discarded clothes and walks down the street to the harbor. Lights are on over at the Coast Guard docks; they are readying a boat to go out, paid fetchers and rescuers, men in trimmed beards sporting tattoos on their legs like South Sea Islanders. Somewhere way out there in the dark somebody lost and wallowing in a big distant rolling trough, and he thinks: no, I still wouldn't go, why would I ever have thought I might.

By the Flagler monument, in a spot where the streetlights don't quite reach, he runs into Dup Randle, a sporting goods salesman from Miami. He'll remember this moment: it's like an ice cube down the back of his shirt. He flinches or thinks he does, he's not sure and catches himself; a thin twist of . . . not panic—discombobulation—slips along his spine. Dup fronts baseball gloves and scuba gear, but he's also a Business contract man. He says he's glad to see Cot—"Man, as I live and breathe . . ."—and offers him a Tums that he accepts but hesitates a sec before putting in his mouth as if it might be poison. The flat, chalky taste of what's left when everything else is eliminated. Dup actually seems glad to see him. He's been walking around alone over by the old turtle pens. "Kraals," he says. "*Corrals.* I never knew what that meant until just this minute." Waving vaguely back toward the docks. "I thought it was just the name of some guy, Kraals."

"Nope."

"How's your mother?"

Cot's sure then something's up, has to be. "She took the late ferry to Fort Myers. Gone to see her buddies in Tampa."

"I met her several years ago. She's a nice lady. Snappy sometimes."

Dup passes a hand over his forehead as if he's wiping

away sweat. He has a round plain face that creases into a translation of happiness when he smiles. He once told Cot he was born in a tent behind a tobacco warehouse in Virginia. It was part of a joke he was telling. Cot thinks of those video games where what you shoot disintegrates as if it never existed. He thinks of walking Dup over to the little byway near the Coast Guard compound and throwing him off one of the floating docks, cuffed with the set of handcuffs Dup always carries, but he decides not to. He doesn't feel up to it just now. Maybe *I* never existed, he thinks. He knows everything about what's happening here; it's not that much of a mystery.

"I'll see ya on the turnaround," he says.

"You going my way?"

"Which way you headed?"

Dup waves halfheartedly toward town.

"Too bad. I'm going over here."

But as he turns away from Dup, whose disguise is accessibility, in that instant, he wants to give him another chance, give him a lead, let him in on secrets that'll help him along. Maybe we could get your house out of hock too, buddy, old duplicitous Dup. The thought startles him, and he knows Dup can see this in his face. Dup starts to say something, then stops. It's not because he's letting Cot off. He wouldn't do that. The street lamp shines in his eyes that gleam with a dark avidity. The situation's one notch too public.

Halfway down the street Cot turns—Dup's still standing there pretending not to watch him—and says,

"I liked that song you made up for the party over at Hal's hotel."

Dup doesn't say anything.

"It was funny."

"Thanks," Dup says.

He walks slowly around the corner and then scoots up Grinnell, cuts over on Thompson Lane and up Francis across Fleming and on to Regent and his mother's house. He stands in the street. No one's about; the lights are off under the house. But he knows his mother is lying awake. She's lying there making up her life, fiddling with the pieces, fragments and unraveled bits, knitting fresh strands of ridiculous makeshift into the fabric, a living example of how crazy we all are. He crosses the yard to the porch, but nobody's under there. Nobody either in the backyard in the little pup tent Jackie's set up under the almond tree. He tells himself they've found a more restful place to sleep. But he really thinks they've been caught by wrongful men. *Help me.* What's the name—the inspector? Pollack—that's it. Like the fish. Or was it Fish? Wilkins. He's known him too all his life—hasn't he? A slow-moving boy (become a slow-moving man) with a ragged purple wen on the back of his neck and a black mole above his upper lip like a beauty spot. Cot used to see him years ago at semi-pro football games. He carried the chains for the yardage markers. He remembers his earnestness, the way he smiled when somebody looked at him. He wants to smash him to the ground and makes a plan for it, the plan wobbling as he makes it. No matter, in the dark ironworks the instruments are already being forged. He knows this. He can smell the burning metal, even at a distance; it rides on a breeze that's found him again.

All this in seconds as he cycles over to New Town. Two short fat bare-chested old men wearing tattoo sleeves walk by laughing softly. The moon's drowning in a small cloud pool. Around a corner he comes on two men in dark caps beating another man on the ground. He stops, wades in and batters the assailants back and forth, knocking one into a tree stump, the other onto his face on the pavement. "You okay, Pop?" he says to the man who was already down. The man's propped on an elbow looking at him. "What do you know?" he says. "What the fuck do you know about it?" Cot remounts his bike and pedals off. The moon has risen from its pool and sails unobstructed across the sky. He pedals past the darkened houses, past the cemetery where he used to lie out at night with Marcella under a bitter orange tree near the graves of sailors who had gone down with the battleship *Maine*. They could hear the chains on the flagpole above the sailors clanking as if the dead were being raised and lowered, for what reason you couldn't tell.

He finds Ella and Jackie up at CJ's, thinking as he climbs the outdoor stairs that he's finally coming to know the woman inside him like CJ's always told him he needs to, coming to love her; it's almost erotic, he can even picture her, sitting in a wicker chair on the beach, wearing an orange tam, picking at the sand with her toes and cursing softly as if curses are a form of singing, a hymn even. As a teenager he'd push his unit down between his thighs until just the V of hair showed and try to get off on that but it never worked. His imagination wouldn't hold up to the blunt fact of him, no homemade woman for him. And no CJ around, but they're sleeping in CJ's bed in the larger of the two bedrooms, Jackie and his quick-minded mother. He sits on the bed and talks them awake, clucking their names and telling them about a pelican he took away from some boys who were torturing it. He's at the part where the pelican kept nibbling his fingers as he pedaled it to the little nature rehab on White Street, nipping his skin with its outlandish and delicate beak. "It was nibbling my fingers so gently," he says. "As if it wanted to let me know everything was all right."

"I like that part," Jackie says, awake but not raising his head.

"You've always been so tenderhearted," his mother says lifting her hand to stroke his cheek.

In another hour dawn would be washing its gray hands along the horizon. "You seen CJ?"

"He's usually over to Dover's," Jackie says. Love never dies, Cot thinks.

"How come you're over here?"

"It's restful," his mother says. Her hair spiky, her face drained of color as if dreams have taken everything out of her; she doesn't ask him why he's scouting around before daybreak. "I'll fix some eggs."

"That's okay. I was wondering—did anybody come around the house?"

"Rajah brought us some candles. It was nice of him—to do a favor on his way to prison."

Later they eat breakfast out on the big back gallery. Neighborhood roosters rustle up the dawn and a skinny yellow cat slinks around their feet and shies when they try to pet it. A tiny, ambidextrous breeze pushes lightly at blossoms in the big tamarind tree in the alley. The white flowers look like lights fading. On the wide flat rooftop next door a homeless family wakes and begins to go about its morning routines. *I'm loose in the world, aflight without design or motive.* This's something he tells himself sometimes, sometimes when he stays up all night reading and then walks out on the beach to catch the sunrise. "Sometimes," he says to his mother who is buttering a piece of local bread, "I stay up all night in a laundromat."

"The same one?" Jackie says.

"One of two or three."

"You got somebody to do that with?" his mother says.

Just then a couple of police in detective clothes come up the stairs. One of them's hand goes to his holster when he sees people up on the gallery. Just as quickly the cop lets his hand fall to his side when he realizes who it is. "Hey, Mrs. Sims." The other's also a local fellow everybody knows, Oscar Kazanzakis, one of the Greek boys from Bahama Village. "You looking kinda musty, Cot," he says.

Cot's heart has already caught on a sticker, his sense of things, local agonies fuming. He can tell in every way but words what's up. A gnatcatcher bird clicks in the top of a skinny palm tree like it's keeping time. "I'm waiting for the elaborations," he says and feels the hollowness shift inside him, the desert island landscape rotate slightly until it shows scoured gullies and tidal washes crumbling under a gray sky—he doesn't want to be where he is, but that's how it is for most folks most of the time he thinks, and almost says: *I feel faint*, but doesn't.

"Well, uh," the first police—David Bates—says. He was on the football team with Cot and CJ in high school. "I'm sorry, Cot—Mrs. Sims, Jackie—but CJ's dead."

Though he hasn't moved Cot loses his footing, sags helplessly, wondering *where is the place*—what place?—and drops into the chair he has just risen from. His mother, looking David in the face, says, "God almighty," in a crumpled way.

Jackie has started for the stairs at the other end of the gallery, but Oscar stops him. "You know about this?"

"I hardly know my own name," Jackie says.

"What y'all doing over here?" Bates says.

"Resting up," says Ella.

They want to know the whyfors and hows of the killing, the police do, and they aren't the only ones, it's a mystery. Cot puts his head on the table, closes his eyes and says no to everything. No I don't know where he went, no on what he was up to, no on his real name, on his height and weight, on his capacity for love, his great human beauty, no on the shriveling and wasting under way in us all. As children they'd walked around town holding hands; it caused a half scandal among the conchs. Later CJ was captain of the football team, then he began to wear dresses in public. He was a good singer, a performer now of old songs. Cot can see his face, slanted a little sideways, the half-rubbed-out pockmarks on his cheeks like tiny excisions, his blueblack eyes taking everything in. He wipes his cheeks with both hands though there are no tears. Nobody, it appears, knows anything.

Oscar says Connie was found on the beach near the White Street pier.

"They'd covered him up with sea grass," Bates says. "That senator's homeless daughter spotted him and called us."

"Buried?" Jackie says. He gives a shake, writhes in his skin and settles back down. "First Arthur, now Connie."

"Arthur?" Oscar says.

"Natural causes," Ella says. Dead of a jellyfish sting (or the heart attack that followed), they'd all attended his funeral in the Jewish section of the municipal cemetery.

The cops look around the place, poking into closets and drawers. They wear white plastic gloves and booties on their feet and they don't want Cot and the others to go back into the house. Cot knows where he put the emeralds, but he has to wait. Then the cops notice the trapdoor in the ceiling and Cot leads the way up there for Oscar and they look around the attic room that is like the room of a recluse who forgot to move anything in but dust. Through the floorboards they can hear Ella and the other cop talking in CJ's bedroom. She's just talking, just yam-

mering. Even at a distance and through flooring it wears
him out quick, not for the first time. Sometimes he wants
to wring her like a rag. In his city life he walks right
by people like her, doesn't even look at them, or maybe
he does, maybe he starts thinking how you can cut loose
from the ones you love—how easy it is to do really—and
then feel the frayed ends of the rope dangling and flicking
and chafing for the rest of your life. Maybe, just catching a
glimpse of some neighborhood shouter, he'll start thinking about her, or about his daddy in Cuba and about all
the absent years and who did what to whom and how life
just piles on, and how the past is like a bamboo thicket you
quit cutting back and just walk around to get to where
you're going—*as best you can*, he'd say to Solly or Goldberg or Chips or Butler, or to any of them up in Miami,
to Spane, to Albertson if he asked, but Big A never does.

After the cops leave Cot goes into the small bedroom
where Connie has an upright piano and a bookcase and
an armchair beside a bright blue Iranian rug. He liked
to sit in the chair and gaze at the rug that he said was
his confidential tide pool. Behind the bookcase is a foot-
board that comes out. The stones aren't there. His blood
races, he wobbles, catches himself. He sees the little island white and green in a pale blue ocean. Sunshine like
a spanking. Now another kind of light's shining on him,
like moonlight through a bullet-riddled door. I'm going
to get it, he thinks, meaning more than one thing, two
things at least, maybe three.

He gets up and bicycles over to Marcella's house and sits on her back steps until she comes out. She brings him a cup of coffee. She's wearing a pale green silk kimono he's never seen before, something only somebody who loved her would give her. Even with Connie just dead he wants to interrogate her about this, but he's ashamed even as he thinks it and makes himself cut it out, and then he tells her Connie's dead—*Connie's dead*—and doesn't know or won't let himself know whether he's said it in this straight-out way because he's jealous or because that's the best way to say it, or he simply can't help himself. She winces, her foot turns half over so he can see the ligament stretch and she grimaces and catches herself on the rail and her mouth opens and she gulps air, grunts, and he can see in her face what she'll look like when she's old, her eyes without their scleral ring, her skin raked and tissuey, the same look of incomprehension she has now, the melancholic confusion as consciousness retreats along worn pathways into some convenience store of the soul with pickled eggs in a big jar on the counter and a clerk fossicking his teeth with a peppermint toothpick, death standing like a shadow right next to her, coughing quietly into its hand. Plus instant tears she doesn't bother to wipe off—her tears not death's. Ordell slides out as if he's been lurking and asks if he wants some breakfast and Cot says no. Their big tabby cat sidles up and curls around Cot's legs, but when he reaches to pet it the animal takes a swing at him, claws out. This seems the measure of things.

2

Connie was installed two days later in his family's big coral stone mausoleum that he'd always said looked like the temple of a small, unlikely religion. Standing around on the thatchy yellow grass under the moving shadows of palm fronds, the whole town it seemed had come out, town minus tourist population (or maybe not completely, since CJ was a favorite: Miss Peculiar), the conchs come out to stand in the late afternoon sun and shadow weeping big loose island tears, someone here or there crying out in a strangled voice for Connie, for CJ, for the boy who had run seventy yards once hauling a punt back all the way to win the Marathon game and caught the passes Cot tossed, boy who'd become the dual personalities, maybe the triple or quadruple, or innumerable personalities, like everyone else, only his were public and unafraid to be pegged, this brave boy, man, now already—Cot knew and Marcella knew—growing old in his tracks, his inexpugnable lover Dover standing rigid and straight by the minister who from time to time placed his hand on Dover's arm to steady him. CJ's old parents wept. His father who, back at the house when he was told, had laughed out loud like a man gone suddenly crazy, and cried into a huge yellow bandana bought for him by CJ on his one trip out of the country, to Morocco where he'd been detained in jail for three months and hurt. Some went to their knees, Cot among them. He and Brady Overhall, CJ's former sidelight, leaned over the gold-toned casket, both of them for a moment unable to get back up, both partially stupefied by the enormity (Cot not really, Cot even then watchful), by the calm, the doggedness, the power and intrusiveness of grief and by the thought of CJ's body stacked in the musty smokehouse under its breadfruit tree that was a descendant of one of the cuttings brought west from Tahiti by Captain Bligh. Cot got up on his own, but Brady had to be lifted up, gone boneless as a cat, so they could go on. White butterflies flittered around the casket and seemed to dance as Childress Purcell sang his special hymn, "See You in the Yonder." The late afternoon flight from Lauderdale coming in low nearly drowned the words out.

Cot stared across the assembled at Pollack. Fish, trash fish—pollack. Ah, well, the man probably had problems too. Afterwards he went over and asked him how he was doing. Pollack cringed, stiffened, his long lower lip pursing a little so Cot could see the creases beside it like little healed cuts and said fine just fine. "Sorry about your mother," he added or remembered to say or tossed in like a piece of meat distraction to a pursuing lion. He was sweating.

"That's what I wanted to talk to you about."

Cot had one of his father's old baseball caps in his hand. It had a New York Giants logo on it. He tapped it against his leg.

"Nothing I could do," Pollack said.

"I know."

"It's regulations."

"Meant to benefit the people of the community."

"What's that?"

"Did you ever find ten thousand dollars on the ground?"

"I found a frozen turkey once."

"Lying around where you could pick it up?"

"It was in Cleveland. Somebody'd dropped a turkey during a robbery."

"D'jou keep it?"

"I would have but my buddy said he needed it. He was the one actually who spotted it."

"Sometimes you find money on the ground you get to keep it."

"I don't know, Cot."

"Treasure all over this area."

"I don't know, Cot."

"You know my mother's sleeping under the house." He didn't want to take the conversation in this direction, but he couldn't help it. This showed on his face and Pollack saw it.

"I'm sorry, Cot," he said.

"I don't want you to lose sleep over it." Tiniest slip

and things could go flying off the rails. Now he wanted to punch the guy. "I'll see you, Wilkins."

"Mama said you came by."

"She lives *inside* y'all's house, I see."

Ordell came up just then with his arm tight around Marcella who was streaming tears. "Would you help me with this woman?" he said, an anguished look on his face. Cot dropped the conversation and took Marcella in his arms. She felt alive and wonderfully intricate. The villains had knocked CJ in the head. Hit him so hard from behind that his skull was broken. A chill jerked Cot; he almost let Marcella go, but he didn't. He was crying too. Way up, in the heat drafts, buzzards circled. The birds were an embarrassment, if you thought that way, especially in a touristical culture promoting everlasting life. Sometimes the birds came down to the cemetery and walked around. Bobby Johnson wandered up, and he pointed at them. "They could get to you," Bobby said as if he and Cot had been in conversation. "Though I guess it's true you never hear of 'em digging anything up."

Cot gave him a look and Bobby slid away, beating his white captain's hat against his leg as he walked.

"Who was that?" Marcella said. She looked up with eyes that looked like they had glue in them. "Oh— Bobby."

Her hair smelled of perfume, as citrusy as ever. Way across the cemetery, beyond the fence, upstairs in the old crumbling house on the corner that was half boarded up and leaning to the side, somebody played music on a machine, gay and heartless and loud. A bony, chlorotic beat stuffed under clash and wail. Then the music stopped, cut off. It was against the law to play loud music next door to a cemetery, maybe somebody suddenly remembered that or had it pointed out to them.

He tries to get his mother to leave town, but she won't. She's one of those old-timers who'll still be sitting in the living room darning socks when the apocalypse blows through.

"*I'll* leave," Jackie says.

They're out back, eating yellowfin sashimi under the almond tree.

His mother, tall and rangy, a jabbermouth her students call her, always up on things and alert as a bird, says: "If I had the money to go to Fort Myers"—that was where her sister, his Aunt Mayrene, lived—"I'd be able to begin to do something about turning this house around," but she's just talking.

Last week—just a minute ago it seems like—he lost everything at the track and walked out into the dusk that seemed a different dusk outside the gates than in and stood by his car as two fat men carrying long horn cases walked by. He tried to get them to blow post time once more, but they wouldn't.

His mother looks at him as if she, sadly, knows all about his troubles and fuck-ups, which, so he figures she does, and she does. A breeze, fresh born, creeps and struggles in the top of the big mahogany tree a hurricane had snatched bald in the crown three years ago.

"I'm going to take a nap," he says and crawls into Jackie's tent and after spraying himself with bug repellent slips off into sleep. In a dream CJ sits in a folding chair in the shade, eating strips of salted green mango. "What a gyp," he says, Cot's not sure about what.

So next morning he comes on Dup sitting on Sutler's Restaurant porch eating shrimp and grits and joins him.

"You know that's not the real way to fix it," Cot says indicating the half-empty plate.

"So?"

"You're not supposed to batter the shrimp."

"So?"

"So I guess you didn't find what you were looking for."

Dup doesn't answer. Instead he takes out his little Walther PPK knock-off and slips it under his napkin.

"Mine's sitting on my knee." Cot means the little Beretta he bought in a Key Largo gun shop twenty years ago, but he's lying.

"I know." He smiles at Cot, a strangely smoky and acquiescent smile. "Your buddy was smart."

"He made a perfect score on his college boards."

"You still remember something like that? What exactly are college boards?"

"Never mind."

"I hate when people do that."

"Yeah."

"Say never mind. Shitheads. Like you don't count."

"Yeah."

"I guess it's your turn to lead the way," Dup says moving the gun about an inch.

They drive up the chain to Kaslem Key and park beside a dirty coral road that runs through the woods. They walk along one after the other, Cot ahead. There are little coral-floored clearings in the woods where myrtle bushes and silver buttonwood clump together under skinny pines. They can see little green tufty islands out in the big bay.

"You went to a lot of trouble," Dup says.

"Not really."

They come to a long low house, a concrete shell abandoned years ago when the money to complete it ran out. Beyond the house a shattered boardwalk leads to a spindly dock built out through the mangroves. "Where we going," Dup says, "Exactly?"

Cot points out to the water. In the distance a couple of small white-lipped islands among their heaped greenery. Even now he feels like he's drifting, floating along. *I've been trying to buy my own head back.* Trying, he thinks, to buy back his soul and time and a few curious memories stacked on back shelves, and situations, arrangements, circumstances, old follow-throughs; rushing out to the track to put money on big horses about to break into their future too, carrying baskets of money still sporting their rental tags. *I'm going to inflate bags under it and float it to the surface,* he says, talking about his soul. But the ghostliness stands with him. *I'm on a fade. I'm being rubbed out.* He wants everything to be a joke and makes jokes with his cohorts, but nobody laughs much. He walks out on the beach after midnight and stumbles over nomads sleeping in the sand. *Perdóneme*, he says. Always he knows somebody who can fix things. But he can't get to them in time. "Circumstances have changed," the doctor says, the one Albertson made him go to. "Whose?" Cot asks, but the doctor won't tell him. He hears the wind in the pines, and even the wind, so simple, has a complicated too much to say.

"You're as suicidal as a bee," Dup says.

Everybody knows what's up with Cot but Cot, it appears.

Here and there a coconut palm sticks up like a flagpole. A small boat with a canvas-covered motor is tethered to the dock. This is Sam Seller's place, a lobster fishing rig he keeps operational this time of year. Cot takes the key from its cubby under the dock and gets into the little boat.

"That ain't a very likely boat," Dup says.

Cot thinks of those round boats Indians used on northern lakes. What're they called? Bull boats.

"I don't want to ride in that," Dup says.

"Me either, but it'll carry us to the stones."

"Let's get a bigger boat."

"Hard to do that without anybody hearing the news."

Dup rubs his gun against his thigh. He's had the pistol out all the way from town. He's a big man with caramel colored hair and sideburns several shades darker. "Let's go slow," he says.

"Fine with me."

"Hold the boat."

As Dup steps from the short board ladder into the boat Cot pumps the gunwale and tosses him into the water. A trick he's done a hundred times since he was a boy. No, not that many; he's no slyboots character. Dup comes up thrashing, gasping, and without his gun. Cot has his pistol out and he keeps it on the big man as he dog-paddles to the dock. Cot follows him back along the trail and then he makes Dup drive the rental car to the courthouse where he turns him over to the sheriff.

"Any witnesses to this, Cot?" the sheriff says.

"The waitresses at Sutler's saw him put a gun on me. Otherwise it's just me and my word. But is this the sort of thing you'd expect from me if it wasn't true? I'm known for my candor."

With the flat of his hand the sheriff pushes the front of his blond crew cut back. "I'll lock him up, but you going to have to swear before Judge Mannix."

"Anytime." Some soft thing in him now indurate and losing its luster. But everybody knows about that. You can't see a gangster without hearing about that at least once or twice a day: the dull, inevitable, unenviable stoniness. Yet a softness remains, supple, slowly undulating, a nexus like a jungle bridge flexing in breeze, a worry and substantiation, anchored in coral rock, humanness, spotty and reeking, still apparent—that's another way of putting it—*Hey, Sheriff, don't you know me?*

He calls Marcella on her cell; it turns out she's in the

courthouse and looking for somebody to have lunch with. They drive in her car to the Rumba Room and have snapper salad and iced tea. From the main room they can see the lagoon, sparkling and winking in the bright sunlight. Out on the beach European tourists in flimsy bathing suits lie in the sun as if shot. The Americans are all fat but energetic; whatever's for rent they rent: paddleboats, boogie boards, huge transparent spheres you get inside of and walk across the waves with, contraptions that leave them stalled in the lagoon making signals for rescue. All the picnic tables have been commandeered by the homeless who gabble and sputter, laughing with a sound as if their throats are being ripped out. At a card table in the shade, Hollis March, the writer, scribbles furiously in his notebook. After his stroke he no longer makes sense, but that hasn't stopped him. Marcella wants to know what the fracas with Dup was about, but Cot's cagy.

"Where'd you hear about it?"

"Buster Goins was filling me in on it as it happened."

"The deputy? I was being observed?"

"Somebody's always watching."

"I owed him money. Or I owed his boss money."

"Doesn't he work for Albertson?"

"Does he?"

"I see."

"Yeah. What was the name of that inspector?"

"Pollack."

"Like the painter."

"And the fish."

"You want to get married?"

"Once is enough for me, thanks."

He rubs the back of her hand with his knuckles. She smiles at him, her old enigmatic smile that isn't so enigmatic anymore. Her face is being recultivated by time.

"I been thinking about farming," he says.

"You would."

It's as if there's now a skin between them, something flimsy but regenerating whenever it's torn and too much trouble to keep trying to rip through.

"You want to duck over here into this little botanical garden and cut us off a piece?"

"I love your way with words. I can't get enough of it."

"Do you?"

"I'm vice president of the garden club."

"Then you probably know the nooks."

"None *on* this island."

When they were children the road just outside the Rumba Room had been a dusty half-paved track running through scrub past a scoured and depleted beach, only a whistle-stop among beaches, of the kind that once you're away from you try not to develop a wistful affection for, now sandy and planted with palms and sea grass.

"I got the fidgets," he says.

"I first noticed that when you were twelve."

"Yes. Up till then I was steady as a rock."

"Let's stop bantering."

"All right."

He bends down and kisses the back of her hand. Each

touch lets loose a mental fibrillation and each one's an excitable Stag-O-Lee ready to knife whatever gets in its way. Or it used to be like that. Now everything between them smells musty, it's stacked haphazardly, it's like old clothes and habits and partial caps and somebody sitting on the side of the bed paring his toenails with a penknife. He can't keep thoughts like these out of his head. It's been going on for a while—since he got back—since *she* got back (from *what* place and arrangement of circumstance?). "You were—" he says.

"When I'm around you," she says, "people can tell what I'm thinking."

He warms, bristles, falters, and says nothing.

They sit just out of the sunlight watching some tourists in Indonesian wrap-around skirts playing volleyball. Down the way a man in very white skin makes gestures at the ocean. Carleton Jiggs who runs the little refreshment stand out in the sunlight looks their way. Cot nods at him, but Carleton doesn't see him or does and won't acknowledge.

"I feel as if I am going crazy," she says.

"I know. It's the same for me."

They've broken up half a dozen times, once for four years. That hiatus ended one afternoon when they ran into each other at a fruit stand up the Keys where Cot was buying a basket of Georgia peaches. She'd come up to him from behind some casuarina trees and without a word exchanged they'd walked away down a dusty white road and made love under the raised first floor of a beach cottage. They hadn't had to fight to get out and they didn't have to fight to get back in. "It's like we got vaporized and then reconstituted," he'd said. "We're just mercilessly hopeful," she'd said. They'd sat a long time on the little beach behind the cottage looking out at the ocean, not speaking. It seemed that they were the absentee landlords of a great property, an inexplicable vastness.

"I've got to go," she says.

He walks her out and pulls his bike out of the back of the Range Rover. "Meet me tonight," he says.

"All right."

"At Smathers. Across from where they dump the sea grass."

He doesn't look back as he pedals away under the poinciana trees, he never looks back—or says he doesn't but usually does—so can't see her glance at him and turn quickly away and touch the face of her phone, look at it for a second and put it to her ear.

He spends most of the afternoon with his mother around the corner from the house, at the laundromat. They sit on folding chairs out front listening to *Jazz Hour* on WCCL in Miami. Jackie has his sketchbook and offers to do portraits of passing tourists for ten dollars per. He rarely gets anybody to pay for what he comes up with. A few mercy bucks, a few insults. Ella writes in her notebook. A journal, she says, of her predicament. "Day 147 Under the House," she scribbles at the top of the page, a number not entirely accurate. She scribbles rapidly and then stops, goes back and crosses everything out, taking care not to make the words unreadable.

Cot wants to discuss the gem situation with his mother and Jackie, but he puts this off a little while because he doesn't want to have to explain anything.

He calls his Business buddy Tommy, his pal, on the phone he bought out at the airport, but Tommy says he doesn't know what's happening. "I heard Dup is in jail," he says. "A's not too pleased about that."

"Is Spane headed down this way?"

"I thought Spane was in Tampa."

Albertson has a cigar operation in Tampa, and Spane sometimes goes up there to smooth out problems.

"We're sitting ducks down here," Cot says. He's having this conversation later as he sits in the Pumper family's bower swing in their garden at the corner of Southard and Fiddler, hidden by foliage he can see through to the street. Tiny anole lizards sporting slick red cravats stare both ways from nearby branches.

"Ducks a'sittin'," Tommy says.

"That's it." Out in the street Mrs. Arey Bonita pedals her three-wheel bike along. It's piled with groceries. Among them her little boy Harrell sits singing his song, "O Beautiful for Specious Skies."

"I'm going to head down to St. Thomas," Cot says.

"Don't tell me."

"Or I might run back up the Keys. Or slip a boat out to Mexico. Maybe I'll take the ferry up to Fort Myers and scoot up into the contiguous states."

"I don't want to know."

Cot calls Albertson, but Albertson doesn't answer. He uses an airport phone and wonders if it's unregistered, wonders if Albertson is sitting in his bedroom staring at the number on his screen wondering who could be calling him on his private line. *Pick up, Gus, slap yourself in the face and pick up.* But he doesn't. And it's as if the room is buzzing with wasps, as if he's in a huge warehouse-like space but all around him a buzzing of alert insects, contrivance of dream and some kind of hurtness he can't describe—but he ignores this and concentrates on the folks sitting on a second-floor balcony across the street. He can hear what they're saying. They're talking about God and how God, as they see him—as one of them sees him—is like a foolish waiter or a boat salesman on a spree, and another voice says you goon and then laughter breaks out. A breeze keeps turning over the leaves of an aurelia bush on the corner, exposing their blood-red undersides and flipping them back.

About eight he rides his bike over to the First Baptist church and waits outside the fellowship hall for Ordell to come out of his deacons' meeting. "Listen," he says when Ordell, burnished and newly slim, comes out of the front door lighting a cigarette. "I was wondering if you could provide a little police protection for my mother."

"Who's after her?" Ordell looks him straight in the eye. It's something he does with everybody. Cot knows, as everybody does, that it's just a ploy or attempted saving grace or a tic or something he does simply to divert attention from how nervous he is.

"Boys from Miami."

"I ought to lock you up."

"You did that already, thanks. Hey, Franklin."

Franklin Purl, scion of Purl Auto Repair owner Marty Purl, gives him a wink and a passing nod of his curly red head. "I thought Franklin had drunk himself to death by now."

"Naw. He's doing very well since he went to AA. Been sober over two years."

"Everywhere I look people are pulling themselves together."

"After a certain age it's either that or the undertaker."

The prosecutor stretches his arm out in the way he does when he's nervous, making and releasing a fist.

"What's bugging you?" Cot says.

"Marcella's pissed at me."

"That all it is?"

"What? She left this morning and she said she wasn't coming back home. You know where she is?"

"She didn't say anything to me." He steps back, as if to give this news room. The freshening breeze edges along in the big camphor tree by the church schoolyard, looking for something it hadn't found yet.

"You brought trouble."

"I know."

"You always do."

"Not always."

"I'll see if I can get them to keep an eye on your mother's place."

"I really do appreciate it."

"You don't know where Marcella is?"

"I haven't seen her."

He pedals over to her family house on Monitor Street, the old coral stone mansion once the biggest and fanciest house south of Miami, if not by much. It has double galleries around all four squared sides. The galleries, and especially the big overhanging roof, make the house look much larger than it actually is. Her mother and two of her sisters still live in it, wandering around the rooms hooting and waving scarves at bugs and ghosts. Marcella's up on the second-floor gallery shooting at bats with a pellet gun. Cot spits into a ficus bush as he passes. The spittle catches and hangs like a star in the bush's firmament. "That'll get you arrested," he calls from the big yard.

"Home defense. Get on up here."

Her voice is soft and lilting. *One day we will be old and skinny and talk in squeaks and yips about silly things.* Was it Virgil said that? Anyway now he won't have to stand around on Smathers's smelly beach waiting for her tonight.

When he gets up there she's sitting on the edge of a chaise with her forearms propped on the gallery rail. The gun is balanced on the rail too. Her older sister, square-bodied and defeated, edges away around the gallery corner. "Hey, Mindy," Cot says.

"Don't tell me anything about it," Mindy says and looks back with a mixed startled and risible look. She has always thought him a ridiculous character, but then so have most folks. The difference is she seems to like him that way.

"Mindy's been keeping score," Marcella says. From where he stands, her face, foreshortened into heaviness, looks like a man's, a sporting and lively man's.

"I can't believe you can hit a bat."

"Look down on the lawn."

In the dark on the lighter lawn lie black items like small balled rags. Maybe they're bats.

"So you're off Ordell?"

"I don't want to talk about that."

"I wouldn't either."

"How's your mother."

"Still pretty hard on life."

"I asked her to come over here to stay but she wouldn't."

"Nobody likes a scold."

"Shut up with that."

"Except me."

They walk down to Dell's and get a couple of canned iced teas. Moths loop and waver in the big capped light over the front door of the store. Down the street the old ice plant that's been converted to a storage warehouse looms. A rooster feebly crows; it sounds exhausted, depressed. Houses poke out of tall bushes like outposts in a jungle. Cot thinks he sees somebody, some dark shape, duck in among the bamboo behind the old Friedlander place—not thinks, does. Whoever it is has the size and shape, the shunted able directed movement of a no-good. "I got to go," he says.

"Oh stay the night."

"I have to check on something for Mama."

He takes off down the street. He doesn't look directly at it but he has the place the shape slipped through locked in his mind. He cuts in under a big grapefruit tree beside the old Cooper house, now broken up into apartments and stops under the outdoor stairway and listens: no sound, nothing unusual. He has his pistol out. A nearby radio softly plays Herbie Hancock's "Testament of a Sinner." A crackling sound comes from the ficus hedge separating the Cooper place from the house next door. Cot waits. He feels like a ghost haunting a house where the slightest weight, the slightest lean toward corporeality, will break him through into sordid life. A shape slips out from behind a big heaped bush and tracks across the lawn right by him. As it passes Cot steps out and hits the shape hard behind the ear with the butt of his gun. Down the shape goes in a pile. It's Bert Lewis, an operator Albertson employs for special jobs, out cold. Without hesitating, Cot pulls the man's clothes off, drags him around to the street and leaves him attached to the lamppost with the handcuffs he took off Dup. Then he walks back to the store, uses the pay phone to call the police station to tell them a naked man is passed out in the middle of the 800 block of Retention

Street. He walks back to Marcella's and rejoins her on the upper gallery. She's still drinking her iced tea.

"Everything work out?" she says.

"Partially."

He has Bert's pistol in the pocket of the old duck jacket he wears. His own gun is in the other pocket. Two guns make him feel worse not better. He takes this as a good sign, a sign that informs him of his own humanity. "I've put Mama in a way of trouble."

"That's nothing new."

He wishes he was sitting in the Caribe Diner in south Miami eating eggs scrambled with shrimp and reading Virgil. *The Georgics* is really becoming his thing. Farm advice, life in the country—these soothe his troubles. Which are what exactly? General reduction of force, confusion, this ghostliness formalizing itself into a story he is telling himself of ghostliness, entropy, slippage, the look in her face adumbrated, only half there, age muddying the water. She says she's troubled—with her forefinger rubbing her nose that always itches—and can't stop lying, but this is not fresh news: both of them, they've always loved to tell untruths. A night bird lets loose a little rounded-off cry, interrogatory, just something it wants the lowdown on. Marcella inclines her head to his shoulder, rubs her face lightly against the cloth of his shirt. "Are you going to do something about whoever killed CJ?"

"I'll settle it, yeah."

"I'm glad of that. I don't think Ordell can do it."

"I guess now Ordell won't know *what* you think."

"It'll be a relief, believe me."

He feels for the cool spot under her hair in back, the one that's been cool since she was a girl, but he can't find it. Her hair like thick silk in back, heavy, smelling like a lemonized horse. The smell alone used to take him to another world. Where he figured prominently and was thrilled by this and safe. "*Mi caballo*," he says. "Or *mi yegua*. My mare? That's not quite right." He can't see if she's smiling and doesn't think she is.

The next morning early he's over at the courthouse talking to one of the deputies.

"He's part of that Miami hoodlum element keeps showing up around here. That's why we locked him up. You know anything about him?" says the deputy, a short, bald young man who you think has a limp but doesn't. "He says you attacked him."

"I was all night over at the Cord house."

"At the courthouse? Nobody here saw you."

"Cord. Marcella's mother's house."

"You heard she kicked Ordell out."

"Yes, I did. Have you seen him?"

The deputy leans to the side. It looks like he's favoring a bad leg. "He might not be in at all today. No—there he is now. I misread the evidence."

Ordell, slumped, his tobacco-brown hair slicked to one side, carrying his briefcase in his arms like a true love, slopes in the door.

"Man," says the deputy, Bobby Briggs, "he's cleaned out."

Ordell acknowledges Cot with his eyes—soft brown, sampling despair—and shuffles down the hall into his office, Cot following.

"Get you some coffee?" Cot says.

"That might wake me up. I don't want that."

"I'm sorry for your trouble."

"Well, you know what she's like. Did you see her?"

"I stayed over at her mother's place last night. She seemed a little winded."

"Her mother?"

"Marcella too."

"I can't stand the house—our house—without her in it. I get spooked. I took the dog and the cat, and we're staying at La Concha."

"D'jou get a room where you can watch her house?"

"Of course."

"D'jou see anything?"

"She was shooting that damn pellet gun, I know that. I should of had her arrested."

"You find out anything yet about CJ?"

Ordell raises his head like a man raising his face out of a bowl of soup and stares at the ceiling, squinting as if the answer is written up there. "I don't think it's local."

"What makes you say that?"

"I thought it might be one of CJ's acquaintances. Somebody with a grievance. But it's not."

"How do you know?"

"The way he was killed."

Cot just looks at him. Out in the street someone shouts, happy to be at US 1 Mile Zero.

"He was shot," Ordell says.

"I thought . . ."

"It was a pro job."

Cot feels a chill down his back. That's what he's been afraid of. He turns away to the window. Down in the street a hen followed by six buff-colored biddies moves along. A shirtless man, a fat man, waves them by like a traffic cop. Cot thinks of his father, leaning over his writing board in Havana. A picture of his apartment shows tall peeling walls, rattan rugs, hardly any furniture. Cot wishes he was there, in Havana, walking down a shuttered street, eating a chicken empanada. No, that's not right—he wishes he was in Miami, sitting on a bench in Flamingo Park watching the tennis players. But not—

"What should I do about Marcella?" Ordell says.

"Nothing much you *can* do," Cot says still looking out the window. *Go over to Solly's for banana pudding—that was something to do in Miami.* "I've never been able to head her off."

"You don't have to," Ordell says bitterly. "You always know she'll come back to you."

Cot turns around. "No, Buck, I don't know that. Nobody can know something like that about Marcella."

He leaves and heads down the stairs. Outside the day is big with itself, full spring in the Keys, trumpet trees yellowly flowering, poincianas ruffling their red spangles, the island plump with life. Sam Butler, the mayor, passes on his scooter, on his way, Cot knows, to get a drink at Passerine Dooly's house, his true love—both drink and Passerine. What is *he* going to do? Maybe it would be best to go back to Miami—draw off the stalkers. They *are* stalkers—right? But what could he do in Miami? And how do they know he'd taken the stones in the first place? *Do* they know that? Had CJ—well, it could be anything. Maybe Jimmy, maybe sensors in the ground, maybe a damn force field thrown around the whole of Florida Bay. A springing misery shivers and clips him as it passes.

He catches a ride on the tourist train back to his mother's house. Buzzy Staples, the guide and driver, is talking to the tourists about sponge fishing when he lets him off, making that sloppy profession seem like a tale of romance and plunder.

Jackie says his mother is over at the botanical garden by Higgs Beach, conducting a class in exterminating vermin. "You never know what she's going to be up to," he says when Cot gives him a look.

He phones Spane, but Spane isn't answering. He starts over to the garden on his bike, but halfway there he thinks he had better go to Miami and pedals out to the airport and buys a ticket. The plane is scheduled to leave at three. He goes over to the garden looking for his mother, but she's gone. He sits under a little spicewood tree and stares at the ocean. A flat pale blue expanse that looks gelatinous in the heavy morning light. He again calls Spane who isn't picking up and leaves a message saying he's got the stones. He's ice cold the whole time he's speaking, a voice not very deep inside saying *fool fool.* "I'm going up to the island to return them," he says. He's making mistake after mistake, first on the list—after taking the stones, after getting Albertson's operative locked up, after running around here like he knew what he was doing, after putting his mother at risk, and Marcella too and who knows who else—making such a call, even if it's on an unregistered phone (they don't let you off just because you put the money back in the bank); sticking his head in a noose. But it's like he doesn't care—or not that exactly: it's as if he's only half awake, only half there. Essentials decoalesce, drift away like scents into the trees. Yes, that's it. His mind seems half gone, private areas looted, policies and imprimaturs faded, old sureties hollowed out, schemes disassembled. *Do you know me?* is a question he could ask himself.

A man in long white shorts is throwing a rubber ball into the shallows for his dog. The dog, a sleek black retriever who knows his business, brings it back every time. *He's* a retriever who's gone off. He wants to put money on something, jai alai maybe, preferably on Zabala and his partner Bidarte, but it's too early in the day. Feelings, like quivering animals, range in his body, nameless feelings on strange errands.

In a minute the phone rings. It's Spane. "You have trouble," Spane says.

"I know that."

"You don't have the stones."

"I know that too."

"The Big says he'll give you forty-eight hours to find them and put them in his hand."

"I'm on it right now. Mikey?"

"What?"

"Thanks."

There's a silence on the line. Through this silence Cot can feel Spane, solid as coral rock, feel him leaning toward him, the shadow of his presence reaching for him, the blank malfeasance, substance without form, no mercy involved. And Spane can hear him breathing into the line, breath traveling through the air 150 miles over water and stubby islands, faint as whispers, signaling to him, even a sigh expressive of everything a life is, sum and parts, and it's as if he can lift the life out of the substrate it inhabits and hold it in his hand and pick at and ponder it and toss it aside when he's done. There's been a wariness between them for a while now, a displacement, a shift, but this changes nothing really.

"Don't call me again," Spane says.

Cot sits in the shade looking out at the ocean, a bleak expression on his face like that of a man marooned on an island nobody will discover for years.

3

He caught up with Ordell at Sammy's Lunch, but Ordell told him there were no new developments in the case.

"Not even whispers?"

"It's a complete mystery."

An orange cat sat up in a lime tree staring at some little black-faced birds flickering around in the top of a nearby manila palm. The birds didn't seem to mind. Ordell's dark thick hair like the mournful pelt of a just-extinguished species, strands of gray setting tiny trails in it, shifted as he turned to look from the patio they sat on at four hugely fat old men in ponytails passing on their Harleys.

"How about footprints and DNA and your CIs—all that," Cot said, tapping Ordell lightly on the knuckles. "How about spoor and signs?"

"None such."

"How about known criminals."

"You're the best known we got."

"Come on."

"We'll catch them."

"Them?"

"Whoever it is. You talked to Marcie?"

"Yeah."

"Does she say anything about me?"

"Not really."

"What does she say?"

"She thinks the world of you."

"I got to elevate myself out of this."

"Okay."

Ordell squeezed a few drops from a greenish wedge of lemon onto his fingertips and patted them on his tongue. "You remember when people in Bahama Village used to raise goats?"

"They say before the big hurricane in the thirties it was a real agricultural paradise down here."

"I wouldn't go that far."

Cot knew that Ordell was slightly homosexual, Marcella knew and others did too, but no one mentioned this to Ordell. Ordell, as far as anyone was aware, never mentioned it to himself. After lunch they walked back to the courthouse together. Cot's phone rang. It was Marcella. "How's he doing?" she asked when he told her who he was with.

"Maybe you ought to come see for yourself."

"Don't be mean."

"He's suffering."

"That her?" Ordell said.

"She's beside herself."

Ordell made little grabbing motions for Cot to give him the phone, which he did.

"Honey," Ordell said first thing, "I will do anything. Honey . . . ," then he listened. Then he said, "But, honey . . ." then silence, then, "But . . ." silence " . . . but . . ." silence . . . "But goddamn it, Marcie, I didn't . . . but . . . but . . ." and then he snapped the phone shut and put it into his pocket. He stood in the street looking straight at the sun. The light sparkled on the lenses of his dark glasses. "God almighty," he said, "Goddamn almighty."

Cot pedaled out to the airport and cashed in his ticket. He thought about taking the flight anyway, taking the one he'd paid for and then another, a string of them, until he wound up, dusty and dazed, sitting at a rickety table in a river café in some Kinshasa of distance, drinking a cup of bitterroot tea and calling himself Frederick Boykins. He reached for his phone, but he hadn't gotten it back from Ordell. He had already talked to Dover, who told him he hadn't seen Connie that night. Told him nobody he knew had seen him. Cot wanted to ask him the same set of questions again. Not because he didn't believe Dover, but because he couldn't think of anything else to do. I could walk up and down the streets knocking on people's doors. Dial the phone book. He pedaled back to town and stopped at a few bars and knockout joints but no one had seen CJ that night. "I saw a pompadour of yellow feathers off in the distance," Randy Bunker said, "but I didn't see who was under it."

"Where was this?" Cot said.

"Over on Olivia. I caught sight of somebody in the cemetery, flitting among the graves."

Just hearing this little bit made Cot's heart beat faster.

"I'm so sorry," Randy said. He worked under the stage name Impressionella, a rangy fellow from Stakelight, Arkansas, sans, so he said, his sack of troubles now. In KW many made such a claim, tiny dabs of shame gleaming like melted sugar in the corners of their eyes.

He walked down Fleming, going slowly, planning to arrive at his mother's and rest a while, but just past the library somebody stepped out from behind a big orangely flowering bougainvillea and popped him in the head. He went down on his face into a jasmine bush. When he came to an older couple was standing over him. "We thought you were dead," the man said, a thin prospector-type holding a large yellow hat.

"Do you know me?" Cot said.

"How could we know you?" said the woman, slim too, a little too much sucked out of her to really wear the slimness well. "We're visitors."

"Do you know yourself?" the man said. He was old. Dark grape-wine stains of age, or eternal night, on the hand that gripped the big hat.

"That's a good question," Cot said.

"Were you on your way to the library?" the woman said.

"I wouldn't doubt it."

"We thought so," the man said.

"We thought you slipped and hit your head," the woman said.

"I did."

He was sure it was last night's stalker, Lewis his name was, Bert, a worker for Albertson, an auxiliary, a friendly person generally. He lived in a hotel on Washington Ave. out at the beach. Bert. Damn. But if he hit him that meant he didn't have a gun. Or did it? Albertson had probably pulled him off the job. But Bert still had a little personal business with him. Well, you could go on and on figuring things out. Cot preferred revelation, as he often said, over deduction, but you couldn't always count on it to show up when you needed it. Clouds, puffed and richly white, had a permanent look about them, high in the center of the sky. He was always falling for something that looked permanent. His head hurt. He went into the library, cruised briefly through the stacks, and checked out a volume of Korean poetry. After all this time his card was still good. He loved how they trusted him in here, were willing, despite everything, to let him walk out with a book, their only copy of poems by Ko Un and Ku Sang, as if they had faith in him. Maybe they'd testify as character witnesses at his next hearing. Down at the laundromat Billy Gomes, a guy he knew, was entertaining some tourists with stories about free diving in the Tortugas, a place Cot felt sure he'd never visited. Cot wondered if anyone ever dreamed when they were knocked out. Last night he had dreamed of jealousy and ordinance. Of Marcella revising her opinion of him downward, of his pulling a trick gun, a gun made of horehound candy, and of being forced by elemental but crazed powers to eat it. Everything in the dream had been a bad sign. He pulled Billy off to the side. Billy was sipping pineapple juice out of a green coconut. "What you got?" he said.

"I need you to help get my mother out of town."

Billy's eyes shipped fear like a summons. It was amazing how that went—eyes instantly alerting the universe to a change in mode. "OK," he said.

"I mean I need you to make a suggestion or two."

"I don't know if I can ever do that."

It was as if they had been talking an hour, fruitlessly. Maybe the head blow had done more damage than he thought. Wright Sunderson pedaled by on his bike, pulling his little cart filled with flowers he'd gathered in people's yards for sale to the tourists. Down the street a large man in a faded orange shirt crossed and climbed the steps to the old Stampen house, now empty so long it looked abandoned. Maybe the house had finally been sold. The man—that was what was sticking to his mind—looked like Bert. "Come on," he said and started off down the street. He wanted to pull his gun but thought better of it. Billy came along behind, apologizing to the tourists as he left—the tourists, decked in tourism finery, looked relieved he was going—and caught up with Cot in front of the Big Wreck Hotel. He and Marcella had tried when they were thirteen to get a room there but the management—Cooper Nutall, an extremely short man in a blond Elvis haircut—had called their parents.

"What is it?" Billy said, loping along. He was wearing white calypso pants, a striped blue-and-white shirt, and a gray weathered sailor cap.

"This guy sucker punched me."

"Just now?"

"Almost."

Cot sent Billy around behind the Stampen house—tall, weathered to a tallowy gray, two-storied with double galleries, rusted weather vanes depicting ships under full sail and lightning rods like spearheads on top—and he ran up the front steps and into the front hall. There he stopped and listened. Nothing but the creaks and frets of an old empty house. Here he had played poker with the Stampen twins when he was eight, on rainy days up on the second-floor gallery, once losing his favorite Aloha shirt to Benny. The twins were gone now, one dead of a blood disease, the other, a drunkard he'd heard, just hanging on, in Panama City or someplace, selling used boats. He held himself carefully and loosely quiet. He could hear breeze fiddling with the roof tiles, the shake and swish of palm fronds. "Bert," he called.

"You want me?" Billy called from out the back door.

"Bert."

"I'm out here," Billy called.

Cot heard a noise, maybe footsteps going down the back outside stairs. He ran through the house to the back side door, opened it—no one there. Maybe a slight agitation in the molecules. Not six feet away a gray-and-white cat gazed at him from a closed window in the house next door. "What now?" he mouthed to the cat who just stared.

He went back into the house and out through the big back double doors. Billy was sitting in an old rocking chair next to the swimming pool that was covered with brown stained canvas. "D'jou want me?" he said.

"Did you see him?"

"Who?"

"Big guy in an orange shirt."

"Nobody came by here. Were you calling me?"

"Your name Bert?"

"I thought you were playing with me."

They walked back through the house, out the side yard and down the lane that ran through the middle of the block. At the street entrance there was no sign of the operative in either direction. Cot was holding himself back for some reason, trying not to let himself think about anything, a practice he couldn't sustain for long. The lane sheltered a bower-like entrance to his mother's backyard. He let himself think about this; no good thoughts. He began sprinting. He dived through the big mass of bougainvillea behind the Colfield place and through the slat gate into his mother's shady backyard. No Bert there either. Jackie was putting mackerel fillets in an old metal drum smoker. She was over at the garden teaching her class in sortilege, he said.

"Anybody come around here?" Cot said.

"Oscar Moreno dropped by to talk to Mrs. Sims." Oscar was one of his mother's lawyers.

"That it?"

"Yep. Except for the figments and cordial apparitions."

Cot felt faint—and depressed, as if the blow had knocked happiness out of him. Billy trailed in through the back gate. He was carrying a clutch of green coconuts. "D'jou catch him?" he said.

"Catch who?" Jackie said.

"This misanthrope been running around."

"Back here?"

"Over at the Stampen place."

"They were camping on the back porch last week."

"Like us."

"Poachers."

"I got to get my bike," Cot said.

When he got back to the library he thought the bike was stolen but the man behind the counter, a skinny man who, Cot knew, liked to stand late at night under streetlights smoking thin aromatic cigars, said they brought it in and put it in the office. When he went to get it the head librarian, a woman with too much emotion for a librarian it had always seemed to him, scolded him and told him to stop leaving his bike unlocked at their door. Cot didn't try to explain anything to her. He had generally quit that by the time he was ten. "I feel a headache coming on," he said to nobody in particular as he pushed the bike down the ramp behind the library. Across the street workmen in do-rags were just finishing removing the last remains of the Crawford house. He had known the house all his life and now he couldn't recall what it looked like. Only an expanse of raked coral dirt containing traces, like an empty gold mine, of what had once been an arena of desire and mortification. He walked over and spoke to Bucky Winters who was pulling a big rake across the surface. Bucky had a small Wake-up Andy doll stuffed in his back pocket. "I found it mashed against the fence over yonder," he said when Cot asked him about it. "Last significations of habitation."

"The Crawfords still in town?"

"Naw. They left right after the fire. Moved to Titusville."

"Fire did this?"

"Drunkenness and bad behavior did this."

"I got you." Despair and shame—terror at the bone—there was a list.

"You want this doll?"

"You don't?"

"It just made me feel bad to see it lying there."

Cot took the limp, goggle-eyed doll from him. He placed it in the basket on the back of his bike. Up ahead, just ducking around the corner by the Simeon Bros. grocery, he saw the flicker of an orange shirt. "I'll catch you later."

He couldn't however catch up with whoever it was, with Bert. Southard was as empty as the morning after a parade. Tatters and bits of what looked like flags fluttered in the poinciana trees—as if there *had* been a parade. Then Marcella came backing her Rover over the hill.

She cranked the big car into a parking space, honked, and waited. "How about a snack?" she said when he pulled up beside her.

"I got to get Mama out of town."

"I know."

"That's what you always say."

"That man who you stripped and sent to jail got out this morning."

"I'm just waking up from where he conked me on the head."

She grimaced—from concern or disgust it was hard to tell. "Where'd you get the doll?"

He told her.

"Entices us into a life of nostalgia and other misrepresentations," she said.

"Not me. I'm strictly a present-moment kind of guy."

"Are you going to get in the car?"

He loaded his bike in back and got in beside her. The leaves of a big kapok tree above their heads rattled and seemed about to break into speech—muddled and distraught speech, he thought.

"Ordell said you got a phone call from Miami. It sounded, so he said, like someone named Crotch."

"Crodge."

"The usual desperate character?"

"We're all desperate characters."

"Existentially speaking."

"I thought you weren't speaking to Ordell."

"I'm not. But we talk anyway. Like you and me."

People, folks who knew her, who knew them both, who had known everything about them since the day they were born and their parents had put a conch shell out on the front porch rail to tell everybody about it, waved or bopped the horn as they passed. Crook and Countess—that was what they had called them in high school. You could spend a lifetime feeling rosy and accomplished about such matters. He leaned down and placed his head against the dashboard, caught himself, and jerked back. She pressed deeply into her seat, looking at him. A line of tension showed like a scar along her jaw. He was losing his sense of the elaborated moment. Thought this and said it to her.

"I'm on my way to get some shrimp," she said.

They drove out to the docks on Stock Island and she bought three pounds of pink shrimp and half a dozen dorado fillets.

"Having a party?"

"An impulse."

Jocko Brainard, the counterman, looked at them as he looked at everyone who appeared before him—as if he knew all there was to know.

"You ever go out on the boats, Jocko?" Cot said.

"You asked me that the last time you was in here," Jocko said, pushing against his bad eye with the back of his hand.

"I can't think of anything else to say."

"You used to be real talkative."

"You seen my mother lately?"

"She comes in here about onc't a week."

"When you see her would you tell her I said would she please go up to Aunt Mayrene's?"

"You going to have to tell her that yoself."

"I would, but she won't listen."

Marcella had drifted out the big warehouse-style doors onto the docks. He followed her, and they walked along looking at the high-prowed shrimp boats rusting under their painted skins. "They still go out," Cot said.

"It's like the Japanese growing rice."

"You mean government subsidy making sure a ritualistic jot of rice—the historic symbol of the outfit's once great mythos—is still grown in-country."

"You bet."

"About a washtub full I reckon."

"It's awful. Birds falling out of the sky. Fishes washing up on the beaches—what few fishes there are. Raccoons wandering into the yard coughing like smokers. Manatees sink to the bottoms of ancient springs, never having uttered a single word of protest. Children rock with allergies. Gunmen stagger retching into the undergrowth."

Her voice almost gleeful, the energy, the synthesis, like a mixture turning red to blue, making her happy.

"That's what's happening to you," she said. Brooks Dublin, fat shrimper captain, stood in the door of his wheelhouse looking down the channel where nothing but a few gulls, tough as old prizefighters, wheeled and complained. They both waved at him, but he didn't wave back.

"It's for the best," he said.

"You always know the right thing to say."

"If only that were true."

"Cot—damn." She dashed a single tear—it could have been a tear—off her cheek, quickly, with her finger tips, as if it were a bug. "You're in so much trouble."

"Ah, honey, it's not time yet to bring out the fun-destroying facts."

She skipped a beat into silence. "I apologize."

"Aren't you supposed to be off somewhere lawyer-ing?"

"There was a bomb scare at the courthouse and Judge Tomlane sent everyone home."

"You mean besides the one I called in?"

"So funny."

"I have to find out who robbed CJ."

"It was some men from Fort Lauderdale."

"How do you know?"

"One of those little lawbreakers from up the Keys told on them, Ordell said."

"That's a fact for sure?"

"Mmm."

"So'd Ordell call the authorities?"

"He said he was going to."

They watched a slender sailboat, a sloop, sails furled, a sunbrowned man and woman on deck, come sliding along, easing in against the next dock over. It soothed him to see such a beautiful boat. The man's hair was sun-blond, the woman's too, they could have been twins, familiar gods from another world. He said, "We get so close, just a step away—you'd think we could make it."

"Are you talking about us?"

"Among other things."

"I wish you wouldn't get portentous—is that the word?"

"Dystopian."

"That's not quite it."

Across the water on the far side of the docks: egrets in the jucaro trees, white fuel tanks belonging to the power station next door, and three cars coming down the unpaved street raising dust—something . . . a feeling as if they were moving smoothly into a silent, secret movie, into still pictures, coming over him. A's deadline hours ticking, a whole day gone—and more, was it more?—like fingernails ticking on a hardwood counter, on the stock of an AK-47.

He grabbed her hand, pulling her. "Let's go."

They ran down the docks, cut through an open storage warehouse and out into the power plant grounds where a couple of men on forklifts were moving bales from one place to another.

She hadn't spoken, she had only run with him, her head thrown slightly back as if she was running in a parade, but now she said, "Are you going to tell me anything?"

"Sorry. In a minute."

Around a corner among the huge exposed parts of old transformers and uncoiled spools of wire they stopped.

She said silently *what what what*, and he kissed her, putting his tongue like a sly one into her mouth, wishing it was long as a snake, that he could sink into her guts among the placards and ruby necklaces and the gushes of untainted blood. "What?" she said.

"This guy. This Bert."

"The one you depantsed?"

"The exact same. Plus a couple of recruits."

"Because you stole from them?"

"These islands are dotted with little crosses where they buried treasure." In his business, he had told her, after you pass the tests, they begin to reveal the locations of these X's.

"Does he know the locations too?"

"No."

"That's his real problem, ay?"

"Yeah. Envy."

"It gets in everywhere."

"Like fly eggs."

So they spoke as they sprinted across the big rumpled yard and entered the scrub woods. Immediately the smell of sea rot—grasses and tiny fishes, abandoned mollusk housing, shreds and tatters—fumed up. There was a path, winding, gray with bony coral outcroppings, and they followed this through mixed buttonwood and acacia past a little stream, really only a sally of ocean water diverted into the woodland. The water was orange from the buttonwood roots; tiny snapper fry darted and frisked in cloudy schools, shirking danger. The buttonwoods creaked and swayed in a jittery breeze. He knew there wasn't really anywhere but Coon Channel to get to, but he hoped Bert didn't know that.

Dodging faded fabric trash, broken fish boxes and such, they came to a clearing. Off there the reticulated sea vista: the old channel, ruffled along the back by breeze. She waved flies away from her face. "We're going which way?"

"Swimming."

He was still carrying the shrimp but now he swung it in an arc and sent it sailing into the channel. She made a muffled cry, half laughter, half scooped out of other sorrows. The shrimp hit the water, followed by gulls that began to nip at the plastic bag. "Salt to salt," she said.

"You all right?"

"Don't I look it?"

"Only partly."

She scowled in a familiar way that didn't really reassure him.

They waded into the clear, lightly soughing current. Across the channel a quarter mile off they could see houses poked out from among bushes and palm trees behind a short flat beach. Okay, he said stuffing his flip-flops in the back pockets of his shorts, and they slipped in, not taking time to say good-bye to land or struggle. Behind them nothing at first but halfway across he looked back and saw Bert taking aim. Saw as well the other two abruptly conjured, miscreant experts, one holding his pistol with two hands, the other crouching among refuse carefully drawing a bead. *Pop, pop.*

The shots weren't close, hit the surface like skids, kicking up aught in the sea's big mitt.

They were both strong swimmers, but he kept himself between her and the assailants behind who were not getting into the water, were not shouting or threatening, only taking—Bert was taking—a long last look, a steadying and fixing look, and tucking back into the smelly boondocks.

A bit later they caught a ride out on the highway from Bubsy Mannix, a local woman who'd run off at sixteen to join the rodeo and come back at twenty-five with a permanent limp and witty stories of livestock and cowboys throwing their weight around, now a seller of fruit pies and bakery goods, a woman with pulled-back blonde hair and a cowboy hat hanging behind her head on a string, who stopped by Randy's Imperial Room and picked them up, two sea-damp escapees, and let them off a few minutes later in front of his mother's misaligned house.

Marcella immediately stepped next door and hooked a ride with Delilah Strake, who had her cab parked out front while she sat under the wheel eating a slice of devil's food cake on her break.

"I have to fetch my car," she said as he followed her over.

"I wouldn't do that just yet."

"I'll get somebody from the station to pick it up." Standing under a big flower-filled flamboyant she called the police on Delilah's phone—hers was wet—explained the situation, and they said they would get right on the problem. Problem of Bert and his confederates. He stood in the shade listening to her talk to the police. It was like somebody talking to one of her feckless and amusing former boyfriends.

"They already have a cordon—that's their word—thrown up around Stock Island," she told him.

It's in the paper that night, Internet version: three men, possible assassins, picked up lost in undergrowth and transported to jail. They are all in jail. Cot goes down there, and they let him in to talk to Bert who as usual is sick with regret.

"I don't know what came over me, Cot," he says.

"You mean trying to kill me?"

"Well, that too, yeah. But I mean losing my head about it. I felt so ashamed when you pulled my clothes off."

"It was the quickest thinking I could do at the time."

"You were always a strange quick thinker, Cot."

"So, Spane sent you?"

"Yeah, well, the first time. Before you had me put in jail. The other time was my own. They say you got to show initiative. Big A's awfully mad at you, Cot."

"I'm getting a little worked up myself."

"I mean they told me to leave you alone. At least until four P.M. tomorrow."

"That's what had me confused."

"Yeah, I know. Would you tell Mrs. Bakewell that I'm sorry."

"She already knows you are."

"But if you'd tell her I'm sure it would be a big help. Maybe she'll take the case."

Out the window Cot can hear children shouting. Or maybe they are only childish adults, frolicking. He feels sick to his stomach.

On the cab ride home he stops to pick up some Chinese food at Chee's and then he has Slocumb drive over to the botanical garden to help fetch his mother. As usual she doesn't really want a ride but because it's him she consents. He explains what the trouble is, more or less.

His mother, who was once a heavy woman with a light step and is now headed in the opposite direction, leans her head against the doorpost and closes her eyes. She has spent the afternoon talking to local women about flowering vines and fortune telling and is worn down by human contact. They sat in a circle up in the grassy space on the garden's top terrace. From there the ocean lay spread out flat and fetching, uninflected and blue as a baby's eye. As always—as almost always—Ella thought of her husband. He was probably lying in his same-time-zone bed in the big tile-floored apartment on Castroneves Street thinking about one of his *gráfico* predicaments, about conjurations, fated charmers. Everyone in his books was some better-realized version, some prophesied and never-found version, of himself, even the villains. He would probably get up and fix himself a big jar of tea that he iced with chips struck off the block he bought from the ice man on his rounds. It would be mushy hot on his side of the Gulf Stream and he would rub a small chunk of ice against his forehead. She could see the gleaming streak of water on his pale, half-Scottish skin. "It soothes the little molecules of remembrance," he would say to the air. Her son, this man she had once told never to come around again, was in trouble. She offers a little prayer, by way of her husband who never seems not her husband, and lets it go, like a small bird, out the window. The sky is jammed in the south with clouds, but the clouds have no threat in them. She wishes things like this were a sign—of goodness, of hope. But there are no signs, only imaginings, she's pretty sure of that. *Oh, Rafael.*

She's almost said his name out loud.

They drive up the beach and stop at Christie's market for some mangoes, imported from Mexico. Christie and his two sons are in back drinking pulque around the large table with a few of their customers. His wife Estella waits on her and the two women exchange looks filled, so it seems to Ella, with fealty and an understanding that contains a timeless wisdom. Lord, what we know about this world. And those running around in it. She no longer believes there is much you can do about any of it. Back in the cab she thinks again of her husband, who, when he made the tea, would drink a chilled jar of it standing out on the little back second-floor balcony looking into the courtyard. The feral cats lived out there during the day. Rafael would call to the cats, whistle softly to them as if they were dogs, and the cats would come.

4

That night they all eat over at Marcella's house, feasting on a second batch of shrimp and dorado the police who drove the car home picked up. Jackie's there along with Arthur Haskel's mother and his brother Hauck. Hauck wanders away down the back lane before supper is served, swinging his crippled left hand as he goes. He says he wants to go down to the store and play a round of pool. It's just something he says, everybody knows that. He probably doesn't know what he wants to do, he only has an itch to move. "Come back soon," Marcella says, and Hauck looks at her out of his hooded friendly eyes as if he's afraid of the pressure she's putting on him.

They eat the shrimp on the upper gallery overlooking the big bamboo patches on Chastain Street. As children he and Marcella ran up and down that dark street waving sparklers. The streetlight on the corner has been put out, and Cot wonders about that and then he doesn't wonder, and he gets up and goes down the outside stairs, around the house and slinks along the big silvertop bushes—

careful not to step in the drained fishpond where twenty-five years ago Marcella's father burned his law books—until he gets under the big poinciana that belongs to the pie-maker, Frank Bacon. When Cot was a boy Mr. Bacon's place smelled of baking pies, but no longer. Now the pies—fruit and custard—are mostly baked in a facility up in Marathon. Over behind the wall of the Church of Holiness grounds children at play shout. It's dark, but they don't want to go home yet, that's clear. A car, sputtering and backfiring, passes: Donnie Cantrell on his way home to explain himself to his wife. Tourists on bicycles, their tiny LED lights blinking, wobble by, moving in a slow motion that must be a feature of the tropic dream they have purchased for themselves. Right after them he sees a figure enter the street, pause, then slip so quickly it's as if it wasn't there, between two dilapidated sheds beside the old Terrence house. A familiar buzzing sets to in his head.

He crouches and angles around to the other side of the pie-man's yard and through a gate that opens into a little fenced-off area where the Hertzels next door used to keep chickens in the days before local poultry became ornamental and consigned to the streets. In a minute the somebody—a man moving fast, carrying something like a long valise—crosses the street and enters a vacant lot. Cot slips around to the right, easing in among and out of big hibiscus bushes massively flowering, and comes around the side of the dark and shuttered tourist house across the street. He waits in the shadow of the tourist house. Crouched in the lot among stacks of loose bricks and boards, the man, darkly clothed, is working on a small, bulky piece of equipment on the ground.

Cot can barely make it out then barely believe what it is: a sniper rifle.

He takes three quick steps into the lot and with the pistol, Bert's pistol, shoots the man once in the head. The sound of the shot is loud, but it is only one shot and a single shot you can always just wonder about and let go. He leaves the man where he falls, a stocky man in a dark shirt, someone he doesn't know. He takes the half-assembled rifle in his hands—for a sec marveling at its compact uncomplicated shape—jams it between two large coral stone boulders, bends the barrel sideways and tosses the rifle into the bushes and shakes the .308 ammo out of its little cartridge holder and flings it into the bushes too. The ammo makes a rustling sound like lizards moving among the leaves as it hits. From where he stands he can see the lights of Marcella's balcony through the still-bare branches of the big mahogany trees behind the pie-maker's.

They're all enjoying themselves, drinking rum drinks and watching a Cuban comedy show flown in each week to Miami. His mother and Marcella look up at him from the couch where they sit side by side, and they both get up at the same time and come to him. Marcella's mother pays no attention. The two women—still his favorites—touch him lightly, brushing little special places that maybe seem out of synch or stained, their hands just reaching him as he crosses the room and goes out on the darkened second-floor gallery with the women following. A throbbing presence inside urges him to keep going, keep moving, even if movement is only a small and futile agitation, but he makes himself stop. Above the yard bats stitch up the night. His mother sits down in one of the big armchairs. Marcella, letting the skirts she has gathered up to run after him fall, pushes unrestrained straight into him in the old way, as if she is setting off on a walk right through and all along the byways of his body. He catches her and gently holds her off. He remembers where he is. "We need more firepower," he says and laughs and looks out into the yard that seems to be disappearing in fog.

"We're all right," Marcella says and runs her hand over his, picking lightly at the skin.

"No. We're not."

"Ordell has the police on alert."

"Concerning what?"

"Marauders in the neighborhood."

"I didn't see any cruisers."

"They're around."

He never really trusts letting others take care of things. He doesn't especially believe in his own ability to manage, but it's familiar and he believes in possibility, in increments adding up if you conduct the affair deeply enough in the shadows and keep at it. Or has. Even this is slipping away. What he believes in now, in this moment—*a sniper?*—has become tatters and figments, outlines drifting like ghosts above where the body'd been.

They bolted the doors and he put Jackie downstairs on a mattress pulled out of a spare bedroom (Arthur's mother slipped out as soon as she got a good look at Cot). He himself simply stayed awake walking around the house in the dark. The clamminess, the polluted sweat, was still on him. His insides shivered and sloshed. If anybody was coming it would be in the blank precedence before dawn. But you couldn't be sure. The house still smelled of rosewood and cinnamon and of bay leaves crumpled in jars as it had when he was a child and Marcella's father, the old padrone, roved the premises giving orders no one minded. He had been knocked dead of a heart attack when Marcella was thirteen. She'd found him on his knees, bent over the bed, his pants around his ankles. And she had taken the time to rearrange him before she called her mother.

For a while she stayed awake with him. He didn't tell her about the sniper, but he talked to her of his crime, of CJ, of the emeralds glittering somewhere, elsewhere, out on the earth, glowing he said like little lit furnaces left over from worlds so long forgotten no one remembered there had ever been such worlds, and, as if answering a question, she said *chain of being* which was a phrase they had gotten stuck on in high school the year before he left for Miami, and they laughed at this and then on the couch in her old bedroom where they had made love for the first time they made love in their rude and troubled fashion, bumping and shoving as if in a locked trunk they were trying to get out of, and she said, only a moment afterwards, that it was the one thousand four hundredth time, a number she made up afresh each time, high or low, depending on how she felt about him, about things in general, and then he walked around the house and sat a while on one of the creaky bamboo couches on the upper gallery, and got up again and walked around the gallery as well, and sat on the glider that he was careful not to set in rusty motion and watched the dawn stumble eventually to its feet out of the ocean's basements beyond the scattered and brushy islands to the east.

When the sun is up finally over the horizon he walks to South Beach and swims for half an hour. There's a slimy mess of seaweed on the rough slab-coral beach, and tourists are out at the old hotel next door talking about it. It's only sea lettuce, and every year around this time there are expected vagaries in the water, but it doesn't look appetizing this dank vegetable wallow and smells bad. The hotel's been freshly painted and looks like a vision of the tropics that anyone would go for. Blinky Borden, the proprietor, comes out as Cot starts up the street and he goes in and they have coffee on the hotel's big back porch. Blinky wants to know how things are between Ordell and Marcella.

"Nothing much I can tell you about that."

Blinky like so many others has been in love with Marcella all his life, but he's never made much headway. It makes him feel good, makes him feel as if he's in the mix and important, to talk about her. Cot sees this. He doesn't mind. Somehow it makes him feel connected to the world, up to something like everybody else, a cohort and celebrant among the multitudes, and this soothes him a little as it's going on, even if it doesn't later. After a while he excuses himself and walks back to the old house. Nobody's there. He runs around the rooms, coldly angry, shouting under his breath, but everybody's gone. The cars are gone. He calls Ordell, and *he* says he doesn't know where they are. He has already pulled the police detail off the job. "Were they ever on it?" Cot says. Ordell's voice sounds weak and Cot wonders if he's been crying. "I'm sorry," Cot says. This is the day he's supposed to produce the emeralds. He doesn't have a clue where they might be, but, as he understands it, he has until late this afternoon before his time's up. He calls Spane on a cell he found on the kitchen counter, first time doesn't get him, but the next, five seconds later, he does. Spane says he'll check on the time. "I'm on my way after them now," Cot says. Just outside the window a bird in a little red vest dawdles in a skinny lime tree. High up Cot can see clouds lined up in dots and stripes as if they're about to become messages. No special telegraph of the astral needed here, thanks. He goes outside and stands in the big yard, one of the last big yards on the island. The sun sprawls yellow and helpless on the meager grass. The big flamboyants on the street side take the breeze in their arms and fling it back, gently, as if the breeze is a bully charmed into sweetness. Cot sits down in one of the white-painted cast-iron chairs under a little pollarded orange tree. The fruit is green and small in the branches. He thinks about where Marcella and his mother might have gone but can't get a reading. Then the phone rings.

A man whose voice sounds vaguely familiar tells him *they*—"Who's they?" Cot says but the man ignores him—are *keeping everybody*—"Who's everybody?" Cot says but the man goes right on over his asking—and the detainees will be *okay, returned to him*—as if he is speaking of lost pocketbooks—when he delivers the emeralds to the mailbox of a house on Scooter Lane up the Keys at Summerford. "You know where that is?" the man says. Cot knows. "You get 'em there by twilight time and everything'll be jim-dandy."

"That the beginning of twilight or do I have all the way to the end?"

"What's that?"

"Twilight lasts a while. Do I have . . ."

"Just bring the fucking stones."

"Okay," Cot says.

"What'd you say?"

"Okay. I'll get them there."

"I thought you didn't know where they were?"

"Who is this? This you, Solange?" Solange worked for Albertson on the administrative side.

But whoever it is, is gone.

He leaves the shade and stands in the full sunshine of the new day shaking. The yard—a corner lot—opens on two sides onto the street. A string of tourists on pink and yellow bicycles pedal orderly by, parents and three young children, dressed up. Natty gray mockingbirds tumble in the big grapefruit tree at the edge of the old, now unused, driveway. Cot tries to redial the caller, but the number's private, not available. He takes Marcella's car that's still in the new garage beside her mother's aged Buick and drives to the police station. Everybody there knows a little something about the CJ affair, but nobody has a really good idea of what to do. "You see," the chief is saying into a cell phone as Cot waits to talk to him, "the only thing you got backing up a hustler is neediness and a yearning for unearned pleasures." He winks at Cot. "He falls apart in a minute."

"Well, nada on top of nada on that one," the chief says to Cot concerning the Cross Dresser Killers as he calls them. Under his right eye he has a small scab from a skin cancer excision that moves as he smiles.

They haven't yet found the body over in the vacant lot.

Cot sits on the station front steps running down the possibilities. Each is fey and shaky, thin, bubbles coming through milky surfaces. Buzzards circle high above the parking lot next door, taking their time. A man in red shorts chases a little boy around the lot and appears unable to catch him. In one of those little abrupt clicks in time Cot can't remember where he is, who he is, which world he's in. Then everything snaps back into place, same old arrangement. What he's done is carved into tablets leaned against a rough stone wall, letters and florid phraseology shining in a dusty murk. You can't miss what the words say.

He goes around to Ordell's office but Ordell isn't in. His secretary says he's taken a leave of absence. He finds the sheriff and asks him about this but the sheriff says there isn't much he can tell him. What about CJ's case? With a silver penknife the sheriff carefully peels a small guava into an ashtray as they talk. He looks at Cot as if he doesn't know what he's referring to. Maybe they *are* in an alternate universe, some place where just now a big poinciana waves its massed orange flowers in the window and a flock of gulls fresh in from sea duty peck at a dead chicken on the sidewalk.

"None of y'all got the heads-up, ay?" Cot says.

"CJ?" the sheriff says again, touching his lower lip with the blade of the penknife.

Maybe it was you, Cot wants to say. *Maybe you did it*. In a moment of blind slippage, of modal disharmony, this traveling second of spiritual beggary, everybody looks guilty. *That's how it gets*, he thinks, *when you won't face up to your business*.

He goes around to Jonny Day's on Front Street and sits in a window seat drinking salted coffee and tapping into a rented computer. He tries one or two of CJ's social pages, but everybody there is in mourning, baffled and without a clue (though some make raging, preposterous claims). He calls Tommy in Miami and asks him to find out what he can about an arrest in Lauderdale. Killers under lock and key for a Key West murder. Tommy says he'll get back to him. Bert passes on the sidewalk and Cot goes out to meet him.

"We probably shouldn't be talking," Bert says, wincing. He wears a straw cowboy hat with a feather crest.

"Haven't you lost weight?" Cot says.

Bert grins. "If I have, it's from worry."

"You know anything about a kidnapping?"

"You into that too?"

"Not me—my family."

"Your family's kidnapping people?"

"No."

"I get it."

"They're gone and somebody called a while ago and said he had them."

"Probably Willie Rollins."

"He's back in town?"

"Got in last night."

"Where's he staying?"

Over at the Sea Farm as it turns out. Bert says he doesn't know anything about Willie fronting a kidnapping, but Cot drives Marcella's car up there anyway. Before he leaves he goes around to the house and packs a few things for Marcella in a bag. Then he goes around to his mother's house to get a few of her things. A street crew is digging up the pavement; the undersoil, a white, jagged marl, looks like the fossilized innards of a huge dessicated body. The men, powdered with white dust, stand in the street drinking Cuban coffee from tiny paper cups. Jackie's up under the house sleeping on a lounger. Cot wakes him up. "I thought you were kidnapped."

"Not me. Not by a long shot." He'd left early and come back over to the house. "I can't get no sleep in a strange bed."

Cot tells him what's happened. Tears fill Jackie's big wide-set eyes. Gray eyes that always looked cloudy—Cot remembers it. Jackie, who used to play small forward on the high school basketball team when Cot was a boy, who said he was leaving for New York to start a singing career. He'd returned a year later riding luggageless in the back of a pickup truck. "How could that—a kidnapping you say? How could it?"

"The usual reasons. You don't know about it?"

"When I left they were all sleeping like babies."

He has half stood up to talk and then sunk back down on the lounger, an orange plastic affair, but now he leaps bent over to his feet, articulating a small series of gyrations and spins, all in slow motion like an old basketball player driving through a transfixed crowd to the basket; it's pitiful to see, sad, sure, but Cot's thinking as he watches that it's a pure act of true love for such a tall man to live under four-foot ceilings. "I got to go," Jackie says.

"You want to ride up to Summerford with me?"

Jackie doesn't want to, but he says he will. They stop

at the Bangladeshi's for Jackie to run in and get a beer. Cot gets out and peers into one of the art papers he pulls from a box at the curb. Delphine Curtis has won another beauty prize, in her forties still racking them up. Bill Butler is running something called the Improvisational Fisherman's Crew. Dottie Harris heads up the Mosquito Control that, so an article says, is being overrun by criticism of their handling of the latest dengue fever crisis. All the old tropical diseases are back. You don't need to go to Africa anymore to catch them. He wonders where Jackie is. The Bangladeshi, a new man, short, in heavy frame glasses, says he's just stepped out the back. Cot finds him sitting on a crate drinking his beer.

"I can't go," he says. His eyes are baffled, a man looking for the key to the lamentation closet.

"That's all right, bro."

He drives through the morning traffic that's still heavy, past the Naval air station and all the way to Big Coppitt. Jets pour out of the Navy confines, rising into the cloudless south. A nervousness is in him. He calls Tommy again but he can't get him. Maybe he's sitting on his little hotel balcony watching the tankers out in the roads waiting for their turn to enter Government Cut. He tries Ordell again, but Ordell isn't answering. Two boys in cutoff jeans and dusty-looking T-shirts wait at the turning beyond the Snapper Channel bridge for a bus. They say sure they wouldn't mind earning twenty bucks. Apiece? Yeah. Cot buys a warmed-up pizza at Harry's. He drives to Cuthbert and turns west on the old road that runs through the pine woods.

He parks down the road from the Sea Farm in some bushes and walks up through the woods. The farm's a former fishing camp that became a county park and then, during the recession, went back to being a camp, this time for general touristic purposes. It has ten solidly built pineboard cabins in side-by-side semicircles behind a double set of docks. Cot sends the boys to deliver the pizza. They get the number from a cabin that has OF-FICE painted on a small wooden sign by the door. An old woman in shorts and a flowery halter gives it to them. One of the boys, tall and slope-shouldered, indicates with his head where the cabin is and the two of them stroll down to it, the shorter boy carrying the pizza box on his fingertips like a waiter. Cot follows after, sneaking along behind the cabins. The bay is still as glass, only a few pelicans, just returned from their winter roosts in South America, sailing low over the water. One of the pelicans rises into the air and drops, suddenly, as if its strings have been cut, plunges headfirst into the drink—thunk!—and comes up with nothing. Unperturbed, it climbs into the air and rows off toward the west. Cot comes sneaking along the cabin row. Big ficus bushes separate the cabins from one another. A man he only knows by sight sits out on the back deck of the one they are headed to. Cot gets close and waits until he hears the boys knock on the front door. The man, heavy with thick hairless forearms, turns his head and gets up. As he does Cot swings onto the deck and before the man can react gets a gun on him. The man makes a face, as if he smells something unpleasant. Cot puts a finger to his mouth. He smiles and comes close to the man who's looking steadily at him out of black, intelligent eyes. Cot walks the man through the sliding glass back doors into a combination kitchen and living room that has a door off to the side. A skinny man in a purple stained shirt is watching a boy with long peroxided blond hair deal with the pizza. Nobody else is in the room. The skinny man turns, dragging a pistol out of a shoulder holster, and Cot shoots him. As the man crumples the blond boy sags and goes to his knees, the pizza sliding out of his hands to the floor. Cot calls for Marcella.

"They have us locked up in here."

"Anybody with you?"

"I'm here," Willie Rollins says. "Fully armed."

"Shit, Willie. Come on out."

"No thanks."

The pizza boys have hightailed it.

A momentary paralysis, stasis, stagnation like cloud shadow stalled upon the surface of an inlet, comes over them. Time falls unchallenged through ten thousand years of struggle and stubbornness. The heavyset man grins savagely at him. *I should ask him to dance. I should ask how his mother is. She probably died in a terrible way and it hurts to think about it.* Cot whips the pistol across his face. The man goes down backwards and hits his head on the floor. The fall makes a big noise, slightly crackling, as if his head has broken wood. The floor is pale blue tile. Maybe laid over wood, Cot thinks.

"Y'all fighting?" Willie calls.

"Dancing," Cot says.

"Who'd you shoot? It better not be Brooks. Brooks!" Willie cries. Brooks is the blond boy, gunless it looks like, Willie's brother from Okeechobee, Cot recognizes him, little birdie flown down to the Keys, shivering now.

"I'll trade you Brooks for the crew in there."

"You doing all right, Brooks?" Willie says.

"I'm fine," Brooks says smiling foolishly, "as long as he don't slap me with his pistol."

" 'D'jou hit him?" Willie says.

"That was Coover stubbing his toe."

"Let me think a minute," Willie says.

"You faithless shit," Brooks says in a loud reedy voice. "Come the damn on."

Another moment of near quiet, only the damp complaining of gulls out over the water, the sound of Brooks's toe scuffing at the pizza box on the floor. *We are surrounded by an ancient world and all of time.* "Mind if I dig out a slice?" Brooks says.

Cot watches him scoop a slice, fold it in half and start to eat.

"Everybody okay in there?" Cot says.

"I'm still thinking," Willie says.

"I mean my party."

"We're still healthy," Marcella says.

"You okay, Mama?"

"Pretty nearly," his mother says in a quiet, firm voice. She has a faint, only slightly Cuban accent, developed, she says, in honor of his father, a memorial, or homage, sustained, more or less, since his early childhood. Sometimes in dreams as a child he remembered her speaking in another accent, rich and sea-blown, an island tone, clement and knowing, sun deepened. It sounded good on her, Cot thinks, the dream accent, overtaken suddenly by a dense and knowing nostalgia, as if a truth has come clear though it has not, tears springing to his eyes.

"He's out here crying," Brooks, the blond, says.

"You got scorpion tendencies," Cot says and looks the boy in the face. A twitch of anger. He could crack him across the skull too.

The boy sees this and chokes on a mouthful of pizza. He tries to get the dough out of his throat but can't, smothering.

"You all right?" Willie calls. *Maybe he knows even the sound of his brother choking.* As Cot crosses the room, stepping over the still out-for-the-count figure of Coover Miller, he wonders about the sort of closeness that could make that possible. Is it what we're supposed to yearn for, tightness like that? Albertson runs the Harvard of gangs, he once said to Marcella, meaning, he tried to get across to her after she slapped him, a home, a refuge, a *querencia*, but she snorted in the way she did and sneered, saying it was not a *home* he wanted but a pinnacle.

"I got you, buddy," he says to the blond boy who's bent double on his knees gagging and trying futilely to hit himself on the back. Cot straightens him up, wraps his arms around him from behind and squeezes. A muffled, half croupy sound. Cot squeezes again, harder. *Crush.* The dough, a surprisingly small wad, ejects from his mouth in a pretty arc and hits the baseboard at the bottom of the wall. The boy lurches to his feet and away, and stands, bent over again, puking.

"What'd you do?" Willie says, his voice easing down a register.

"Pizza went down the wrong way."

"Y'all got pizza?"

In another minute Willie comes out with his pistol at his side. He flips the gun and slides it across the floor at Cot. It catches on a tile, spins, and comes to rest against the leg of a chair. Cot makes him pick it up and drop it out the front window.

"I never had much confidence in none of this anyway," Willie says smiling amiably.

They head down the Overseas Highway to Jimmy Lawrence's airport on Sunset Key. Jimmy, so says his wife, a short freckle-faced woman, is down at the dock. "The other dock," she calls when Cot starts toward the plane, tied up at a short square platform bobbing just the other side of a stand of casuarina trees. He walks down the little coral path and finds Jimmy standing among tick runner vines casting a line in—after grunts, he says. He says he doesn't know if he will ever want to go flying again. Jimmy gets that way. It usually isn't difficult to make him change his mind, but this time a wariness, a sense of the futile and ineffective, has settled on him. It's part of life, Cot thinks, to from time to time feel betrayed by your heart's delight. But Jimmy looks off from Cot in a lying way, his gaze off-loading misery. *He's been reached.* "I'll give you a gemstone when I get my stash back."

"I can't do business on promises. Especially with the shape I'm in."

"That how you get when you cross-run your friends."

"Shit, Cot."

"I got to carry my mother up to the mainland."

"I just don't feel like it."

Cot doesn't want to do it, but he doesn't think he has a choice. "Jimmy," he says, "I could put a gun on you—and maybe I should, you weasel—"

"Cot, I got to live—"

"Okay—or I could beat you. Or I could tell Doris about that time up in Homestead. But I won't."

Jimmy looks out at the bay snapping and clicking with light under a fresh breeze, little rips showing the white underneath. The islands like beginners too small to make much of themselves lie shaggy with green life in the stupefying sun. "You don't even have to mention such a thing," he says.

"I know and I'm sorry."

"It really bothers me that you would."

"I'm sorry."

"Sorry doesn't really cut it."

"The Christian thing would be to forgive me."

"Now you're trying to use the church against me. Nothing after that but a gun." Jimmy's puffed up now and high on his righteousness. "It doesn't become you, Cot."

Cot feels latches and loosened hinges give, just slightly. "I need your help here."

Jimmy lets a moment of silence fume up between them. The jointed needles of the casuarinas whistle softly in the background's breeze. "Okay."

Jackie—who is again a member of the crew—who has thrown up out the window on the ride up from KW—helps Jimmy gas up and generally prepare the plane. He isn't coming, he says, and he is both sad and glad about it. "I can't be of any real help," he says. "I want to make that clear from the beginning."

"You've been awfully good company and I'm sure grateful for that," Ella says.

Marcella says she isn't coming either.

"Well, damnation, May."

"I'm an officer of the court," she says, ducking her head as she speaks. "I can't be riding around the skies with a fugitive."

"I just saved you from the damn fugitives."

She's pulling Coca Colas out of a big ice chest as she speaks—ice slivers crusted to her hands, fingers wet so they gleam in the tropic light—and carries on a conversation with Doris who wants to know where she does her shopping when she goes up to Miami. Cot's uncomfortable talking to her with Doris there. "Let's walk outside," he says.

"That won't change anything."

He knows she's scared of flying, especially scared of flying in planes where she knows the pilot. *I picture his inadequacies*, she once said to him.

"I think I can get the stones back."

"Those emeralds? What did you want with them in the first place?"

"I thought I told you." The wind skips across the tops of some mangroves up the shore, picking at leaves and letting them go. She's dressed in black rodeo clothes with bits of orange highlights here and there like a cowgirl villainess.

"You didn't tell me anything that I can remember."

"I wanted to pay Mama's house out of hock to the city. I still plan to do it."

"If you didn't give all your money away at the horse races you'd have a little."

"I know that already. I don't have to be shamed by you to know it."

"I'm not the one shaming you."

He wishes his whole life could simply stop—so he could sneak around behind it, work on it and if he couldn't fix it escape out the back. "My appetite," he says as old desires crawl on his skin, spiral up from the inside, circle his heart like an abashed tribe that's lost everything, and he can't remember what he wanted to say.

"Appetite?"

"Agreed. Yeah. Foolishness. I still need you to come with me. And I expect—I'm sorry, sweetie—I expect Albertson'll look at you as a part of all this."

She squinches up her face in aggravation, in sadness, in several other load-bearing ways, but says only, "Yes, I guess so. Maybe so." She looks out at the bay where the breeze is chopping bits of light off the wave tops. "I keep meaning to say good-bye to you, but I forget."

He laughs his crackly, off-key laugh, his jokey, shamed laugh.

She says "I wasn't saying it to be funny," and turns away leaving the words like tiny signals or remnants cast aside as one walks off down a path. He can tell something else is on her mind, maybe Ordell, maybe the whole rattled beadbasket of her life, the one with him. "All right," he says, knowing anyway—by osmosis, telepathy, by spirit consciousness or the cast of her eyes, by her face and the movements of her body, by guesswork or deduction, by the tiny, loosely shaped stillness in her—that she's already agreed.

The pilot—wearing a Cincinnati baseball cap and rally gloves—hurries everybody along as if it's been his project from the start, which is his way. Cot and Jackie haul a small ice chest and some clothes stuffed in plastic bags and put them on the plane. Jimmy skips along behind jotting a flight plan in his little blue book as he comes. "Where we going?" he calls to Cot who stands on the dock looking vaguely out at the water.

"Anywhere you like—no, how about Madeira, or Joe Bay?"

"Okay, I got you. But where *are* we going? Just so I'll know. We going to the mainland, or just up the islands?"

"The mainland. West side." Naples, he thinks—where they can catch a bus up to Fort Myers—but he's feeling vague, feeble, and doesn't want to say. "We need to get there in a hurry, if you don't mind."

And sure enough Marcella comes along too, and Jackie who wouldn't desert his mother, and his mother who has her own reasons; they troop up the steps, enter the cabin, and settle in.

As the plane lifts smoothly off the light chop, the sound of the rushing water ending as if they have flown off the edge of the world, he sees from his seat in the copilot's chair a boat veer out from behind a small, tousled island in the bay. They're going to be too late, he thinks, but he doesn't say anything. The plane rises, climbing steadily as the little white boat comes on at high speed. A man gets up in the bow and raises a small machine gun. "Better turn," Cot says.

"What's that?" Jimmy says looking up from the dials in front of him. "You know them?"

"Just barely."

As the plane comes suddenly upon them the man in the bow opens up with the machine gun. A string of holes smack through the bottom of the plane and into the cabin. One of the bullets catches Jimmy under the chin. He sits back in his chair with his eyes suddenly red and bulging in his head, still pulling on the wheel. Cot can see he's dead. The plane starts to slip to the right but Cot straightens it out with his wheel and continues with the take-off, already almost complete. He calls out, a sudden grief saturating his voice, asking if anybody's hurt. The answer comes back in bleats and shouts that they are all right. He glances back at Marcella; she's gnawing at the inside of her left cheek, looking out the window, but not down, just out.

They are up high by now, rising into the clear blue sky. Behind them the man with the gun stands in the boat watching them go. There's blood on Jimmy's chin and dribbled down the front of his white shirt, but not much. Marcella gets up and squats behind them. "Ah, Cot, look at Jimmy." She sinks back but immediately re-appears, her head and shoulders beside him. "Poor oh nos," she says in a thin, whistling voice. She looks past Cot's face. "Can you fly this?"

"Sure. Sure." Thinking: *about half.*

"I know *all* your shortcomings. I don't even *have* to imagine them."

"Don't fall to pieces."

"I'm not."

He can get them to the mainland—he figures he can—well enough. He tests the pedals and the plane slides sideways, to the left. "It's kind of loose," he says.

Marcella disappears and comes back with a beach towel she folds up partially under Jimmy's head against the side window and laps over his head. The towel is one with a big color map of Florida printed on it.

"Now we won't lose our way," he says, but she doesn't get it and he waves the words off.

Ella comes up and looks at the situation. She smiles at her son, there isn't much else to do. "We're okay back here," she says, meaning she and Jackie who's crying mutely into a large blue bandana. He raises his head. "I knew I never should have left home."

"You're doing fine," Ella says.

Cot turns the wheel to the right, pressing slightly on the left pedal as he pulls back a little on the throttle. He's scared but as he pets his fright he senses a clear space opening inside him. He returns the wheel to a steady position and holds his feet quiet on the pedals. The plane levels out and then they are flying north toward the Florida coast. They have a hundred-mile-wide stretch of coast to set as their mark so they should be able to grope their way to it all right. Down in Colombia he has done a little cub flying—taking off, setting down under Johnny Cutler's steady hand, handling the stick in clear weather—a piecemeal, jokey apprenticeship, only a pastime with him, it'll have to serve. His hands are shaking so the plane jigs slightly, and he forces his hands to stop and then he's calm again or half calm and even though he really wants to bring the plane down low enough so he can jump out he makes himself sit steady, feeling the panic heaving and gushing under him, and smiles.

"Would you get me a Coke?" he says to Marcella.

He can tell Marcella wants to sit beside him but neither of them want to deal with Jimmy. I don't want to, Cot thinks, and then he does.

"Can you move him?" he says. Marcella ignores him,

gets the drink, opens it, sets it on the console. "Can you move him to the back?" he says.

She asks Jackie to help but he won't. He looks steadily out the window where little green islands float like bobbers in the wide clear bay. The water is so shallow it looks like tapwater running over a sandy brown floor. In the channels the water is blue. Farther out in the deeper channels it's a stronger, steadier blue, but then abruptly it's shallow again. You can see the pleats and patterning of the sand. It'll be like that most of the way across.

Marcella and Ella manhandle Jimmy to the back, prop him half–lying down on the back bench and cover him with the Florida beach towel. The arrangement looks not like respect for a dead man but a poor game Jimmy's involved in. His face is under Daytona Beach where a woman rides a surfboard over a high-curling wave.

Marcella slides in beside Cot. "When I'm with you I get stretched pretty quick way out past where I intended to go."

"That's good, isn't it?"

"Only rarely. And then only briefly." She hooks a straggle of black hair away from her face. Her wide forehead is clear, unmarked by trouble. Only around her eyes, netted in fretting lines of capture, can you tell living's getting to her.

"I never met anybody as worried as you," he says now.

"I have cause."

"That you do. How's Ordell?"

"Weirdly evasive."

"About what?"

"In general—and particularly—about all this business."

"Us?"

"CJ—and those gems."

"You told him?"

"I had to. He didn't seem very surprised. He said he knew it was some foolishness."

"I wanted to pay Mama out of trouble."

"You said that." She looks out the window. "How high are we?"

He studies the dials: RPM, Torque, Oil Pressure, Fuel Flow—he understands Air Speed, Fuel Quantity—ah, there: "1200 feet."

"I'd feel safer if it was . . . maybe four feet."

"We're going eighty-five miles an hour."

"Who were those people?"

"Poachers."

"Tell me. The ones firing guns at us."

"There was only one shooting." He knows him. Buster Brane, originally from Tampa, son of a cigar roller, ex-semi-pro ballplayer, now an Albertson machine gun artist who lives at the Tradewinds Hotel out at the beach and likes to sit out front with the old folks on his days off and make remarks about the tourists. "I don't know. For sure."

"Who maybe?"

"Don't pressure me."

"Pressure you? For Christ sake, Cotland. All the

hoodlums in Miami are after you, and you don't know who they are?"

"Why are you talking this way? I told you Albertson was after me."

She slumps in the seat. "This paradise," she says.

"Don't pity yourself."

"I can express an opinion."

"You're my panacea. *Mi querida.* That's what I meant to say."

"When?"

"Just now. Every time I look at you."

"You probably can't see how disappointing that is." She has always loved his dash, his stubbornness even, his hesitancy most, but not his tendency to see her as saving him. "I can't," she says.

He looks at her as if he understands. "I know." But she knows he doesn't, not quite.

They fly over the tip of Summerford and over the kidnap camp. It looks deserted. The crew already on the way back to Miami. The land dribbles out into the bay, the scrub pines giving way to buttonwood scrawl and wax myrtle bushes, then to mangrove. The original flora has never been anything much. Even the Indians probably hadn't been proud of it. Once there'd been a little topsoil, just enough for sweet potatoes, peppers, melons, other truck crops that could grow between the cracks in the rock, but storms scoured it off the coral bed. His mother used to plant tomatoes and bell peppers in buckets on the front porch. Like a country person, his father said. She wanted him to let her cut down one of the big trees in the backyard to put in a garden but he had shrunk at the possibility. After he returned to Cuba she could have done it, but she didn't have the heart to then.

The view opens up to the north, clear skied all the way. There's hardly any breeze over the water. He laughs out loud.

"What?"

"I thought I'd come down here and . . . well . . ." He doesn't finish the thought.

"Lord, and you were born here."

"Hilarious, ain't it?"

The fuel is draining too fast. He touches the black-faced dial, lets his fingers rest on the glass. Brane must have hit one of the tanks. She looks at him, her blue eyes more smokey than blue, just right, for him, he's always thought, just his color. "What is it?"

"Nothing. I'm just plotting."

"A course. Or an escape?"

"Is there any difference?"

She leans in and kisses his cheek. Her lips are thin but soft. Her breath smells of oranges. "You're scared," she says.

"That's not unusual."

"What is it?"

"If you haven't noticed yet I can't explain it."

He glances back. His mother is reading one of her books, her pamphlet of stirring passages, Marcus Aurelius, Thomas Browne, and the like. She doesn't look frightened. Jackie has his head leaned against a rolled-up shirt pressed against the window, pretending to himself that he's asleep. "It's going to be all right," Cot says, the words passed back like stale snacks.

"For everybody but Jimmy," Jackie says without opening his eyes. "For everybody but us," he adds more softly.

"You were always the brainy one," his mother says smiling her slightly off-center smile, the one where you can't tell exactly what she's thinking but have hopes, and drops her gaze into the remarks of the great. Time was he would have spoken sharply to her, time was he would have blamed her for his father leaving, for predicaments raised like corpses from a marly deep, time was the savagery between them was like a sickness in them both, their words cutting and forced in like knives, but now there are only slurs and asides, quirky bits the other can only half make out. They go by feel, by memorization, by heartbeat. It's getting late, he thinks to resolve things. He's been thinking this for years. Sometimes you wake up and what's capsized has righted itself. Sometimes the other way around. Hope like grease on your hands if you even can bear to hope. *What a crock.* Nobody can ever tell for sure what's coming, he's sure of that.

Then the big islands are behind them, trailing off to the right, hazy in the morning sunlight. The bay is clear mostly, little islet stubs every few miles, then these peter out and they're over open water. Nobody talks much. Cot holds the plane steady. After a while he can make out the mainland, a thin yellowed strip ahead, then, soon enough, the shapes of the swamp, humped trees pushing up out of the grass. The fuel is still draining, but maybe they'll make it. He turns toward Chokoloskee, toward Naples and the highway north, the plane sliding, sinking and rising again in a mushy, reluctant way, and leveling out.

As they fly over the first of a string of coastal islands the engine begins to cough. He jiggles the fuel switch, tips the wings and the engine fully catches again, but they're losing altitude. He doesn't want to say anything about it, but the look in Marcella's face makes him. "We're going to have to set down."

"Lord God," Jackie says, pressing his hands flat against the ceiling. "I'm like a crab stuck in a shell."

Cot looks at Marcella. She smiles like somebody with nothing else to offer. He smiles back, but he can feel the skin of his face tight as if it won't go along. She told him once that he had the face and body of a squat man who got stretched. He's taking the plane down. The engine keeps running, whacking and kicking a little. He knows to keep the nose up. Then they're right over the water. The country looks deserted off to the right. A few tall native palms stick up out of scrub, a few big trees front a shallow bay below a beach and a large, listing, empty-windowed house. They're a hundred yards out. The plane seems to be settling, drifting down, time inside the cabin holding back, expanding into an apartness and stasis that seems filled with a quiet movement of some other section of him, even as he watches the water, black as pitch, stained by roots, rush along beneath them.

Then they hit and then they are skiing across the flats. He pulled up with one hand on the wheel and one on the yoke just as they hit. He presses back in his seat hard and he can see Marcella out of the corner of his eye pressing back too. He can hear Jackie moaning. The plane continues in a straight line, slowing as it goes, and then, without his hands moving the wheel, turns slowly all the way around so they are facing the stretch of ocean already passed through, and comes back to itself, and stops. They rock like a baby in the waters.

An instant of faintness gives way to exhilaration. He yells. Marcella leans over and presses her face into his chest. His mother bangs on the back of his seat; he can't tell at first whether in anger or relief. It's relief. He leans forward and presses his head against the dash. *Half saved, maybe more than half.* On a re-dump into the deep—the shallows, little numbers in his head spinning by as he thinks this, rushing over cliffs and plunging into the dark, numbers of the dead he knows them as.

Passing it along through the shallows they're able to hand-walk the plane in to shore, to a little hump-backed leafy island with a broken-down house on it.

5

Spane drove back from Channel Haven Gardens where through his big Nikon Monarchs he'd watched transient birds just returned to the trees—redstarts and warblers, even an oriole—and had lunch at Sappy's with Albertson who was trying to pin back a waitress's ears with complicated repartee when he walked in. Albertson was scary and he was tall and massive like Spane, but he was no good at repartee; he was too concentrated. The waitress as she veered toward the kitchen was laughing at him, something Spane hoped Albertson didn't notice. "So where is he?"

"Trying to scrap his way out of the Keys."

"Shit. I'd a'been in California by now."

"Not Cot. He always thinks he can fix things."

Albertson laughed his croaky, sharp-witted laugh. "For a smart boy, he's awfully stupid."

"Persistent though."

Albertson had a big shovel face and sharp black eyes placed a little too close together like an athlete's. Spane was thinking about Cot. He'd started on the run finally. But there was no telling what he was really up to. Spane ordered a drink and talked with Albertson about the shipments coming in over on the west side of the Everglades. It was spring outside, a remarkably subtle and unconvincing season in Miami. He wanted to take another walk in the gardens and look at the little buds of frangipani and court St. Susan flowers just coming out, maybe drive down to the Everglades and sit in the car looking at the grass prairies that always made him think of Africa. This girl—this woman who'd left him sorted and frazzled, bit down to the quick—he would think about her too and about what he could do. Albertson droned on about business and then the food came and they ate and Albertson tried again with the waitress but she told him she would call the manager if he didn't shut up.

"Something's wrong with me," Albertson said.

"What do you mean?"

"My groin. I got some kind of growth."

"Like a tumor."

"Probably not only like."

"I hear these days they have robots can cut those things out in two seconds."

"That's as terrifying as a tumor."

"What you doing eating a steak?"

"I don't want to give in."

"I understand that."

"Where the hell is Sims?"

"We got the eyes on him."

"Bug eyes? Fish eyes?"

"Mortal eyes."

Last week he'd tried to explain to this woman about how he loved the flowers in the gardens around the city, about how the big gobs of orange blossoms popping out in the poincianas looked like the flower cloaks of Aztec kings thrown up into the trees, about bloodflowers and tickseed, sea daisies all coming into bloom on the dunes, but she wasn't interested. "I came up here to get away from flowers," she said.

On the way to Spane's hotel she said she'd decided to start making other plans.

"About us," Spane said in his dry voice.

She didn't answer.

"That's the end of this then," Spane said. Secretly he called her Ceci—his favorite name for a woman—and he almost called her Ceci now.

"I didn't say that," she said.

"I don't know any other way to take it." But he didn't believe her. It was a quirk with her, such declarations, a stabilizer that cut the nervousness. She wasn't going anywhere.

On Dixie Highway traffic was backed up, so he took another route, dodging in among the neighborhoods around Kendall. A guy was selling shrimp from a sky-blue van, and Spane stopped to get a couple of pounds. Pink sweet-smelling shrimp the man shoveled into a plastic Walgreen's bag. He recognized Spane and asked him for a tip on the horses.

"If I could give you something like that I wouldn't be buying shrimp out of a truck."

"These shrimp you would," the man said. He had salt marks on his forehead and spoke with a slight Jamaican accent.

"Ceci" sat in the car working on some papers. She looked like a dark-haired, specious, aging princess, but she was a workhorse and sharp as a whip, and she was disappointed that somebody as smart as Spane had become such a dud. She was tired of herself and tired of vegetation and maybe even of life, and she didn't yet know what to do about it. Maybe Spane could tell her back at the hotel where he lived in a suite overlooking Government Cut. She liked being up high in hotels. It made her think that the world had opportunities she'd never considered, fresh approaches like the big cloud reefs piling up in the west. She dreamed all the time of a new life. It was the kind of dream you could put anything into: love, children, wrestling matches on late drunken midnights, kisses like flower petals falling from a tamarind tree, friendly usages, complicated plans taking years to come to fruition, the smell of rain on a sunny beach. In any version of it she would hate to be called Ceci.

Albertson looked Spane straight in the eye. The look was like a bar of black steel connecting them. Neither of them had to say a thing.

It was late afternoon and they were still on the island. The old wooden house, half fallen in, stood among pines back from the little wrinkled beach. Scarred level patches, places where hunters built fires, railroad vines stretched out to their skinny full length dotted with blue blossoms, excavation holes, stacked moldy boards. A place of history maybe that you would have to be local to know about. The gray sand beach ran up into grass, then scabby pines and a couple of tall cabbage palms, then the house facing the cut, then the heavy bristle of the Everglades. The house's front galleries, top and bottom, were intact, as were the front rooms on both sides of the door, but the back had been torn off, a single bite for the right hurricane. Visitors had built fires and part of one of the rooms was burned. They set their belongings on the porch and Ella went off walking around the property. His mother was good at outdoor business, business Cot had never learned very well. His ambition, he had told her when he was eight, was to be a city boy, discrete, he meant, solitary on a street corner, unknown by the populace. The back of the house looked into myrtle scrub that a few twisted poisonwood and caper trees poked up out of and a few senna bushes too, bent down with brushy flowers. Old outbuildings now mostly bits and haphazard piles of sandy sticks were knocked back against the bushes.

Ella returned after a while with a couple of papayas big as dopp kits. She gave him one of her offhanded smiles he could see the weariness in. He was impatient with her, as he'd often been as a child, such old times were back, for a moment. He put his hand on her arm and as she folded around, hugged her. She hardly hugged him back, and that was familiar too, both of them disjunct and shy, waiting for some indecipherable impossibility to relent. Suddenly ashamed he grabbed Marcella who was walking by, aloof, spying maybe. She swung around in an old cartoon skidding and leveling way she had, smiling at him, and attacked him with a hug. For a moment he clung to both women at once; it was like a picture, in life and in his mind, a gallantry, a needfulness that was both aggrandizing and humbling. The women broke away, separately, looking as if they didn't know each other. Marcella stayed closer. "I got to . . . ," she said and threw up a smile that was tinged with regret or something like it, fatigue maybe, this strange askew way of her lately. He thought he understood. "My phone . . ."

His was still back in KW, but Marcella had one. She hadn't been able to get a signal over the water and the one she got now—stepping back from him to make a call as if he might interfere with reception—was weak—*calling who?* he wondered—but he took the device from her and got through like a charm to Tommy in his room at the Orange Blossom in the Grove. When he answered Cot abruptly didn't know what to say. He couldn't ask for retrieval. He listened to Tommy's voice speaking from the barrel of distance asking what he wanted. "Come get us," he wanted to say anyhow. He wanted to go on in his ordinary rapid-fire way throwing out ideas and pointers, laying down a handline of talk, but he didn't have a turn now. Tommy, in a few chopped sentences let him know what was up: there was no longer anybody he could trust in Miami, including him. He broke off the call.

"We got to bury Jimmy," Cot said.

They had an argument about that. They had walked the plane around through the shallow water to the stobs where the old pier had been and tied it up, but they'd left Jimmy propped in the seat.

"They won't like it back in town," Marcella said, meaning Key West, meaning culture and life, and his mother agreed.

"We can't just leave him lying out."

"Someone'll probably be by here soon," Marcella said.

They agreed to leave him in the plane overnight but then Cot thought that would be a bad idea, and he talked them into getting him out. He and Jackie carried the body up onto the porch and wrapped it with one of the crinkly silver blankets in the plane's emergency kit. Near dark they saw a boat far out in the bay and tried to hail it, but the boat didn't stop. The twilight filled in around them. They sat by a fire built in a three-sided brick fireplace out in the front yard. Supper was the sandwiches Ella had prepared, onion and chicken, and banana with mayonnaise. Jackie wanted to sing songs and they did that. They had only a couple of six-liter bladders of water from the plane, but there was a catchment in back of the house. Cot walked with Marcella along the shore. The beach wasn't wide and gave way to mangrove scrub and bushes before they could go far. Lines of trickley vine ran down from the grass. A little brown-backed plover skipped along the waterline and was gone, headed for the roost. After a while Marcella asked what he was going to do.

"Deliver you to Aunt Mayrene's in Fort Myers, I guess."

"As soon as we get up to town we'll be all right," she said rubbing her arms.

"I don't mean you need me to haul you. But I'm nervous about who might be lurking between here and Mayrene's."

"You're always nervous."

"I know about these things, matters, frolicsome killers, you know, all that." The words like used-up chewing gum he was hooking out of his mouth.

"Your kidnapper buddy said they were going to make you say where those jewels are."

"Rollins—Jeez." He looked sideways at her. "I'd tell 'em in a flash if I knew." He wanted to say that won't be the end of it, but he didn't, the words in his head poised to take on weight if issued to the air.

"I'm not going to criticize you."

"That'll be a first."

She swayed against him, cocked her head to look at him, looking barely up; she wasn't a lot shorter than he was. "You used to have freckles on your face, but now you don't have any."

Standing before the slithering quiet surf they kissed, not deeply. Little blinks and cohorts of darkness, of something that promised an endless supply, skipped and went on by. They sat down on the sand. There were lights far out in the Gulf—shrimpers probably. "At night," he said, remembering something his father told him, "when it's really dark—"

And then he forgot what it was and stalled in the gathered dark. He thought of himself in that moment as simply waiting, but there was something else.

"What?" she said. Her voice was changed in some way. A hollowness, a new channel cut down into her heart through which came sounds and alarms almost too faint to hear.

"I don't get you," he said.

"Get what?"

"You."

"I'm glad you finally admit it."

Even her face, oblong of un-sun-changed whiteness in the edging-away twilight, like some apparitional aspect revealed now, as if she had all along been a ghost. He looked away, not wanting to see.

"You already know everything," she said.

"About what?"

"About me."

This too was contrary.

She leaned over and spit in the sand. "You're still getting up in the middle of the night, aren't you?"

"I ever was." Since he was a child he'd waked restless in the dark, wanting to get into things.

A nightbird called, maybe a chuck-will's-widow, checking something that'd stuck in its mind, the cry slipped like a note under dark's door. The moon this night had come up while it was still light. Now it westered out over the Gulf, leaving a splashed-in trail to follow if you were fool enough. He figured everybody at one time or another wished he was.

She got up and stepped away from him, listing, edging, sidling, and straying, her head up as if sniffing a scent on the breeze, like somebody trying to disappear before they got out of sight. He watched her go. Each footprint laid in sand was sculpted, a faint chinked line. She sang under her breath, something personal, only for herself. Across the channel the mainland, the sprawled and tangled swamp, was as black as absence itself. It chittered and rustled, setting itself up for night work. Then a scuttling, thrashing sound from bushes across the strip of water only as wide as a country road. Then something else—the cry of an animal, unfamiliar and scary, a scream, set in opposition, whining, thin at first. They both knew what it was: a panther, letting loose a complaint that slithered and coarsened as it came, breaking into a scream that was almost a howl. It was a noise set against the weave and busyness of the swamp. It stopped them both, stopped hearts everywhere nearby probably, stopped breath, stopped everything but the faint undersound of breeze. It was a fresh take on things. He could feel his blood draw up.

She could feel hers too that had already shivered. *There's nothing to do about it now.* The thought came to her fully formed, like a new law. She swayed and would've fallen, but a breeze, the same old one, caught her—so it seemed—and held her, just enough for her to catch her balance. She saw again how thin he'd become, tightly and muscularly composed, but pared down, hardly, even now, looking to be much more than a boy. She had noticed the lines in his face, the harrying.

Small waves, fresh born, chipped at clearings, soughed in the mangrove banks. "Cot," she said under her breath. "You don't know, Cot." The panther—it could be *her* screaming out in the dark. She said his name again, softly; and again: she wanted to see how long it took him to hear her. But he was looking straight at her. He had caught her right off.

He got up and crossed to her, the sand squinching and shifting under his bare feet, and took her in his arms. They embraced hard. A nightbug banged against his arm and he brushed it off without thinking. She let go and side by side they looked westward out over the Gulf. The moon had been there all day, like the panther, waiting behind the blue. Half of it was gnawed out. Brane, he thought, and who else had been in the boat? Albertson scattering men like seeds he spewed from his pockets as he walked. They should have stayed in KW. This thought like a dab of unwanted color in a picture. He rubbed it out in his mind. *We're where we are—that's it.*

A breeze trailing smells of distant burning oil wells passed by. She'd been talking all the time, in a low troubled voice like a shuffling noise. He wanted to accuse himself. But he only rubbed against her, ran his hand up and down her bare arm.

"I can hardly even feel the mosquitoes," she said.

"That's something."

"Don't be glum."

"How can I help it?"

"Mental gymnastics."

They laughed.

"I'm sorry," he said. "What were you saying?"

"When?"

"Just now."

Her eyes that even in the dimness he could see, angry for just a second. "Other things."

"We're supposed to be sitting on Aunt Mayrene's screen porch, drinking Long Island iced teas. Sorry, Sweetie."

"I don't mind that much."

"Well, I expect you do. But thank you for saying it."

They watched his mother coming along the beach toward them.

"She's still a sport," Marcella said.

He didn't say anything. His mother, slight—wiry you could say now, lean like a deer in the woods, ready for most anything, but not everything, not so much anymore.

"Did you hear the panther?" his mother said.

"Yessum." He kissed her on the cheek.

"It's got Jackie scared to death."

"I'll go speak to him," Cot said. He wanted to get away.

"I'll go," Marcella said.

Ella smiled at them. "Both of you go."

But he stayed behind. Guilt held him, close like a crippled brother. *I'm sorry* was the first thing he said.

Ella just looked at him. Strange how you went on loving what was hurting you, she thought, what was twirling misery up out of the ground onto you. As she loved her husband, loved Rafael sitting at his kitchen table working on his stories, neglecting everything else. "We make mistakes whatever we try to do," she said.

"That's pretty philosophical."

"It's hard to forgive ourselves," she said, gazing out at the Gulf that moved toward them in long smooth swells that changed to nubbin waves flopping over like weariness itself at their feet. She was barefoot.

"I hate it about Jimmy," he said, words from the formula you used with civilians, but words that now had some feeling pumped into them, just a little. *Sorry, sorry, sorry* scratching over the other words, brute sounds. "It was bad."

"All of us will have to grieve on that a while."

"I didn't expect any other group to come at us."

"You should have, son."

"I was just saying that, Mama."

The panther cried again. A low, moaning sound, halt at first then almost liquid, flowing under the scrawled brush, oozing from dark cuddies. Yet this time it was a little easier to listen to. The cry sometimes, so Cot had read, meant the panther was coming to get you. He said this, and added, "I find that hard to believe."

"You sure, honey?"

They both smiled. Something between them was always tipping slightly one way or the other. "You get old," she said, "and pains—bald aches—rise up in ways, in styles, you never imagined. Aches like memories."

"Memories?"

"Catcalls from death."

"Mama."

"—and whatall. If you hadn't already got a means to calm yourself, it can be kind of difficult to start trying to find one."

He said you're all right—or didn't say it—and felt the rasp of an old shame that sometimes took hours to pass. He wanted to plunge headfirst into the dark. She stood beside him, her weight on one leg, like a woman waiting at a bus stop. Time was, her familiarity grated against him, the private knowingness, the burden of attachment enraging him. Silent now, he endured the burning of his own recklessness. Times past he couldn't have stayed in silence near her. Now he could, just barely. Then he couldn't.

"You're all right, aren't you?" he said.

"In the way you think, yes."

"I'm sorry, Mama."

"It's not really something you can be sorry about."

Stars to the south, a jumble, straight overhead the double wings of the Milky Way, prickly like the sore spot a patch was just ripped off of. In the west, lying low, clouds in gray bunches. Just another few feet farther south and they could see the Southern Cross, now less than itself Spane had told him once, as one of its point stars died. The Indians here—the old Indians, the Calusas, the Tequestas—what would they have called it? Not a Cross. *The Crisscross.* He used to know some of the Native American constellations, but he'd forgotten. Marcella told him that to the Australian Aborigines the Southern Cross was Two Brothers Sitting Around a Campfire Eating a Fish They'd Caught. A couple of local boys.

The cat cry came again. Now it didn't seem to be a panther. No cat or critter. A human cry—not just in its style or mimicry, but actually. He didn't say anything. His mother stood silently looking out at the Gulf. The waves made faint sizzling, then flopping sounds. In KW they lived too far up the hill, with too many structures in between, to hear the ocean. "Let's walk up to the house," he said.

There he told Marcella about the false cat cry.

"Are you sure?"

"Near 'bout."

It was full dark now. They had the light of a couple of candles they'd found in the plane's emergency kit, the only lights outside those of the dying fire.

"How could anyone be after us out here?" she said.

"Maybe it's a fresh group."

"What does that mean?"

"Local freelancers."

"Cot. Gee."

"I know."

They decided to let Jackie and his mother sleep. They would take turns keeping watch. "First or last?" she said.

"Which do you want?"

"Either one."

They flipped for it; a quarter that seemed as he showed it to her an artifact from a vanished civilization. She got first. He walked with her to the beach where she snugged herself up under a soursop tree, in its long, glaucous night shade. He gave her one of his pistols, the one he had taken from the boys at the camp. He knew she already knew how to use it, but he showed her anyway. It was easy. He lay on the sandy ground beside her for a while. "I get itches all over me," he said, "when I stay outside."

"I wish we had some bug repellent."

"Well, you're in luck on that one," he said drawing his mother's little bottle of bug juice from his back pocket.

"At last my love has come. You sweetie."

She turned her whole body to him, put her hands on his shoulders and kissed him. He had been waiting—it felt as if for months—for her to do that. He drew her nigh, and closer. Her body still felt like some kind of map he'd chanced on, his good luck, proof that the world wasn't just a mixed-up lostness.

"See you later, agitator," he said getting up.

"After while, crock of style."

He waked before the alarm he'd set on Jimmy's phone went off. In the darkness there was only the slow, poised sound of the surf. A stillness behind this. Then a nightbird call, low, interrogatory, unsure. " . . . *bless the rains down in Africa*," he whispered. Words from a song, one of his favorite non sequiturs. He felt good. It was odd but not unusual. He had slept on the ground, a little ways from the house, in shadow under a senna bush. He had waked knowing just where he was, no strangeness, or none extra.

He walked down to the plane. It bobbed lightly on its tether. He put his hand flat on the surface of the water: cold, spring still a ways to go before the Gulf was really warm. Someone from up north would remark on how warm the water was. You got used to your own gradations, fluctuations. Truth was you could die of hypothermia even in warm water. Eighty degrees, given a few hours, would bring your temperature down to ninety and then you were gone. A screech owl over on the mainland whinnied, a small, woeful sound, childish almost, trying to strike the right note, the one that would settle things. The moon was down already. Above the earthly night that had contracted to a closeness the stars were full-bodied, eloquent, spewing; he could see the shape of the islands, the smoothed-off tips of the little waves winking.

He found her asleep, her head lying on her arm. She woke as he reached to touch her, coming to even out here in the bush country with an ease, a lack of elaboration, that impressed him. "Sorry," she said.

"It's a pretty night."

"Up until a minute ago I was enjoying it."

She couldn't find the pistol. With a hand on her wrist he stopped her searching for it. Her face, even in star gloom, looked stricken. A grimace, a cast-off look, returned to her, her thin eyelids drooping.

"Stay here."

He stepped from under tree shadow into the shadow of yaupon bushes piled crooked and more than head high along the inner shore. He had his own pistol out, but he didn't think about it. He ran along under the darkness around behind the house and crouched beside two large jumbie bean bushes at the edge of the backyard. Scent of the decayed remains of an outhouse. A little breeze, careful and shy, circulated and dropped off. Under it the faint sounds of the night: a bird, rustle of small beings, shurrs, loose wavering pickup of breeze, a coon maybe off to the right, worrying some reluctant bit. The coon sound—what was it exactly?—checked him. Off ahead, at the grassy edge of the yard, he made out a shape: someone crouched. He pulled back, sank further into shadow, and ran low through sandy grass toward the shape. Whoever it was had his eyes on the house. He reached a low bush just behind the watcher, stopped there and held still. He could smell the leathery odor of the man—it was a man—saw the dark hair sticking out from under a bandana, the collar of his shirt, jut of bony jaw, the rifle cradled in his arm. All in a second. He took a step and put his pistol under the man's ear. The man, loose, lean, jerked forward, wincing as if the gun burned him, and fell on his side. He tried to squirm away but Cot was quickly astride his back, pressing the pistol into his cheek. He had man and rifle both pinned. "Awk," the man said and coughed.

"Take your time." He pointed the pistol in the man's eyes.

The man held his tension close, squeezing it; in his eyes a guilty knowledge. "Okay, mister."

Cot slid the rifle away and got up. The man raised himself on an elbow. He coughed, hacking, and spit to the side. "Flu," he said. "I shouldn't have come out."

"For what?"

"For what what?"

"Did you come out?"

"Bats."

"Don't kid me."

"Yeah, bats, sho. Fruit bats."

"I'm from around here. I've never seen that."

"Must not have been around here for a while."

"Yah?"

"Exotic pets—you don't know about *them*?"

Everybody knew about strange species that hurricanes had let loose from their cages. Maybe bats too. He'd read about fruit bats. Big as cats, roosting in leafy trees, snacking on papayas and mangoes. "Good eating," the man said.

He was an Indian, Cot had seen that right off. From one of the walled and padlocked villages probably. The Seminoles were like everyone else down here: driven to the hot areas by government, by clamor, by a need to get a little peace. They too weren't really native to these parts. He used to call up Marcella and talk to her about it.

"A hunter," he said.

"You done hit right on it."

"What'd you swim the channel?"

"Got my boat."

First he took Marcella's pistol back, "Hunting, huh?" and broke the breech of the rifle that was not a rifle but a bolt-action shotgun, an old Colt.

"I come on her sleeping—that your wife?—and took that gun. It scared me, her having it, so I took it."

"I'd have done the same thing."

"What y'all doing out here?"

"Camping."

He had the man walk ahead of him to the place where Marcella waited. He didn't see her at first and his heart tightened. But there she was, down at the water, sitting on the gunwale of the man's boat. The boat was a little canoe with a small outboard raised above the squared-off stern; a paddle propped against it. Marcella got up, listing a little as if cramped, bent. "Hello."

"Hidy, Mrs. Bakewell."

"You know him?"

"I do," Marcella said, smoothing her hair back from her forehead. "How's your family, Choky?"

"They're just fine, 'cept for Mama's rheumatoiditis. And Jimmy's got him a hernia from baseball practice, and Lorene, she broke her foot running from some police wanted to talk to her about a still or something."

"How's Longman?"

"He says he's gon go to college."

As she explained now, she had gotten Choky Rough's older son back from the state for him, some years ago, when people were still being arrested for alligator poaching. "Well that's a mighty fine thing," Cot said.

He shook hands with the man.

"I saw y'all's plane," Choky said.

"Local charter," Cot said. He still didn't trust the situation, still held his frets close. A breeze trickled through the brush, stroking leaves. "You really hunting bats?"

"Sure. Why not?"

They walked around to the house and sat on the front steps talking. Choky said he would get a larger boat and ferry them over to his house on Cold Press Island and carry them to Fort Myers. Everybody seemed delighted. Like real castaways. His mother had waked and she sat in an old rocker on the porch listening to the conversation. Her streaked gray hair was loose, and it swung against her face in a way Cot remembered from years ago. "What about James Lawrence?" she said. Jimmy, wrapped in a crumpled survival blanket, unsurviving, who this day would begin to smell. Cot could *already* smell him.

Cot mentioned this situation to Rough, told him a little of what had happened. "Maybe hunters," he said. "No way of telling—or just fools." Everybody knew about Cot. Anyone, in any circumstance, could see in his face that he didn't really want to say anything. But he had to say something. A harshness now in his look, a waywardness too; he didn't want to inform, even on loss, even on death. Rough looked off toward the darkness of the cross-channel woods. The false dawn, gray as if already tired of the day, had tracked up, and was already going, slick and inapplicable, brushing the shoulders of the real thing as it went out.

"You want to bury him?" Rough said.

"Ah. Not really."

"I guess we can haul him out."

Cot could tell Rough didn't want to get any of Jimmy on him. Cot knew about this. You had to protect yourself—from the slow shell-shocking that life was giving you. Death brought it on in leaps sometimes. People sensed this and backed away. Even the police, and the doctors, the surgeons who wore suits and big crumpled green hats and masks—to keep it off, the dizzy spin and crumpling, the waking in a lost place without a clue, somebody yelling at you to *come on, come on*, it was like that.

But they were too many for a small boat.

"I'll set with him," Jackie said, his hair spiked around his head, his eyes still gummed with sleep, come up as if just revived from the dark floor.

"You don't know who's coming," Cot said.

"Ain't nothing but the rangers," he said. "They always show up down along here. They got rounds to make."

They agreed, Cot agreed. It bothered him that somebody was left dangling, dead or alive, but he was careful not to let the others see.

He walked back into the house with Jackie and

thanked him. "You got everybody in a mess," Jackie said, his arm tense under Cot's fingers.

"I know." There was a ringing in his ears, something new or fairly new, circles of flat sound like an alien surf.

"That's only *almost* the worst of it," Jackie said.

The cell towers in Everglades City as usual weren't working, and Marcella wasn't able to make a call to the Collier County sheriff until they were already inside the Naples city limits. She told the 911 operator that a man lay dead in the islands, his plane abandoned. She called Ordell and asked him to go speak to Jimmy's wife. She began to cry as she hung up the phone. She looked at Cot who was talking to a woman. He had a tense mouth and he seemed to be trying to convince the woman of something. They were standing in front of a curio shop on Merrywood Road. One side of the road was stuffed with housing developments, the other a sprawl of raw and skimpy-looking, neglected woods. Down here it was like that, she thought, looking at a couple of brown cows standing under a big lime tree: development or nothing. Cot crossed the bit of concrete apron and took her in his arms. She could feel the hardness in his back muscles, the stiffness she took as a refusal to mourn, thinking: Why would I think that?

Over her shoulder Cot could see his mother sitting on a bench against the shop's front wall. She was writing in a small notebook. Maybe working up a story, maybe putting together one of the island bulletins she published occasionally in the KW paper. *Been on a murder party and a plane ride. Retrieved from the swamp by an able young poacher whose mother I once had over to the house to trade stories with. The dead continue to speak to us from every bush and patch of shade. They remind us that we are never free to do what we want. There is only affection and service to a higher . . . and all such as that.*

6

All the live oaks in the yard lean toward the water. The little clearwater spring Mayrene's dammed with a single concrete wall to form a pool makes a faint gurgling noise where the runoff exits through an algae-stained gutter into the canal. Beyond the pool the canal widens in one direction into a baylike area. Boats and houses sweltering under big oaks and cabbage palms are parked along it. The other end passes out of sight in a jumble of old warehouse buildings over which on this afternoon big piles of cumulus gather. The afternoon is like a familiar stranger, someone you observe taking walks in the neighborhood who nods as he passes, whom you wonder about without nervousness. Thin gray squirrels chatter in the tops of the palm trees.

Mrs. Stanford, the next-door neighbor, an eighty-year-old widow and fortune-teller, comes over bearing a plate of freshly baked cornbread. She reads his mother's and Marcella's palms, but Cot won't let her read his. "Shoot," she says, "I can read yours from across the room."

"I don't want to hear it."

"I wouldn't either."

"Hey," Marcella says wagging her finger.

She's talking on the phone to Ordell. The fortune-teller has said a number of items are fading from her life and—nervous, spindly in her heart—she wanted to call home to check, ha ha. Ella sits at the kitchen table (they're in the big kitchen that opens onto the screened back porch) writing in her notebook.

"I expect my fortune rides before me carrying a sign," Cot says.

"That's a way of putting it," the old lady says sourly. She has faded orange hair from the special old people's dye only they can get, you see it everywhere. Her hands look like knotted rope stained purple—with leukemia, Mayrene's said. He wonders what fortunes she tells herself. Likely they blare at her from the dark, cocksure and smug. He feels a faded, estivating sadness for her, irritation too. They are wearing bathing suits, he and Marcella, both of which, men's and women's, belonged to Mayrene and (that is) to her deceased husband, a former bandleader on the Cornwallis circuit. Mayrene, his mother's older sister, had been his chanteuse. "My girl singer," Harry called her. "My canary." He's buried in a cemetery over in Cape Coral, under a cement slab with a clarinet stuck bell down in it. The clarinet, Mayrene says, looks like an erect penis.

They walk in the shade of the big live oaks that never drop a stitch leafwise, winter or summer, feeling on their bodies the cool shade buffed by a sea breeze. Cot knows they aren't particularly safe, but maybe they will be as soon as he leaves. "You need to run north," Marcella says. "Or west."

"I don't shine particularly to being tracked."

"That one of your sayings?"

"Half and half."

She twirls a papaya leaf, frog-footed and yellow, in her left hand.

"It was because you were crippling my nerves," she says.

"That you married Ordell," he says picking up the thread. "I know. It was a good idea."

"The fact you think so's always bothered me."

"It's just another way of my refusing to accept responsibility."

"That and a host of other things."

"I get bogged down."

"Most people call that living." She makes a motion with her hand across her eyes, involuntary but characteristic, as if wiping a small gathering of gnats away. "You'd overworry about me."

"I'd sit up nights."

"Don't you worry about me now?"

"Off and on." It's already crossed his mind that he's traveling with people he might have to die for. He's not really been in that situation before.

She waves the leaf at him, almost a swat, that misses. "I don't really want you to worry about me at all."

"Likewise, sugar."

Ordell tried a case against her only once. She beat him so soundly the judge dismissed the charges. Cot doesn't like to try anything against her either, even though he knows he has a jimmy, an in: she loves him.

"But I love Ordell too," she said when he told her this.

"I know you do," he answered. "I love him myself, but it would bother me if I went up against you and you gave me a break, and it'd bother me if you didn't."

"I already figured that out," she'd said.

As they reach the pool a boat, speedboat, appears from behind a large ocean cruiser upstream, and begins to run down toward them. Cot watches it come. It's blue, open-hull and he can see three men in town clothes. "Get in the water," he says.

"_____"

He shoves her into the pool, crosses the little fore-court to the oak tree nearest the canal, and as the boat comes up at speed raises the pistol from under the towel he carries. The boat roars right at them, at the last moment swinging broadside. Two of the men rise, and as they level their little Belgian machine guns he fires. His shots catch one in the throat, catch the other in the shoulder. Both men go down, but not before one of them fires a burst into the top of the oak tree. The shots scatter some grackles among the glossy, almost black evergreen leaves. The boat continues down the canal. Cot kneels and fires a shot at the driver, but he doesn't really want to hit him. He wants the boat to be able to leave the area. All this in choked seconds. The clouds over the warehouses haven't moved. The day continues in its brightness.

He pulls Marcella by her arm out of the pool and gives her a moment to gather herself. She sits on the concrete shivering.

"This isn't my end of things," she says.

"It's pretty alarming, yeah."

"Alarming? Jesus, Cot."

He puts his hand on her sleek black hair. "I know."

He helps her up and they jog back to the house. There they gather their things. Mayrene tries to laugh it off, but she's just faking it. He tells her to pack a bag. She doesn't want to, but his mother quickly convinces her. She wants to stop long enough to make a thermos of limeade, but Cot tells her she better not. A solemnness, like a sticky shellac, covers everything. They lock up the house, take her two goldfinches over to Mrs. Williams's, and leave for the airport in Mayrene's big Lincoln.

On the way to the airport his mother talks on the mobile phone, something unusual for her. "Who is it?" he asks. She is sitting in the back seat, turned away from them as they pass a line of muscular royal palms before a huge pink mansion. "Your father."

He wants suddenly to speak to him. He holds out his hand for the phone, but she doesn't give it to him. "Mama," he says. "Come on."

She hands the instrument over. A big red pickup passes. In the back a gang of Latino boys yell and shake their fists at them. Have they done something they don't realize? "Papa," he says. There's silence on the line. "Papa."

"You need to slow down, son," his father's faint reedy voice says, as if he's been watching him.

"I will soon."

"Won't you come to visit?"

His accent, urban, Cubano, has deepened, and he sounds weary, distracted, caught maybe by his lifelong contemplation of his troubles—*mis aflicciones*—always unnamed. The last time Cot visited he had been weighed down, his thin arm waving to him from the floral armchair like a man waving from a bog. "I'll come soon," Cot says.

"You come soon," his father says. "Mrs. Sobales will make some of the stew you enjoy."

Would he become like this—or could he if his life were only slightly different—like this fey wanderer among the possibilities? He doesn't believe so, believes as he has since he was eleven that he has evaded his father's life. He knows this isn't really true, but it helps him to think it. "Do you remember your father—*mi abuelo*?" He's asked this before. His father's father, the ship's captain from the English Midlands, a seaman who knew the names of all the flowers that grew among the hills there, went to sea, and washed up in Cuba. "You take care of yourself—and take care of your mother," his father says.

"She's doing fine."

The phone goes dead; maybe he hung up, maybe the connection, always feeble over the strait, had been doused.

At the airport he puts Mayrene and his mother on a flight to their—to his—great aunt's house in west Texas.

Halfway across the state, at a spot she once measured by odometer, riding in a cab on Alligator Alley, I-75, the longest piece of perfectly straight road east of the Mississippi (so she believes), Marcella makes him stop and gets out. She hurries across the parking lot of the little pull-off and vomits over the barrier into the grass. Beyond the barriers on both sides of the road empty grasslands stretch vastly away. They could be in Africa. Tawny, currents of breeze circulating like rivers among the grass, hawks riding thermals high up like they have not a care in the world, its spaciousness has always loosed something in her, something daunting and encouraging and shapely. She retches again, violently, shaking, her face white as paste when she looks up at him. He's holding her by the shoulders. A black-water canal runs alongside the barrier, a few Miccosukee boats are tied up. Otherwise there's nothing human about but them, except for the cabbie.

"You got too much strain on you," he says.

"Who wouldn't have?"

"Some don't notice it."

He sits on the barrier, a silver steel fluted railing. He wants to lean back, fall into the strip grass by the canal, and sleep his life away. Time, time. He can feel it slipping away. The past gurgles in the gap it leaves. Some while ago the slippage started getting to him. He hates it like a limp. So what if he can remember when in KW you could address a letter to "Marcella Cord/City" and know it would reach her?

"It's this sense of imperfection bugs me," he says now.

"I know." She licks a smear of yellow effluvium off her lower lip. Her tongue is greenish. She looks to him—white-faced, weary—like the heroine of a nineteenth-century novel.

She says, "I don't want to go on with you anymore."

"Yeah."

"No," she says. "I mean it."

"Yeah."

He helps her to her feet, and they stand with their backs to the highway looking out across the great expanse of seemingly untouched terrain. It's a national park. The political version of a sacred place. But they both know people won't keep from putting their hands on it. Like them, like who they are together, like them to each other: sacred places they can't keep from poking and tromping through. It irks them both.

"Still a ways to go," she says.

"Yeah."

The cabbie lets them off behind the courthouse in Lauderdale and they walk upstairs to the sheriff's department where, after she follows a deputy into a corner office, Marcella returns to say she inquired about the disposition of the boys caught in CJ's killing. She's got a funny look on her face. She's holding her phone.

"What is it?"

"I don't know what to say." The look isn't funny, it's sad—a look you could call *infinitely* sad, as if she'd been shown one of the black mysteries, the submerged and lifeless facts at the bottom of things—and she's working her jaw in the way she has, chewing on nothing. Two deputies, who look like twins, sit at side-by-side desks eating sandwiches. "Who you think you fooling?" an African American voice from down the hall says loudly.

"What is it?"

"I don't know what to say."

"What do you mean?"

"They're holding—not for CJ—they're holding two men for burglaries up here. They don't know—"

"About CJ?"

They look at each other. It might really be nothing he thinks but doesn't believe. Her eyes hold a blankness like a film, and she's squirming internally he can tell.

"Didn't Ordell come up and talk to them?"

"He talked to Pickens—the sheriff—but it was just to pass on information. He wondered—the sheriff wondered—why he didn't just phone."

She sits down on a long upholstered bench against the wall. The upholstery—black plastic—bulges like muscles.

He catches the drift from the look on her face. *Unusual, how even the looks you've never seen before, you get, when it's like this.* He checks with the desk sergeant who tells him they aren't holding anybody concerned with a killing in Key West—or anything else down there.

He sits down beside her. "Maybe he was just making inquiries."

"They said he didn't ask about it." She scratches the back of one hand, hard.

"What was he doing?" He already knows. A sudden rage catches in his chest and sputters there, burning.

He pulls her up, and they hurry down the stairs. They take another cab down I-95 to Miami. The cost of cab rides is mounting, but Marcella says she doesn't mind paying, even the two hundred dollars to get them across the state she didn't complain about. He wants to take her to the airport, send her back to Key West, but she says no. "Then I'll just have to throw you out of the car," he says. "I'll open the door and kick you out to the Redcaps."

"No, you won't."

"I'm going to kill Ordell."

She gives him a hard look, her blue eyes like stones. Looks, dips in scale, poses—it's one of the ways they fight. He doesn't say anything back. It isn't that kind of fight.

They check in at the Castaway Hotel in the Grove and ride the elevator up to the seventh floor. When he first got money fifteen years ago he stayed there for a year, living quietly. He swam laps in the pool with Billy Brent, the writer, both of them young and mad about the women in their lives. He saw Billy around town sometimes now, across the floor maybe at Swan's Show Room, Billy, his eyes popping as if a noose around his neck had just pulled tight, who never seemed to recognize him.

They don't speak going up. Don't speak until they are in their clean yellow room.

"I don't know," she says.

"Okay," he answers. They're both beat.

She walks out onto the balcony and stares down at the pool in the big courtyard two floors below. He follows her out and stands beside her. They don't touch. Large silver palms grow in big pots back from the pool and flimsy orange-striped cabanas are set along one side. There're only a few people around the pool.

"You want to swim?"

She says yes.

He wonders if she's pretending about Ordell; he knows she holds special info to herself, she always has, and something's not right. He makes himself stop thinking about it. On the way down in the elevator he strokes her hair, kisses her expertly on the cheek. They'd almost stopped to make love in the room but held off. They both wanted to be in the water. With them, making love's sometimes a contrariness they can't overcome, a shadow on the floor in a sunny room (and vice versa), an instance, insistence, a raillery posing as the genuine article, and sometimes only the brisk notion they sup from; occasionally it's all they have to hold on to, at other times, nothing much; mostly it's an essential, like salt, humble and tasty. They've never had the easy swing of routine life, the ordinary days piled with coffee mugs and laundry, dinners sitting before the TV. There're times when this has bothered them, times they see what they're doing as ridiculous, as strange and cowardly, but they don't hold each other to any set of principles.

Only a raddled honesty, he thinks, grazing the smell of her as she turns toward him in the elevator, unoccupied except for an extremely small gentleman dressed in a pale blue linen suit. Even honesty's nothing they've really believed in. Maybe they only believe in the freshness of their coming together, the newness of it, rejuvenated by time apart. That's probably closer to it.

He lets her go ahead of him out of the elevator and across the courtyard to the pool. He's always loved the high-risen hotel pool, its formal fifth-floor isolation and bounty amid the coarse limestone walls of the Castaway. In his days here he came to know maids and bellhops, he became friends with one of the assistant managers, a Cubano who, like his father, had fled Castro—but, unlike his father, stayed in the US, Joan Montoya, now no longer assistant but the manager. They swim in the cool water under a sky half filled with clouds that look torn along the tops, as if some force from inside has blown its way out. She asked him in the room what he was going to do, but he said he didn't know. This is true but only in the sense that he's waiting until the next action comes to him. He wants to be in the water first, then sleep, then it'll get here. They swim laps, side by side. She's faster even if he really pushes it, and he doesn't. After a while he lets go (he can feel it happening, like a swimming inside his body), opens his eyes, and drifts to the bottom. She swims down to him, touches his face, runs her fingers over his short-cut hair. As children they would speak to each other underwater, it was how they met, in Francis Mockermound's pool, talking, then yelling at each other six feet down, after that time she saved him. They do this again now. "Everybody's dying for a piece of the action," he says, half-remembering a passage in *The Georgics* or something Tommy quoted one afternoon in Flamingo Park, "We all feel so unsafe and . . ." His breath isn't long enough. Before the end, before he adds codicils and reparatives, new, fresh aspects that if they would only hold still would contain the key to their future—to life itself, anchored in the tars and sunbursts of time—before this, his air runs out and he has to push for the surface.

She follows, touching him along his body as she comes.

"It sounded like a telephone ringing," she says.

"One of the old ones."

"Ours was in the hall."

" 'Miracles can't be left unclaimed,' " he says, closer to quoting—Virgil he thinks. He knows by now long passages of *The Georgics* by heart, half-heart. "I know."

"You look panicked."

"I try not to, but I do."

"There're other things I want to point out, later, but go on with your speech."

Hurrying, he pretends he doesn't hear her. They shake out a few of the heavy orange towels, wrap themselves in them, take the elevator up to the room where in the bed she's already chosen as her own—"It's okay, since you're the one paid for it," he says—they make love, tensely at first then abruptly and with a rolling feverishness. To both of them they seem to be climbing up out of deep coverts. Despair threads quickly through him; behind it an emptiness, a ghost town. He senses how far off she's gotten; it's as if he can see her standing on a bluff looking out at dusty, parched terrain that goes on forever. But they're workers—earnest, faithful. One then the other finds a way, hauling and heaving and falling back in a retreat that's sweet and inevitable, and is what, as they give in, they both know they're after, the cudgeled humility of it, their flesh sweaty and maculate.

They turn off the air conditioner, crank open the windows, and lie back dozing in a hesitant, salt-smelling breeze. His mother must be in Texas by now, eating posole in Mamie's kitchen or standing out in the chaparral letting the dry wind blow on her face. Everything'll be all right. He tells himself this in the half-light of half-dreams, the following seas of calamity and shame still somewhere behind—for the moment behind—his body for a moment like a shield against loss, half-lit dreams like a proof of no loss, the woman beside him, whom he senses in her fullness as she turns against his body, exemplary for a sec of a world without loss. He snugs against her, pressing his chest against her long broad back, pressing his lips into her neck that smells of pool water. They haven't showered. Then the phone rings.

It's Albertson. His breathy thin wheedling voice. "You resting up?" he says.

"Partly."

"I can tell at the first word that you're mad."

"That's because I honestly reveal my emotions."

"It's one of your shortcomings."

"So they say."

"You want to come see me?"

"I might like to."

"Come on the boat. Bring Mrs. Bakewell."

"Ms. Cord. I'll ask her if she wants to come. She doesn't like boats much."

"You put too much store in what people like or don't like."

"That what they told you?"

"Mickey'll meet you at the dock," Albertson says and hangs up.

Cot knows A doesn't have to say that last bit, about Spane meeting them. He's trying to make a point—which one wasn't clear—but his having to make any point tells him something. He has a sudden urge to go to the track—go, or call his bookie and lay some bets. He sits still until the craving passes. It turns gradually to a wisp, to a thin, miserly, tailing notion and then fades. Behind it comes a small, terrifying sense of lostness, of emptiness, like that of the barrel you look into after the treasure's gone.

Marcella runs her fingernail lightly along his hair. "I do too like boats." For a second or two, hardly any time, he lies still, gazing up at the pale orange ceiling. You got what you wanted, he thinks: his plan unfolding. A gull cries, far away, busy with its life. He remembers years ago walking along Miguel de Cervantes Street in Havana with his father, on the way to the market. People knew his father as the creator of the picto-novella *Felix y Consuela*. He could feel them looking at him, looking at the guitar his father carried slung over his back. He asked his father, who did not play the guitar, why he carried it. "To ease trouble," his father said. To be part of things, his mother said when he told her. But it wasn't only that. It was that and something else.

"You probably won't like this boat," Cot says.

"I don't guess it's something you either like or don't."

She gets up with him, and they stand on opposite sides of the bed dressing. Her body is wide and rangy both, sturdy, still firmly muscled, a body like his own, female version. He hardly looks at her. They ride down in the elevator in silence.

On the way to Albertson's building on the bayside Cot has the cabbie detour into the old Crosswinds neighborhood where at a sporting goods store he buys a gallon of gasoline in a little can. At the grocery store down the street he buys a clear glass quart jug of Martinelli's apple juice and in the alley pours the apple juice on the ground—all but a cup of it poured into the collapsable silver mug he carries in his coat pocket—and refills the jug with gasoline. He screws the top and pours juice over the jug to make it smell of apples. He takes a taste of the juice, strong and fragrant, and hands the cup to Marcella. "Bent all the way backwards and still here," he says. She smiles her slightly off-center, hectic smile. Her face falls back into a somberness, and she takes a full swallow of the juice and hands the cup back to him. He drinks the remainder down and puts the cup in his pocket. He has the driver stop at a card shop, and he buys a small white tag with a thick red string attached. With a pen the proprietor lets him use he writes a note to Albertson: "Thanks for the many benefits." He really is thankful for everything Albertson has done for him. The Big Man took him on as an enterprising boy who misunderstood instructions and blundered. Cot sits down on a bench outside the shop and slips the red strings into the jug, soaking them, pulls just enough of the string out of the neck and lets the card dangle.

"I got it," he said when he slides into the cab's back seat. He's okay as long as he's moving, as long as he's enterprising.

"A big flight of parrots just flew over screaming like crazy," Marcella says. "We don't have those in Key West."

"Screams?"

"I almost jumped out of the cab and ran away."

"I hoped I'd given you enough time to."

She regards him with wise, vaguely risive eyes. "This is more mischief."

"In a way."

She can see what he's doing. He's about to render something—that's the way he would put it if she asked. He's been like this since she knew him and she has never gotten used to it. But it excites her. Sudden nimble actions that knock a window in things. But then you want quiet and he can't keep at that, not for long.

He has the driver pull over a block before the big white waterfront building.

"I think you better hang back," he says.

"I knew you would say that."

"I hate it when you say *that*."

"But not so much you don't listen."

"No, not that much. I mean it on the hanging back."

"I thought it was just pro forma."

"Only partly."

"I don't want to miss your stunt."

He pays the driver, and they get out of the car. A hotdog vendor on the corner is in Albertson's employ. "Your mama get those place mats I sent?" Cot says.

"She did and thank you, Cot," the vendor says. "How you, Miss Marcella?"

Marcella smiles at him. They haven't made a decision about her coming up, not one that Cot sees. It's the way things usually go. Objections registered, statements made, ploys attempted. The deed developing. He knew she was coming.

There are two large Egyptian date palms out front and a couple of big hibiscus in pots. He picks a red flower off one of the bushes and gives it to Marcella. She puts it in her hair. In Havana, the girls wear hibiscus and plumeria blossoms in their hair. He thinks of his father and then instantly of his mother, wonders what she's doing right now. Probably walking along a dry arroyo collecting plant specimens. She had been an anthropologist when she went to Cuba with her father for the first time, but she fell in love with the mountain butterflies and gave up anthropology for biology. The red flower is like a big butterfly in Marcella's hair.

Inside they all know him, the factotums and skill men and hangers-on, the rumble boys and the slack, ruined characters kept around by Albertson to remind him of worlds and episodes most men would want to forget. There're a few smooth types, able guys who in other lives would have gone on to highly paid selling jobs or medico positions where they went in fast and cut. "How's it going, Cot?" they say. Ralphie Modine says it looks as if he's losing weight, but he means it as a compliment, the only one in his repertoire. Mostly they're quiet. Albertson owns the building—eight stories on the bay—but the offices he doesn't use he leaves empty, except for the flower shop and the pharmacy on the first floor. Through the pharmacy's interior glass windows Cot can see Spane standing at the counter talking to a man in a pale blue smock. He might be the pharmacist, he might not. Spane nods and smiles in his taut, half-smiling way. "Pride'll get you killed," he likes to say. He could be saying it now to the possible pharmacist, who's new. He doesn't come out, but he glances at Marcella who doesn't look at him. A man at the round lobby desk, standing beside two men staring into monitors checks him in. "I like that kind of apple juice," he says. "It's my favorite."

"I'll get you some," Cot says.

Two men Cot doesn't know well accompany them down the long front corridor and out the smoky glass-fronted doors to the back patio that's covered for most of its length by a large orange awning. The boat, a ship really at more than a hundred feet, is tied up to the big dock, its only occupant. At the foot of the gangway a man sits at a small white table. He gets up, and then the two men accompanying pat Cot down and take away his two pistols. One pistol they recognize.

"Bert's," the shorter man says knowingly to the other, a hatchet-faced hombre Cot knows to be secretly afraid of thunderstorms and travel by air.

"It's kind of mournful," the taller man says. "Bert not being attached to one end of it."

"Guess he went around to look at the *wrong* end."

A memorial moment, of silence, death wrought, death depending, drifts through. The short man looks up as if he's caught sight of something distantly passing. An expression flees across his face, of pain, of surprise and hurt, too fast for anybody to keep up with, even him. "He wadn't nothing much," he says.

"Yeah, Bert . . . ," his partner says.

"Bert's fine," Cot says.

The man at the table, a man with short, carroty hair, wearing a green eyeshade like a figure in a gangster movie, studies Cot and tells him to sign the register. Cot signs his name and Marcella's too. Then Marcella leans down and signs her name again. "She's my lawyer," Cot says.

"We know who she is," the man says cocking his head like a mockingbird. He has marine blue eyes and a spray of freckles across the bridge of his nose.

"I hate plastic boats," Marcella says and smiles.

There's the outline of a big door in the side of the hull, a door they could have been let through if Albertson wanted, but they have to climb the steps of the gangway. That's all right. Cot looks back and up along the front of the building to the long balcony on the top floor, a balcony men not Albertson are looking down from. They have weapons, Belgian Minimi submachine guns, in their hands. Above them, puffed white clouds hold their shape, practicing for summer. This winter he walked Albertson's fields west of Homestead, poking blackened tomatoes with a stick. "A shambles," Albertson said when he told him and looked as if he might cry. But he didn't; he sometimes looked as if he would, but he never did. "The beans might make it," Cot told him, but Albertson asked in his wispy snake's voice how the hell somebody like him would know—he didn't want to hear about it.

A fattish man in a puffed white cap looks down at them from the flying bridge. "That what you wear on a sea voyage?" he says. "Farm clothes?" This is Bales, Albertson's unlikely brother, a distracted killer that being brother of a hoodlum mogul has given leeway to. Always the skittish malefic brother around in these assemblies, the one scared he won't be violent enough. Bales counters his panic by uttering vituperatives and mashed-up malignant thoughts out loud. Some admire this. Most are just forced to. Cot feels oddly close to the man, brotherly. It's all right, he says to him sometimes, fondly, as if speaking about nothing. He climbs the outside stairs ahead of Marcella and meets Bales at the door of the main salon. Cot shakes his swollen, mole-speckled hand and introduces Bales to Marcella which he likes. "Great hat," Cot says.

Bales smiles, half abashed, half murderous.

Sailors at the bow and stern have already called for the dockside boys to cast off the lines. The gangsters clumsily unwind the heavy gray ropes from the concrete bollards, fumbling and joking and squeezing the rope as if it's the sliding muscles of a pet snake. Through the open windows Cot can see across the salon to the bay blue as a blue eye and beyond it the half-tall white buildings of Miami Beach. Albertson has a house out there, raised on pillars among mango and ceiba trees, big trees with aboveground roots erupting from the coral like huge gray tumors. The salon is empty. Bales walks them in. "You want a drink?" he says. "You want some of that shit apple juice?"

"It's for the Big Man," Cot says.

Bales scowls. "Maybe I ought to sample it first then." He pauses, waiting for Cot to give him the jug. Time like slivers of cold blue glass drifting in space.

"That would worry me. It would probably worry your brother too."

Bales looks to him as if he has pronounced the answer to an intricate, distasteful riddle. "What you want, Mrs. Cord?" he says.

"A gin and tonic would be just right," Marcella says. She's studying a clear glass bowl filled with cowrie shells. Mixed in with the shells are what look like human knuckle bones. "Y'all sit down," Bales says, but Cot ignores him. "You ever tried to swim across the bay?" Bales asks, mostly to Marcella.

"I think it would wear me out," she says smiling her winning smile, the one that carries a stinging rebuke just a couple of microns below the surface.

"Oh, no," Bales says making crabby swimming motions. "It's stimulating."

"Exercise is the key."

"To what?" He cocks his head as if it has slipped slightly on his neck.

"To a full life."

"I never heard that," he says earnestly.

Cot looks at Marcella as if to say *see what I mean about nobody to talk to?* though he's never said exactly that and doesn't really want to. She looks back a friendly puzzlement that isn't puzzlement at all but is something else he can't get straight in his mind and for a sec he feels alone in the world. It's a feeling guzzling along like a hag fish, chronic. *I live in a dent in time*, he thinks, something that came to him in the last few days, maybe on the bus ride down, but this doesn't mean anything. Mobsters are sometimes friendliest just before they kill you—he thought that too on the bus, cupping a hand under his chin so as not to drip the orange he was eating above his lap. A moment of freedom from a lifetime of restraint.

The friendliness clumsy and overeager. Later it's what they're most ashamed of. He's probably already said all this to Marcella, but he isn't sure. I'm running a tab on my life, he thinks and almost says. "Mobsters are often friendliest . . ." he says in a quiet, conversational voice and stops.

"I'm like that too," she says and smiles a simple home-made smile.

"So where's the maestro?" Cot says to Bales.

"Down in the innards."

Cot knows that Albertson likes to go down to the engine room to watch the big turbines work. He likes to wear a stained khaki cap like that of petty officers in the Navy. Not like—a *real* Navy hat.

"I'll go down and talk to him," Cot says.

"Maybe you better wait."

"Why don't you check the view out at the rail," Cot says to Marcella.

"Where you going?" Bales says to Cot as he starts out of the big room.

"I've got a present for your brother."

"Besides that apple juice?"

"Something he'll like."

"You better have something mighty special."

Cot descends into the interior of the ship. Double doors open into a long room containing large blank-faced engines. The turbines turn huge driveshafts that lie like great dragontails in their beds of power. Albertson leans over a rail, so far that he's partly balancing, looking down at them. He's a large black-haired man with a wide, slightly pockmarked face that is roughly handsome and seems just barely to conceal a figuration of the spirit, a domesticity and warmth, that has never been known to come fully to the surface. Cot walks toward him through a humming silence. Bales hasn't followed him down. Being that deep in the steel makes him seasick; Cot's counted on that.

Albertson watches him come. *There's something about me that has never been touched*—Albertson tells himself. His soul, he thinks, wedged like a stone deep inside him. But that's not it, he doesn't mean that, he means some bit, some startling indestructibility, alive, that always swims just out of reach. He's almost fainting. Fainting? The engine room is air-conditioned so it can't be the heat. Maybe it's the tumor. Cot, this Cot advancing, has worked for him for eighteen years. He's grown like the grass in the field. Now it's time to cut the grass and toss it into the fire. *Whyfore have I exalted thee . . .*, he says to himself, believing it to be part of a great quotation. Albertson thinks Cot looks tired. He sees something else, something that has lurked nearby for years, and he knows it for what it is, but a power he doesn't understand stalls him. *What's it going to be?* he thinks as he watches Cot take a lighter from his pocket. *Is that a jug of apple juice?* He's familiar with the brand.

In no time Cot's back on deck. Heads, already turned, minds already reeling. A man in whites on the other side of the ship—Cot can see him through the salon windows—is loudly yelling. Another man has two pistols out and is waving one of them as if directing traffic.

"Something blew up down there," Cot says. He's shaking, grimacing into a close-by nothingness. "Oh, man."

"Something you had a part in?" says Bales, white in the face. He's pulled his pistol and he jerks it at Cot. "You stay right there." He runs down the passageway.

The ship has already pulled away from the dock and is headed out into the bay. Marcella leans her back against the rail gazing at him. "You look a little frosty," she says. She clasps herself in her arms and lets herself go, slaps the rail with her open palm. "Cot," she says in a low voice.

"I know," he says. "But it won't always be."

White clouds solid as giant figurines hang above them in the vast blue placidity. Concussive, dark with a louring yellow eye, the blast knocked him against the bulkhead, even though he managed to get one of the steel doors slammed shut between himself and the engine room.

Hurrying Marcella along he climbs to the bridge where he tells the captain to maintain headway. The captain knows who he is and does what he's told. Then Cot goes down to Albertson's cabin, offers his hand to the man standing outside the door and when the man—Jackie Harris, owner of a new Mercedes he likes to wheel triumphantly down Ocean Drive—goes to take it he brings his fist sharply up and slams the back of his head against the bulkhead. He takes Jackie's pistol and locks him in

Albertson's suite. The other men with guns are out on the fantail watching the ship get under way, waving—or were until a few moments ago. The alarm, the dread, is still in their faces when he takes them, which he does by sending a steward out with a tray just before he comes around from the side with a gun on them. He makes them throw their pistols overboard, all but a little Sig .38 he keeps for himself. He herds the men downstairs and locks them with Jackie in Albertson's stateroom. He knows them all, has eaten steak dinners with them at Johnnie's, lied, goofed, come nearly to blows—all but one, a kid from Texas who has come by way of Wilkie Wilkes into the organization, an encumbered thinker, too quick to anger, but eager—and he tells them he's sorry, it seems the thing to do, about this.

"About what?" Marvin Chek says. "About *what*, Cot?"

He finds another gunsel washing his hands in a restroom down the hall, de-guns him, and puts him in Albertson's suite as well. Finds the last one—he figures—groaning in his bunk in the crew's quarters where a couple of sailors are arguing over a book of recipes.

"Done in?" Cot says to the groaner.

"Oh, God almighty," the man says, a slender fellow with a slight lisp, another new man, who, week before last, walked out of the cane fields with Jean Paul Loess's head under his arm.

"Joined the Sea Brigade," Cot says.

"What's that?"

"Sea Brigade."

"I can't talk."

Cot makes him get up anyway. The man throws up on the floor and tries to get back in bed, but Cot makes him come along. He puts him in with Albertson's crew, drives with the butt of the Sig Sauer the thick-bladed oyster knife he'd taken from Jug Melson into the door's steel lip strike, jamming it, and leaves them.

By now Bales is on his way back topside. He's come on the carnage in the engine room. The turbines were sooty but unhurt, but the men down there—three of them at least—had been burned. Two killed, one being his brother, Gustave Lorian Albertson, Master of Miami Ganglia, as he liked to say. His body burned naked and peeled to flush and char, stinking of gas. His face hanging in strips. (Cot had lit the lamp of Martinelli, held the jug a moment in his palm, wondering even then if the idea would work [if all the years could come to this, if Albertson would know what was up, if he Cot could possibly get out of there], and then he threw it in a high and—it seemed to him—slow arc that he never caught the end of because he had already ducked back through the companionway door and slammed it behind him. The wall seemed to bulge and a radiance, a force he had not expected, knocked him against the opposite bulkhead. His ears rang and he could smell gasoline. There was a layer of black smoke feeling its way along the floor. It curled, writhing, around his legs. A thumping in his chest grated and lunged, as if his heart was being hurled repeatedly against bone.)

Bales comes up the central passageway crying, with his head down, the shock of seeing his brother dead reared like a shrieking ghost in the center of his mind, and he doesn't see Cot until he has his pistol leveled at his face. "Ah, you squat," he groans. "How could you do such a thing?"

Cot takes his pistol, an ugly, squared off police Glock, and backs him into the salon. He hands Bales a napkin from a stack on a counter and tells him to wipe his face. Bales looks at him as if he doesn't understand. Marcella takes the napkin and wipes his face for him. "It'll be okay," Cot says.

"No, it won't," Bales says. He stands on the dark blue rug trembling like a winded dog. It's the steadiness, the rationality in Cot that makes hatred thicken in Bales. Cot makes him go outside to the rail and wave to the boys still on the dock—now concerned, now wondering, now hoping no disaster—he doesn't want to but he does it.

Marcella goes with him and she waves too. She calls the name of one of the boys—Gus Boland—even though they are too far away by then for him to catch it.

She's a good-looking woman, Gus thinks, getting a little age on her, but still crisp.

There're only three or four men on the patio. A couple wave at Marcella or maybe they are waving at Bales. Marcella, a pistol held in one hand and covered by the other, keeps Bales out there until the men have gone back into the building. It isn't unusual for the boss to head out to sea. From where they stood the explosion was only a muffled metallic cough—who knew what went on in the bellies of ships?

Cot makes Bales sit with them in the salon until the ship has made its way into the roads. They come up the back side of Dodge and slip into the channel and through to the Cut and out. Cot sends Marcella up to the bridge to ride with the captain and make sure he doesn't worry about anything. These are the new days, not the old: the captain doesn't have to speak to the engineer to get more, or less power. The explosion sounded like dropped crockery. But the captain wonders where Albertson is, maybe he knows, maybe it's like a coup that everybody senses, that gulls and ants and highwaymen sense and turn toward as to the discovery of a new sun moving in. Marcella calls Cot to tell him the captain's nervous.

"Tell him the Big Man's taking a nap."

In the salon he drinks a glass of ice water. Bales doesn't want one. Cot feels sick to his stomach. His blood's hard banging has subsided, but he feels crashed into and knocked around and dumbfounded partially; he feels as if maybe he's going out on his feet.

"I'm about to be sick," Bales says. His face is yellowed with gray patches under his eyes. Cot goes with him into the restroom, and while Bales vomits into one of the toilet bowls Cot vomits into one of the sinks.

"Make sure you clean that up," Bales says when he comes out of the stall. Cot is already wiping down the blue marble countertop, and it annoys him that Bales would order him to do what he's already on top of. But he understands—Bales is crushed. He would be too if something happened, say, to Marcella.

After they're out in the inky blue deeps, after Bales has begun his elegies and trifles, his death song of stories about growing up on the north side, up in Hialeah where he hung around the track cutting up and extorting cash from the big shots, where he cut his first shag as he puts it out on Raymond Canal, under a big yellow flower bush, his fuck bush, as Bales puts it, and, after he keens and cries out, his voice straining in the sunlight, perspiring as he yells, his face flushed and in his eyes a despair Cot has never seen there before, after Cot who's in and out on paying attention thinks about how he rarely pauses to see how a shot man falls—unless he's only wounded—rarely any more than glances at the body pitched on its face like that of a drunken man, say, who would wake the next morning with his face stiff and numb but still alive, after the gulls, side-sliding and cawing like crows, depart under a sky briefly clear even of clouds, after this he walks Bales down to the loading area in the stern, opens the big doors that look out on the oily Atlantic, takes Bales by the hand and leads him out onto the small platform where in port they would board the runabouts and jet skis, and without saying anything to Bales by way of exculpation, accusation or commentary, throws him into the roiled and frothing wake. Bales goes straight down as if he has important business on the bottom. Cot squats and then sits down on the platform and gazes out at the wide blue ocean that's as empty as on Earth's first day.

After a while he gets up and goes to tell Marcella what he's done. She's lying face down in the salon on a couch she gets up from and slaps him across the eyes. The water in his eyes runs down his face like tears. They stand in the big room, each on a separate bar of sunlight, looking at the other. It's the third time in their lives that she's hit him. He's never hit her, not yet. He thinks of this. The blow seems to've knocked something out of him; there's now a space inside. He expects this space to fill quickly but it doesn't. She looks him in the eyes with a ferocity that doesn't scare him. He feels as if he's in a separate circumstance looking back at this one. Marcella feels this too. But she also feels the ropes and binderies that will soon enough haul her at great speed and force back into this place. It's just what she was afraid would happen. There's no mystery, she thinks, and no solution, and hauls off and hits him again.

7

Ten hours later and just outside the reef they took the runabout in the six miles to Cow Channel, entered the canal below Roosevelt Drive, and ran down to the boat ramp on 11th Street. There they were met by Jake Muster in his cab and Jake drove them to Marcella's family place where Cot took a bicycle and peddled over to his mother's house on Regent. He had a feeling, he told Marcella. His mother was sitting barefoot on the front steps. Mayrene's car was parked out front. Ella was eating a small papaya, scooping curls of yellow flesh out of the hull with a salt-corroded spoon. "I'm like an addict," she said grinning. "I can't stay away, and every minute without it I draw closer to it." Cot stood in the yard looking at her. He didn't quite get what she was saying. "Look at this spoon," she said. "All my things have been spoiled and rusted."

"I'd sue."

"I'm not sure that's the thing."

High up, buzzards, small and tending to their business, rode the island thermals. Gulls, those busybodies, raved and cut along, headed for the beach.

"It's stormed," his mother said.

She looked down at her long feet, long slender toes that her husband on the beach at the fort, or between Cuban sheets, liked to take in his hands and hold. "When I was wading over yonder where we plane-crashed," she said vaguely, speaking like a country woman and pointing in the wrong direction, "when I walked out of the Gulf waters, I could feel the rheumatism in my ankles. The bones hurt as if somebody had whacked them with a stick."

She hadn't meant to say that, say or think the trailing thought. But that was what age was, wasn't it, that tendency toward expostulation?

From the little yard, under a half dead, peeling gumbo-limbo tree Cot looked at her. "They let you back in?"

"I borrowed on the house."

"And did what?"

"Paid off that little squirrel."

"I don't believe you."

"I'm sitting here, aren't I?"

"I'm not sure you should have done that, Mama." Thinking, well, she could have done that all along—thinking, now they'll just take it from her in chunks of blackmail and scurrilous doings and put her in the street.

"Why not?"

"I don't want to see you living over in the park."

"That isn't likely." She thought she might go to Cuba, rejoin her husband, learn afresh to live in his unacknowledged version of failed glory. That had been the trouble before: unacknowledgment—hadn't it?

"I have a phobia about it," he said.

"You don't live in a park. And don't you mean a precognition?"

"I live in a hotel. And I can't stand the thought of sleeping outside."

"Is that a non sequitur?"

"No, Mama." He *did* have a phobia about it. He waked in the night sweating from fear of it. Sweating from fear of losing Marcella, his father, CJ when he was alive, even Spane and his cohorts in Miami snug in their hotels. What conceived shambles wasn't he scared of?

Jackie came out the front door. He was eating cereal from a bowl. He grinned broadly, a smile that mashed up his face in long rubbery creases. "I drove that car down here myself. Didn't get stopped nare a time."

"You seen Ordell?" Cot said.

"Not lately," Jackie said. "Miss Ella picked me up at the bus station in Miami and I drove the rest of the way."

"How'd you get up to the bus station?"

"Jokey Bivins carried me."

"What about Jimmy?"

"I had to leave him."

A mist of complicatedness, confusion and mischance was forming in his mind. "Let's drop it," he said.

"I didn't bring it up."

His mother said, "I expect you'll find Ordell over snooping after Marcie."

She seemed fey, shy, almost indistinct. A breeze lifted a reef of flowers in the poinciana tree by the street and set it back. Spring had stuffed the town with new blooms. He wanted to tell his mother to lie low, wanted to force her onto a plane or a ship, but he knew it was no longer any use to try. "I think you need to go to Cuba, Mama."

"I've thought that myself."

She could see in his face he meant what he said, that he was scared, peeled back from his sureties. But there was something else. He tapped his cheekbone with his foreknuckle, an old habit. She could not always read him now. Was there more, more than she could know? As with Rafael? It was as if a part of them had moved into shadow. She felt a chill.

"You got any more of that cereal?" he said.

She smiled and got to her feet and they embraced. She smelled differently now, he thought, slightly sour, bland, sunworn, the old strong odors of childhood become snips, faded flares. Her body was not frail in his arms but pared down, sinewy. He tipped her head back, placing the heel of his hand against her hairline, as he had done as a child, smoothing skin and hair both, and kissed her lightly on the lips.

"Memory lane," she said, her voice creaking, and disengaged herself.

Out in the street Johnny Lowery towed his sister Ronnie, a slow-minded skinny woman, in a wheeled seat attached to the rear of his bicycle. They were both over fifty and, so Cot knew, inseparable. Johnny gave him a severe nod of the head. A mockingbird in the little lime tree by the porch made a mewing sound. Just then, down the street, police cars turned the corner. Cot stepped back into the yard, whirled, and ran along the side of the house, through the backyard where Jackie had the drum smoker going and into the lane. Mrs. Cranson, in a blue pinafore, was shaking out a small owl quilt on her front porch. She waved and as she did the quilt, in full fling, collapsed over her. He laughed out loud and was suddenly happy and crossing a tiny space in which happiness was stuffed in every corner and you could snatch it loose as you passed, and this passed—it was clear—but still you carried the traces and perfumes of it as you went. I won't tell anybody, he thought and almost shouted, barreling along in big strides. He walked quickly down the lane and out on Constance. A couple of tourists in matching muscle shirts were putting their bicycles into a rack outside the Sponge House hotel.

"I'll get those for you," he said taking the blue racer from the larger of the two men. The man didn't want to let the bike go, but Cot insisted.

He pedaled up the street, turned left on Harden and took the shortcut through the municipal cemetery to the Bakewell house up a little shaded driveway just past Knockout Lane. He went around back, past a large red bougainvillea draped over a big stake frame, and entered the house through the back door. Ordell was sitting in a pink banquette built into a little nook off the kitchen before a clumped mess of pancakes. He was reading the paper that had a picture of Jimmy's plane in color on the front page. Ordell looked up, unsurprised it seemed. He pushed scarlet reading glasses up his forehead.

"It's too bad about Jimmy," he said.

"How about CJ?" Cot said. He hit Ordell with his fist in the side of the head. The punch sent him sprawling down the bench. He slid under the table. One hand was still on the surface, groping at the spilled pages. He came up with a pistol in his other hand.

"Come on, Ordell."

Cot batted his gun-hand away, knocking it against the back of the booth. Ordell dropped the pistol. It fell under the table. "Damn," Cot said. Ordell made a face. Cot dived and snatched up the pistol. Ordell tried to climb over him, scrabbling for handholds on his body. He kneed Cot in the side. Ordell had played on the line in high school football. He was clumsy and slow but played with an insurgent bitterness that made him dangerous. He kneed Cot again, this time in the face. Cot's head banged against the strut holding the table up. He went out for a second, coming almost instantly to, and for a flash thought he was in his mother's garage playing with plastic soldiers in the dust. Ordell was suddenly right beside him. Where did *he* come from? Then he remembered and tried to swing around, but Ordell was stabbing at him with a table fork. The fork struck him in the cheek. Cot cried out. Ordell was stabbing him. The points felt like bee stings. He ducked and got hold of the pistol that he had dropped when Ordell kicked him. He rolled onto his back under the table. Ordell was suddenly out of sight. He felt the blood on his face. He fired twice through the table top. Then, for a moment, as if he had just waked upstairs in the bed in their guest bedroom, the one with the yellow candlewick spread he had always liked and the window that looked down onto a yard filled with blossoming ruella bushes, he rested.

A voice, one he almost recognized, a woman's voice, said, "Throw the gun out, Cot."

"Or what?" Cot said.

"Or I'll shoot you."

The voice, familiar but unplaceable, sounded as if it was a small distance away. Probably hiding behind something. "Okay," he said.

He slid the gun out onto the yellow tile floor.

"The other one too," the voice said.

"Is that you, Isabella?"

"It is indeed. How you doing, Cot?"

"I'm a little worn out to tell the truth."

"Slide that other pistol out on the floor."

"You handling things for Ordell?" Isabella was a police detective, younger than them, a woman with coppery hair she wore tucked up behind her head, smarter than the men around her.

"You shouldn't have come over here bothering the county attorney, Cot. Slide the gun out."

She would shoot him, he knew that. He slid Bert's gun along the floor. There was one more, his, tucked under his shirt. "Can I come out? It's kind of cramped under here."

"Come out backwards," Isabella said. Isabella Mouson. Ex-goalie on the state champion girls' water polo team. Former student of classical languages at FSU. She was the one recommended the translation of *The Georgics* he was reading.

"You know he killed CJ, don't you?"

"We'll get to that."

Cot shuffled butt first out from under the big table. The room smelled now of cordite and maple syrup. Ordell was leaning through the hall doorway talking into his phone. He issued a look at Cot that had no friendliness in it. Cot got to his feet. Ordell grimaced and glared at him, his wide Carpathian forehead unwrinkled.

"Oh, come off it, Ordell."

"You prick."

There were many choice rebukes Cot could apply here, but he held his tongue. He remembered that he wanted to ask Ordell if he was still an animist. He wanted to tell him he could see how in a place like this—seaswept and lonely among the mangroves—you could go for a religion like that. "Did you know the pythons have made it across Seven Mile?" he said.

"I heard that," Isabella said. She pulled a large blue bandana out of her back pocket and tossed it to Cot. "For your face."

He caught the bandana with one hand and with the other pulled his pistol and shot Isabella in the shoulder. She sagged against the counter and fired a shot that broke a windowpane over the booth. Her face went white.

"I'm sorry, Izzie," Cot said. The policewoman tried to shift the pistol to her good hand but Cot was quick and plucked it from her. Two of the knuckles on that hand were scarred where she'd smashed her fist against the side of a pool years ago. He helped her to the floor, gathered up Bert's gun, hers and the extra. He poked hers down the garbage disposal and turned it on and then off quick; the noise was dispiriting. "You sit still," he said and kissed her on the forehead. She had pulled into a fetal position and lay softly gasping. He was sorry, yeah, sorry lathered with a sadness like an animal's, as he saw it, a fox, say, lying under a bush waiting out the end of the hunt.

Ordell had quit the premises. He never liked guns. The adrenaline had made Cot giddy. He raced down the hall, making kicky little dance steps as he went. He hadn't heard the front door slam, so maybe Ordell was still in the house. A sudden conundrum. Was there time to check upstairs? "You there, Ordell?" No answer. "What'd you do with the stones?" he yelled, not so loudly the police force hurrying to this spot might hear.

He checked the front porch. No sign of him. Wind shoveling itself out of a young poinciana. He yelled back up the front stairs "I'm going to shoot Isabella if you don't come down."

Nobody answered. Shouts, appeals, statements of fact—none of that would work with Ordell. And it wasn't just Ordell—you never really got to run your plan out as devised. The measure was in what you made up when it haywired. Some guys pulled a gun, some sneaked, some waited, some got out of there, some capered and yelled, some prayed, some just kept cooking. He simply moved, glancing off a hunch. It was getting late. Shadows, mixed and pliant, clotted under the big mahogany tree, closing in on dark. A skinny breeze, almost not there, slid up the driveway. He crossed the open space, took the little path that ran through senna bushes around and past the Lovelaces' yard and stopped at the street across from the cemetery. A lone cyclist, balancing a child-sized rocking chair on the handlebars, pedaled slowly up the street. The light from the laddering sun seemed stalled among the tallest grave markers.

He crossed the street and entered the cemetery though the unlatched side gate. His cheek had stopped bleeding but he dabbed at it with the bandana anyway. In the distance a few tourists were taking pictures of the Kagle's big ziggurat tomb. He wished he was carrying a cat in his arms, or maybe he was thinking of a baby. He and Marcella rarely talked about such as that—small, bustling enterprisers, offspring, making irresistible demands. She said it would make her go blind if she did.

He crossed the cemetery to the far side where CJ's family compound rose in its stones among a small stand of coconut palms. A large ficus, once carefully trimmed, now shaggy, loomed over the large coral stone chamber. The black iron front door was locked with an old-fashioned Scandinavian padlock that Cot had known how to jimmy since he and CJ were eight years old. Nobody about, the grounds empty of the living. He let himself in.

Before he closed the door into darkness he looked at CJ's casket, a golden metal vessel with recessed handles set on an upper shelf to the side. Cot had no illusions about CJ's ghost being in the room with him. A mournfulness curled around him softly, running its spiky teeth across his skin. The vault was a shadowy station between the living and the dead. An intense pressure like something trying to come through subsided before it could. He burst out sobbing, so hard that he bit his fist to stop. But he didn't want to stop. After a while he let the dark back in. He sat on the rear bench and leaned against the wall that was warm and dry. In the quiet, unallusive lightlessness he settled himself to wait.

For a time Ella drifted through the rooms of her house like a spirit returning to its natural form. She touched the curtains, the counters, the bedsteads, the dressers, the huge cabinet in the hall that Cot liked to hide in as a boy. Each seemed to rise out of a massive stillness. She saw how time could stop and rest in these simple places and thought how there must be many other such around the world, disused buildings, forgotten stretches of road, houses in cutover fields, scrub meadows, caves, ruins in deserts that themselves were quiet spots where time lay like an old cat sleeping. She hardly wanted to wake the silent rooms. But she could not stop herself. She lay down on the yellowed sisal rug in the living room and listened to the little house geckos chirping like docents. She folded back the old blue spread on her bed and lay on the clean sheets underneath. Dreams almost captured her there, but she shook them off and rose and moved on. In a pool of sunlight in the hall she knelt and said a prayer, offering it like a fingered rosary to Whatever might take it. She did not wish to hurry the sleeper, but her movements became more purposeful, more engaged with the beating of her own heart. *Arise*, she said silently, *the Redeemer has come*, and stopped in the kitchen—that still held its faded bundle of afternoon light like a sheaf of yellow seagrass in its arms—and laughed out loud. *Arise! The Redeemer has come!* She drank a glass of water straight from the tap, the chalky, dust-tasting island water that she disliked. She found a broom standing straight as a soldier in the closet and went through the rooms sweeping the dust ahead of her. She stripped the beds, the couches, pulled down the curtains and sent them with Jackie to the laundromat. She raised the rugs off the floor and hauled them to the backyard where she beat the old dead dust out of them. She washed the floors with oil soap, washed the walls, got down on her knees in the bathroom and cleaned the floor, tile by tile, careful to excavate the curdled dust from the little grout troughs. She washed all the dishes, the pots, everything in the kitchen that could be washed. She dusted lamps, polished tables, carefully wiped the books in the old red-painted bookcase. The house took on a brightness it had not known since the early days of her marriage. Time started up again, roved like a hunting dog into the lost fields, and returned, headed out to the new lands. She danced and capered. "Carry me!" she cried. "Oh, carry me!" It was as if the world, or life itself, would snatch her up and swing her around dancing in the charming sunlight. She sat in the east window seat looking out at the pale purple flowers of the frangipani tree. She ran a bath and got into the tub and listened to Bach's oboe concerto on her little player while she lazed in the cool water. In the spaces between the notes she thought she could just hear Bach's wife calling him to supper.

She was thinking of an old bathing suit she loved as a girl, picturing it draped over the back porch rail drying in sunlight when Ordell Bakewell walked into the bathroom. He was wearing his pinstriped suit pants and a white shirt and carrying a black pistol. For an instant she wanted a cigarette, something she'd not tasted for thirty years. "Hello, Ordell."

"Hey, Mrs. Sims."

His face looked raked back by wind, or by a hard hand, strained and pressured, the pale shining skin worn nearly through. "You look tired," she said.

"Actually I'm feeling pretty fit."

She thought of her son, of the brightness in his eyes that as a child had been like a promise that nothing terrible would happen to any of them. She remembered her husband and pictured him leaning over his work table bringing lovers to life in pictures. She blessed him, blessed Jackie, blessed her son, and experienced a declining and simple tenderness. She never heard the shot, and the bullet entering her brain burned too briefly for her to worry about it.

A little after midnight Cot slipped through a section of bent-back fence that let out onto Conover Street, walked up to Cromartie's All-nite Store, and got a *pernil* sandwich and a cold can of ginseng tea. The Bangladeshi man behind the counter had a family resemblance to Cot's friend Rajah, his brother, who was on his way to jail on a tax dodge—probably already there—but Cot didn't know his name and the man didn't know him. He bought half a dozen postcards and stamps and standing at the counter wrote messages to people around town and one to the boys up in Miami, addressed to Spane. Sending postcards was a habit he'd kept up all his life. "Gus said he thinks the world of you," he wrote to Spane and the boys. "*Perseverent* was the word he used. 'They're game,' the Big Man said. I miss you too."

To Marcella he wrote,

> *"You touch the tenderest parts of me with a gentleness that would make the meanest cut artist shiver. This has always seemed miraculous to me, like waking for the first time on the beach to the sunrise shining in your face."*

He scratched the last line out and wrote over it:

> *"I'm feeling a little tentative right now, but truth is I'm making progress on serious matters that concern us both. Maybe we should have a baby after all. Or—forget it—I don't mean to bring up a worrisome topic. Love you lovable you."*

To his mother he wrote:

*"Dear Ma: you extend my thinking always. I never
could quite keep up with your curiosity about life's specks
and illuminata, but still it tugs me on. I really enjoy
our discussions about the why of things but I wonder
sometimes lately if life isn't mostly just taking life in
without thinking much about it. I'm dreaming these days
of Mexico."*

He wrote postcards to Jim Willys, the police chief,
and to the mayor, explaining briefly what Ordell had
done. What had he done? Killed CJ and taken the emeralds.

*" . . . and unleashed a string of emergencies from here
to Fort Myers, Miami, and back. I realize I have had a
part in this. You might even say it's all my fault. But if
Ordell hadn't raised his greedy hand against CJ I think
things would have gone a lot smoother."*

His handwriting got smaller and more rushed as he
went. He was careful to make it legible, a problem that
went back to his grammar school days. There was always so much to say and such a pressing need to say it.
Sometimes these days he looked over his rushed cards
and couldn't make out a word he'd written. He needed
a translator for his own scribblings. *" ' . . . easy quiet, a
secure retreat / A harmless life that knows not how to*

cheat' " he quoted, adding in small printed letters: "Virgil, *The Georgics* 2." This in a card to Winky Gold, the county mayor, chief of everybody who lived in the Keys outside KW. As he finished and stacked the cards—five minutes of his time that he was aware was like gold dust draining from a bag—two drunks, no, a drunk and an older man, not the drunk's partner, came into the store. They both went to the counter, and the drunk took up an argument with the counterman that had clearly begun earlier. As he spoke the man behind him, an older man in a red satin vest and white shorts, pulled change from his pocket. The change got loose and scattered on the floor. Cot and the drunk helped the man pick the silver up. Cot could smell the drunk's fruity and preservative-saturated breath. He knew him slightly, a man he had chatted with one rainy afternoon a year or so ago about mincemeat pies. They both had favored lard to make the crust flaky. The man didn't seem to recognize him. Cot handed the few cents back, and the older man thanked him. He got another postcard and standing at the counter wrote his father.

"You once told me that your parents' heavy hand had worn out all familial feeling in you. Well, it's never been that way for me. My love for you, Papa, keeps winging over the waters. One trade item that no embargo can keep out."

He paid for the cards and for the tall can of iced tea and the sandwich and went out into the night. The air was clean smelling and cool. He mailed the cards at a box on the corner. As he lingered a moment leaning against the big metal container inhaling sweet airs of night he realized he had known the other gent too, the man in the vest: Rev. Buckle from Grace Episcopal church; the rev'd taught him the Nicene Creed when he was twelve. Back then the priest had been a stocky man, the flesh stretching the skin with health, his glittery blue eyes snapping shrewd looks at him as he recited. Now a man grown old. Discrete swirls of white hair, loose jowls, a dark patch above his lip like a phantom mustache. The old man hadn't recognized him either. Maybe he too had lost some essential identifier. As Cot mused by the mailbox the reverend came out. He raised his face to the light from the overhead mercury lamp and sniffed the air. Stood a moment looking vaguely around. Then leaning forward like a heavy object tipped out of its inertia he plunged ponderously into the dark village night. For an instant Cot wanted to be the sort of person who spoke to aged benefactors. A plug of sadness had lodged under his breast bone. Old malarkies that took on unforeseen resonances. He had forgotten the creed the old preacher had taught him. Did it include the part about resurrection of the body? Yes, it did. Not zombies walking around but reanimated souls in their best clothes. His mother had once been Episcopalian but had changed her religion to Catholic to please his father, and then his father had repudiated the Catholics. She was left dangling among the papists. But not really. She had climbed down and walked away through the scruffy ecumenical streets of Key West.

He massaged a place in his chest that hurt. Maybe only a little muscle that had been over-stretched out in the Gulf.

Two tall men on bicycles, the bikes sporting plaques identifying them as tourist wheels, passed by in the street. Both men, as if they were a team, pedaled in the same stately manner. Both were barefoot. It was great to come down to the tropics without ever having to leave the country, everybody knew about that. And good to ride a bike at night in your bare feet. The sea winds blew the stinks of the addled republic away. Not just the beefy and chlorosulfuric stench of the cities, but the funks of the ruralities as well, the crotty smell of cornfields and the coal oil reek of mountains. He laughed, whispery and low. Green growing crops—skinned deserts, elevated scenarios where you had to climb and look out over territory— the natural world, made him uneasy. Dirt. Sap. Fruit rotted black and mushy. Coconuts could drop out of a tree and kill you. Plains, deserts, country roads were clogged with snakes and horrible biting bugs. He'd stopped his car once and fired a full Uzi clip into bushes just to keep the swamp back. He knew what growing things wanted. *Yeah, so why Virgil?* he thought. It was his way—he knew it. Cross-grained to the end. It was homage and hope, it was the little boy trying to become some strange and special thing. Farms! Where you had to go to bed early and everything smelled of cow shit! Mountains hard to climb, hard to climb down from! Fields! Tomatoes with stony green fruit hanging like tiny grenades in the armpits of the branches! *He* liked to sit on the curb outside Smacky's Fin up in Miami eating shrimp salad with his fingers. He liked that, Virge. He liked to squeeze lime juice into his mouth, Marcella liked that too. Christ! He wished she was here.

Back in the mausoleum he lay on the bench sipping the cold tea. The air in the tomb was dry, comforting in its dryness. A faint dust on everything. He got up and ran his hand over CJ's casket. He would like to look at him once more, but he was reluctant to break the seal. Maybe he was only shy, same old Cot, letting opportunity slip by. Except at work, and as he could have said once, except for on a football field. People had always been a little blurry to him. He got up and went outside. Stars everywhere like bristly bits tossed aside, crumbs. He crossed to the other side of the cemetery and entered the small compound where Marcella's people were buried. Oleander bushes flowered along one side of a low rusty iron picket fence. Cot lay down under one of the bushes and went to sleep and dreamed of dogs running ahead of him across a stony field somewhere near the ocean.

Marcella found him there in the early morning, curled up, his face pressed into a tuft of bahia grass, dreams, rusty and creaking, scurrying for the exits. She told him Ordell had shot his mother. Cot sat in the grass in the fresh soft light and listened, but what she said sounded stupid. A flock of crows wheeled above distant bushy trees, unaware of what had happened, but maybe they too knew, he thought, maybe they had seen it all and the flycatchers too and the cats and the bugs and the goosefoot grass and hibiscus flowers and stray elements of breeze and creation in general had seen it. An insufferable sense of humiliation filled his body so suddenly he was choking on it before he could even think what was happening.

"How do you know this?"

"He told me."

"Where is he?"

"He said he was going to turn himself in."

"Will he do that?"

His mother's life an evacuation, a country, a race just wiped off the map.

Marcella's face was marked with tiny seeps and abandonments of fatigue. A small, disamplified breeze, breeze in a minor key, brushed by them carrying the smell of jasmine.

"I better find him," he said.

For a single moment that was almost more than he could bear the full weight of grief pushed against him, bland and featureless and solid. He wanted to run away. Spring from that place, fired like a shot into another world, but he couldn't move. The moment passed as it came but it left a sensation as if he'd been entered by a nothingness, a feral slow-wittedness without design or purpose or connection to anything else, inevitable and vast, tasteless, formless, a grinding stupidity and ignorance older than the world. He felt suddenly emptied, tossed aside, beyond rescue.

He got up and stamped his feet on the scruffy, salt-gray grass. Buried in the grave he nearly stood on was Duffy Holt, Marcella's great grandfather, a schooner captain, a man left bewildered, so they said, when the wooden sailing ships became only curiosities. He had been buried in the uniform of blue and braid he had devised for himself and walked around town in, beached, a ridiculous and touching figure. Cot started to move away but a fatigue beyond his late weariness stopped him. He sat down on a gravestone, above the last resting place of Oscar Cord, child of Hattie and Homer. He looked bleakly up at Marcella. He wanted to ask her what to do. Where should he go?

She took a step and touched his face, upturned to gaze at her. He pushed up the front of his hair with a hand she hadn't realized was (recently) scarred across the knuckles. Rumbling, growling, screeching, the morning flight from Miami passed overhead, a heavy jet that seemed to wobble and sway as it went. The plane disappeared beyond the buildings and trees and he waited for the crash that didn't come. He leaned back, away from Marcella's dry fingers. Her hand hung a moment in the air and then went away. He cupped his hand over his mouth. Grasped his lips softly between finger and thumb and let go. He slid to the ground and curled up in a ball on his side. Then he relaxed his legs and turned facedown into the grass. He could smell the chalky coral earth, smell the juice in the grass. As a child he had imagined embracing the earth in this graveyard, this largest open field on the island, and somehow swinging the planet in his arms. Everywhere around him all his life had been a vastness—of sky or ocean, wildernesses that were continuously running changes. No two days ever the same. But here, in this place, was some sort of unification, of lastingness. One of his grandfathers here—one of the great greats— had been a pirate, before, during the War of 1812, being commissioned in the US Navy as a captain running the British blockades. He had lived to 106 and was buried under a stone that praised him for finally going straight. Cot didn't care about that. Through a haze he looked up at Marcella. He wanted to thrust his hand right through her body into the sunlight on the other side. You could tear through the fabric of the universe if you wanted to they said and knew how. But he didn't know how. Ah, dog. He turned on his back, a movement that took every bit of his strength. He would have to be moved from now on by derrick, raised by davits and lowered into whatever mischief was ready for him. The thought made him laugh out loud, a short bark.

Marcella looked half at him, half startled. She was afraid of what he might do. She wanted this to go away, wanted *all* this to go away, even as she pitied him. Him too. It was okay to leave a bare patch. A raw, rubbled patch where nobody could remember what had been there before. Same for her. And for Ordell. For Ella Sims, the former Ellarese Jax. From space you could see little patches rubbed bald by grief. She knelt beside him. She wanted to touch him, to calm him, help him, but she didn't dare to. Her hand went out, her fingers brushed lightly over his chest. Nobody knew how brave she was—except Cot, and now he didn't anymore know.

He smiled at her. Her face, eroded by what he took to be sadness, looked expressionless, as if the whole array of feelings had been erased and now there was only a single, thin, and diminished specie left, a faint denomination that made her face seem the face of an over-corrected child. He pushed up on his arms, turned over and got to his knees. Marcella touched his hair. Her fingers slid down along his neck, found his face, his lips. He opened his mouth. She slid her fingers in, and he sucked them. The taste was of mangoes, and faintly of hand lotion.

He pulled away and got up, snapping off glances, looks, regards like a ticket punch. "You were about to say?"

"We have to get out of here. Get out of the daylight."

"Where's Ordell?"

"He's in his car, riding around the island."

In a cotton sack with a picture of a chimp in a pirate's hat on it Marcella had brought a change of clothes, a sandwich (egg salad), a ripe mango, an apple, a copy of the Rule of St. Benedict, a box of .38 caliber bullets, a thousand dollars in fifty dollar bills, and his mobile phone. "I have another idea"—which he told her about as they walked back through the grave plots. They stopped at CJ's family vault. The sun caught in the leaves of the almond tree above it. "Would you rather come home with me?" she said.

"I don't see how we can work that."

"Maybe I can think of something."

"The funeral will probably be tomorrow."

"Yes. Ella left instructions with me."

"Are you—were you—her lawyer?"

"You know that."

"I forgot."

"A day for the funeral home business, the viewing—home style now—"

"Jeeze—"

" . . . viewing . . . and contemplation—"

"Contemplation?"

"That was her word. She wanted people to have time to think about her, maybe sit with her awhile as they thought."

"Is that contemplation?"

"Don't start that."

"I'm sorry."

"You haven't gotten much sleep."

"I wish you'd brought an air mattress."

"My innards feel hand-wrung," she said smiling bleakly.

Beyond the far end of the cemetery a man was raising a Florida state flag in his small front yard. The man ran the flag smartly up the silver pole, tied it off, stepped back, saluted, whirled, his blue shirt opening off his pale belly, and ran into the house. Every movement he'd made had been with the rapidity of anxiety, of alarm. But he hadn't looked their way and anyway they were too far off for him to be sure who they were. Over there was where Marcella and Ordell lived, their yellow, biota-embraced house hidden behind its huge trees, its crowding shrubs. You couldn't know for sure what people were seeing or what they thought about it, until later.

8

He mostly spends the day inside the mausoleum reading by flashlight, sleeping and burrowing into feelings he doesn't have a name for, sunken, louring, caved-in-on, spumed up out of deep vents and seeps, those feelings. Twists and false appellations, a meandering spirit, chilled and shrunken, and a sense of the looseness of time, the unavailability of recompense, of shallowness in desire, of the trivialization of all things through calling them by names and even spending time with them are upon him. He wants everything to just stand there. He doesn't even want to touch it. The close air of the dead world is all around him. This pseudoeternity. He gets up and lies by the door, breathing in, but not enough outside air gets through. He cracks the door slightly, letting in a sliver of light. He sits in this light nodding and patting his face, leaning forward like a drunk man at a bar, talking silently to CJ, to the faded dead, to his father in Cuba bearing down on his big pages at his table, to the surroundings themselves and the appetites and calamities he draws small reckonings upon as they pass through his mind, but not to his mother. I'm crazy now, he thinks but that isn't the word for it. He knows no word that will do and leans back into the darkness as if into the cupped hands of absence itself.

Just after dark Marcella slips into the cemetery and calls to him, and he staggers out into the sweet-smelling world and they lie on the grass inside the little family compound where his maternal grandfathers and grand-mothers are buried. She has brought a blanket to ward off the bugs. Clouds hide the moon but they can see by the leftover starlight. From out in the streets murmurs of living passersby drift in. He feels a loneliness as if they're on a big dark ship sailing silently past the resting fleet. World of business and affections, of focused intent. They don't comment on what she said back in the Big Cypress prairies about leaving; she's spoken such as that many times before. She lies on top of him in the grass and they work their clothes loose enough to hook up. They of-ten fucked without looking at each other's bodies, the smells, the broad range of being and pressure enough. The stars wobble in their sockets. Bats tack the night into the heavens. He cries for his mother, at one point gets up and starts dumbly off. He wants to disappear into one of the big wildernesses, not this one of weeds and dirt, but he comes back.

He doesn't mention desires of this nature to Marcella, but in the afternoon he goes out and stands with the gravediggers as they scratch out his mother's grave with a little backhoe. He looks out beforehand to make sure he doesn't know them, and then walks around and comes on them from past the little rusted loggia of the Floret's Cubano graves. Two men work there. One scrapes and cleans the grass off the rough coral marl the backhoe brings up. The cemetery is the highest point on the island, Solares Hill, the place people will flee to if a hurricane blows the ocean over everything else. A real Cayo Hueso island of bones. He stands there looking into the hole. The backhoe's big dinosaur teeth are streaked gray. "Precious spot," he says to the man working the shovel. The man, short with stubby, strong arms, hasn't looked at him until he speaks.

"How's that?" he says.

"Last resting place."

"One hole's about the same as another on this island."

"Unless it's yours, huh?"

"I won't let them deposit me in this rock, no thank you." He plans, he says, to be buried back where he comes from, in a farm cemetery out in Kansas. "We got a little rise among some cedar trees where you can look out and see the house and the fields. Got little groundcherry bushes planted all around."

A pang that's more than a pang, a new condition, robust and dry, sweeps across his consciousness, takes up its motion, banging at him, and this is not so bad. Even a punch is life, even calumny and persecution—still life. He feels slightly faint—or as if he is entering a new state, a queasy wakefulness without precedent or alteration. A panic surges and subsides. I take everything back, he silently says, touching with the tip of his flip-flop the little tufts of hawkweed and cumberland daisies by the grave. Flowers like sports, show-offs, as if they were encouraging life, the dead surrounded by uncaring really. With one finger he knocks a tear off his face, turning away as he does so and catching sight of a large high-flown hawk dipping a wing into breeze. What's next?

He takes up a shovel—"May I?" "Sure, sure, buddy."— and helps the man shape the scattering of dirt odds and ends into a pile on a blue scrap of tarp. The grave looks more like a slot than anything else. He's been to many funerals, it's one of the rituals in his line of work. When he was younger he'd been on the crew sent to clean out the dead man's domicile, usually in a hotel, often at the beach. He sorted the cheesy and futile remains of lives lived in single rooms. Into cardboard boxes picked up behind grocery stores he placed the starched shirts and carefully hung pants, the trinkets and pornographic tracts. Men kept odd and familiar things. Varnished chicken feet and statuettes in contorted poses, calendars with the dates inked out— key rings holding keys abandoned by their locks, smeared wine glasses, a copy of the US Constitution once, rusting electric razors, an empty hornets' nest, shoes with curled up toes, brassieres, trusses like bits of parachute harness looped over coat hangers, studs, medals, coins on which were stamped the faces of kings. The oblate, rounded phraseologies of the funeral services, the blatting words written out on a piece of paper or memorized or come up with on the spot, the preacher's or priest's or rabbi's issuing of the sanctified confidentialities, were lessened, pushed into trivia before the sturdy facts of the photos and rusted diving trophies and the carved coconut doorstops he had placed into cardboard boxes and taken to the Goodwill store (that took them only because he insisted). As far as he was concerned the words were an insult to the gummy razors and the cowboy boots with their tops folded over and the lists of emergency numbers taped to the little refrigerator door. He thinks of this now, these stipulations of grief, and they don't really make much sense. It doesn't matter what you say or don't say, doesn't matter how seriously you do or don't take the bleak mementoes of lives no longer in this world. He wants to explain this to the grave diggers but he knows it's trivial, not much to tell anyone, certainly not a grave digger.

The other shoveler and he—both soon to go, if the little man's cough and his own . . . jam, *I'm in a jam, Ma*, are any indication—work silently for several minutes. Cot stops and picks up a clod of the crusty earth. "You guys must have run most of the dirt in this place through your fingers, at one time or another," speaking like a tourist, like a man without depth, the clustered clod falling apart in his hands, his face flushed; he can feel the blood moving in him—as if it wants to get away.

"Not me," the man says. "I just started here last week."

After a while the men load the little backhoe on a trailer behind their pickup truck, cover the grave with another scrap of blue tarp, and drive off. Cot squats by the grave and reaches in under the tarp, pats the accurate side. The man working the hoe had been a craftsman. Yes, and he, Cot, the Finisher, knows graves that are only a bed of leaves, a saltwater ditch, a slough, ocean deeps. He feels as if he's suffocating. Tiny yellow bees buzz among the foamy blossoms of a little geiger bush. He offers his hand. A single bee, tiny as a pumpkin seed, lands on the back, between the knuckles. It walks around, its skinny legs lifting and lowering the velvety body. The bee dips its rear end and stings him. He flings his hand out, shaking the bee loose. It leaves a dab of guts on the head of the stinger, a dot of fire pinned to his skin. He feels lightheaded, then this passes. He rubs the back of his hand on the grass. Clouds to the south look like white reefs before the invisible continents of space.

Marcella returned shortly after dark to tell him she had a boat. They left the cemetery and walked in the darkness down Custard and turned up Windsor and then into Cutpurse Lane to the little duck-by and entered the house. She said she didn't know where Ordell was. "Just riding around," she said. She had spoken to him on the phone, a few phones. All landlines. He was still in the Keys. "Looping around," she said.

"How do the police know to come after him?"

"Jackie. He saw him run out of the house."

"Jackie was the one found Mama?"

"Yes."

"That's good."

"Yes. And he ran down to the store and called the police. They'd already figured out about CJ. Or knew Ordell had put them on a false lead—I'm not sure. It's going to be a big scandal."

"Maybe I'll be the hero."

"Except for your shooting Isabella, yeah."

"Is she going to be all right?"

"She's got a big pain in her shoulder, but umm, yes, they say she'll be good as new."

"Except no one ever is."

"I'm surprised you know that."

"I need to make amends to her."

"I'd say so. You can do it as soon as you get out of Raiford, if you ever do."

She explained about the boat and he said it's just the ticket—just saying it was—but before they got started he wanted to be there for the funeral.

"They're pretty committed to running it without your participation."

He made a mocking face. They were up in the orange and yellow second bedroom that she had taken to sleeping in since she and Ordell stopped having sex. (*Completely? Without prejudice.*) She went downstairs to get drinks and he lay back on the bed. The room smelled of apples. She liked to keep them around, an exotic fruit in the tropics. *If she had money to give me, why didn't she give it to Ella?* But even as he thought this he knew the answer: *Ella wouldn't take it.* She probably wouldn't even acknowledge the offer. So as not to be the agent of embarrassment to Marcella for having made it. She wouldn't have taken it from him either. *Which was why I had to steal the emeralds.* Only something irreducible like gemstones, something too pretty, would have worked to pry the inspector—what was his name?—away from his principles—his scaredy-catness. *Mama would have looked up from whatever challenging moment she was passing through to find the deed done, her son bustling around the kitchen making breakfast.* He'd wanted to see the look on her face. His act of meretricious special pleading she would have seen through as who wouldn't. He had other motives.

When Marcella reappeared at the door carrying a tray with a pitcher of fresh gin and tonics on it she was crying. He jumped up from the bed and took the tray from her, set it on the big table at the foot of the bed, and eased her into his arms. They lay down together on the bed. She turned away from him, but he drew her back, almost roughly, moving along the edge of what was permissible. He pressed his nose deeply into her intimate, unwashed smells; she had been too busy, too distracted to bathe, and this touched him. They rolled and jolted, whispering their smudged enchantments. Afterwards he opened the two big bedroom windows and let the natural air come through the screens. Tiny birds flitted around the big traveller's palm off the gallery. He thought of *The Georgics*, that kept, each one, circling around through planting and breeding, through star charts and rolling hills and honeyed comforts to the fearsome deadly world and the crash of battles, to chaos and trouble that this life in the ruralities was supposed to be a shelter from. *Help me, help me* was the undercry. Everybody, since the beginning, so Virgil knew, crying it.

He lay back in the bed and slept. When he woke he didn't at first know where he was. He lay on his back remembering a dream: of the time the Albertson company drove out to the Everglades in two cars and fought the Campos—or intended to—a family of car thieves and disassemblers who had tried to break into the drug smuggling business. In the dream the gangmen were all there, as they had been in life—the shooters and the grim-reaper types and the clowns, the steady hands—all ready to gun down the Campos. But there'd been no shooting. Not by Albertson's troop. As they pulled up in two Land Rovers before the big unpainted house, old Mr. Campo had come out on the porch. They had sat in the vehicles, waiting to see what he would do. What he did was this: he walked down the wide plank front steps, knelt in the yard, put a gun to his head, and pulled the trigger. This was in life. In the dream the old man didn't even have a gun. In the dream he drifted down the steps on light feet and in the yard, instead of kneeling, lifted off the ground and flew away. Cot stood by the car watching him dwindle into the clear sky. He wanted to rise too. An anguish, harsh, unpulverized by time, poured through him as he watched the old man dwindle until he disappeared. He felt as if his heart was being crushed. *Oh no*, he cried in the dream, *oh no*. He slept again and in another dream

Marcella appeared in a pointed green hat like the one Robin Hood wore. She didn't seem to know him. He fled into tall golden bushes and fell.

He waked with her lying beside him clothed in soft white pants and linen shirt, kissing his face. He told her about the Campo dream. "What happened in real life?" she said.

"Mr. Campo cleared the matter up."

"I'll bet."

He touched her face. Every part of it, subtle shelving, patch and stain, was beautiful to him. Nowhere on her body was an ugly spot. Still, he always saw her imperfections. The abraded nest of acne scars on her left cheek. The dent in her long nose. The tiny healed-over rip in her left earlobe. She was getting older and age was not being kind to a face raised in tropic sunlight. He sensed the sadness she felt about this. She wasn't like his mother who moved through her life as if there was nothing beyond the passing lashes of loved ones that could harm her. Cot knew that Marcella often stood in front of the long mirror on her back porch appalled and overcome by her disasters. Bursting squalls of disillusionment and failure. They were both like that and both shied from admitting it.

In the night he woke, sure someone was in the house. He slipped down the stairs and walked through the rooms with his pistol in his hand. If he came on Ordell he would shoot him. But he found no one. He tried the doors; they were all locked. He went out on the front gallery and sat in the glider looking down the lane. The big sodium lamp out on the street cast a diffuse radiance back into the bushes. A big, slab-sided cat crossed the lane, returned his look, and slipped into the shadows. Ordell, he thought, come and gone. He went back upstairs, dressed and re-entered the cemetery, made his way through the intern-ments stacked like casket condos, and let himself into CJ's mausoleum. He lay down on the bench and slept.

★★★★★★

On a hot afternoon when the air is filled with the scent of almond blossoms they bury his mother. The crowd spreads out in little clumps from the grave site across other plots, so it looks as if whole families have come to observe special ceremonies for their personal dead. The priest begins the service with a flourish of turning pages. He finds what he's looking for and peers deeply in, strain-ing to make out the print in the bright sunlight, and reads a passage that promises eternal life. Cot sees this. Wear-ing a black baseball cap he's taken from the hall closet at Marcella's, one of Ordell's, he slips from the mausoleum and enters the sunlight. He hasn't shaved for several days now, but he doesn't really think this will disguise him and on this he's correct. Arnie Davis, city editor at the paper, spots him right off. Arnie flicks a waist-high wave that Cot acknowledges with a nod. The air has the bril-

liant and uncomplicitous, wild-eyed feel of a sea breeze
that has blown steadily all night. Everything but the oxy-
gen has been swept out of it. Clouds like puffs of cannon
fire hang distantly in the southwest. Bill Nolen, a silver-
smith who makes trinkets he sells in stores around town,
recognizes him. He speaks to his wife, a short unfriendly
woman who has for two years pretended she has cancer.
She scowls at him, tugs a sleeve, and word moves on.

Then a cop, Frankie Garcia, known as Friendly Frank
when they were in school together, sees him. He punches
his phone and speaks into it. Cot moves into the crowd.
He sees some of Albertson's men over beyond the low
iron picket fence surrounding the Beauchamp plot. The
priest hovers over the grave, hanging above it as if over
a precipice. The boys, Scofield and Buster, among others, catch sight of him. They shy off to the left, moving
slowly, but with purpose, past a line of soursop bushes.
The cops catch the news like a scent. There're plenty
of them, a few dressed in their formal uniforms of dark
blue and white, others in their workaday pale blues, all
well armed. Cot keeps moving, slipping along the ragged
edges of the crowd. There must be two hundred people
standing around. The priest dives cleanly into the eulogy,
words like aces dealt off the top of the deck. The casket is
a dull, unpolished gold, half covered with bulls-eye daisies. The breeze blows the priest's forelock into his eyes.
There's a quiet bumping and shuffling among the gangmen, noticed by now by members of the police force.
Barky Wilson, an Albertson shooter from Opalacka, son

of shrimpers and river folk, pulls his pistol. Cot watches in fascination from half behind a large tombstone that has words from the Temptations inscribed into its cherry marble: *It Was Just My Imagination*. Mine too, Cot thinks. The cops are pulling their guns too. The boys are getting theirs out with the same picky familiarity and nervousness as the cops. High above the cemetery the little buzzards circle, draped and ready. Cot has his pistol in his hand, a pale yellow bandana covering it. *You keep doing irresponsible, dumb things*, he thinks, but the thought doesn't really bother him.

Marcella is standing next to the priest. Jackie and his friend Morty Smalls are beside her with their hair slicked down. Cot slides off toward the east gate, a narrow opening between two brick pillars. The street beyond is littered with white almond blossoms. Old Mrs. Lazarus is out in the street sweeping flowers off the pavement. Cot slips through the gate and sprints down the street. The two outfits, gangsters and police, make their way, at first at creep speed then with swiftness and alarm, after him. He runs straight down the middle of the street the block and a half to his mother's house, cuts in through the yard, crosses the lane, cuts behind the old Mosley place, nodding to sunbathers lying in pink plastic loungers around the tiny sliver of a pool, dashes across Fleming and around the corner, and sprints for the docks.

The cops and gangsters come behind running. They're slowed down somewhat by the cops' attempts to make the Albertson employees quit the chase. Captain

Barkley orders the gangsters to cease and desist, to disband and head out of the area, but the gangsters, mostly led by Pointy Mizel, laugh and order *them* out. There's much yelling and the cops pull mace and tear gas which does not particularly impress the gangmen. The shooting starts about halfway down Margaret Street, as they pass under a huge mango tree. Pops, cracks, the clap of Glock pistols, even the tattered metallics of a machine gun. Bullets whap trees, thunk bodies, and skid off the pavement leaving silver marks children will touch in awe. Men stumble, pitch headfirst out of life.

At the bottom of Margaret Cot picks up the boardwalk that runs along the waterfront. A large sign offers day trips to the Dry Tortugas. Dusty sponges hang on strings at Mary Harris's shop on the corner. Manly Soledad, son of a Cuban farmer, waves to him from the door of Coupole's, a fish bar. They were briefly in Cub Scouts together, before Cot was kicked out for over-arguing. Manly is just back from Raiford where he has done two years for laundering fish money at his father's restaurant out on Stock Island. Cot dashes down the boardwalk, the boards popping and clanking as he runs. A tourist family yells encouragement as he goes by, as if they are spectators at a race they know all about. The boardwalk jags right and Cot runs along past the old turtle corrals and along the docks. Sloops and sport boats are racked in long rows. Somewhere along here is Justin Peoples's Mako. A mingling panic shivers him. Then he sees the boat, sees Justin sitting in it with the motor running.

Marcella went over this with him yesterday. She's supposed to be here, but he's already realized there's no way under the circumstances—cops, reporters, townsfolk everywhere—for her to accomplish that. Grief bites like a small ugly insect. Justin stands up in the boat. Cot scrambles down the little ladder to the floating dock and crosses quickly past the flotilla of dinghies in from the mooring field off Wisteria Island. He cocks a look back and sees Marcella. She's coming fast on a scooter around the corner from Elizabeth Street. The scooter wobbles and nearly goes down. A sudden disfigurement of alarm appears and vanishes in her face. "How is it, Justin?" Cot says not taking his eye off Marcella.

"Sorry about your mother, Cot." Justin says, a speech Cot figures he's rehearsed.

Back a ways shots bust and whine. Voices of the wounded or the shot near to death raise their cries.

Marcella pulls up, letting the scooter slide like a heavy seal to its side, and comes down the ladder at a skip. Justin makes one-handed grabbing motions at her. Cot and Marcella don't bother to hug or even acknowledge each other. But he's waited for her—*I should have gone on*—and he scrambles behind her into the boat. He's put his pistol back under the green Hawaiian shirt he wears, but as he gets in the boat he takes it out again and waves it, per arrangement, at Justin, yelling at him to get out of here.

They're almost out of the inner harbor when the pursuers arrive at the docks, one or two at first, then in clusters. The groups are no longer shooting at each other (eight down) but they haven't made a truce. The pursuers don't see Cot's party until, just as the Mako speeds past one of the big yachts tethered at the outer docks and into open water, a shout goes up. Somebody fires a few shots but the firing is brief and futile. The escapers are out past the island headed west toward the flats before anybody can do anything about it.

Soon enough they're in the Refuge. Green-topped, brown-topped islands lie around them in their ancient scattering. The water that's as clear as if from a tap looks yellow from the color of the bottom sand. They run fast along channels only a few feet deep. Justin spends his life out here making his living so Cot leaves the divagations and nautical finery to him. Twenty minutes later they come to Ordell's sport fishing boat, a fifty-foot Cooper Sea Cruiser he bought up at the boat show in Miami, bobbing at anchor, and Justin hangs the Mako next to it.

"Don't you want to knock me on the head or something, Cot?" Justin says as Cot starts to leave the sleek little flat-decked boat. Without a word or any other sign Cot turns and catches him above the eye with the butt of his pistol. Justin crumples soundlessly into the well. Cot scrambles back into the boat and picks him up. Marcella looks down from the Cooper deck. In her eyes is a hard knowingness but no alarm. They have barely spoken on the way out. Blood pours from the cut above Justin's eye. He's groggy and he doesn't know where he is. "Shit, Justin," Cot says. "I'm sorry."

Marcella hurries along the deck and dashes inside to start up the boat. Cot scoops water and bathes Justin's face. This takes only seconds, but in that time that seems to stretch out from them flexibly as a cast line, he feels a deep and sustaining affection, for Justin, for Marcella, for the world around them. With a fine cold tip grief touches a spot. Justin coughs and comes all the way to. His eyes wander, but then he catches what's up. He jerks like a puppy gone to sleep in your lap. "It's me," Cot says.

"Jesus, you hit hard."

"I keep stumbling on my way."

He tries to help Justin to his feet. "Naw," he says, "Let me sit back down. I'm gon rest a while and then limp around out here for 'em to catch up with me."

"Sure." Cot finds his hand and shakes it. "You got my thanks, man."

"Glad to do it," Justin says and lies back with his head hanging over the side of the boat.

"You sure you're all right?"

"Spectacular."

A jittery, a fine glassine sparkling on the tips of tiny waves. As if the whole sea world is touched by alarm, by tension and nervous collapse.

The big boat engines start with a clap that subsides into a heavy gurgling. Cot climbs the ladder and heads for the wheelhouse. Marcella has already gotten under way by the time he gets there. "Go down and fix us a couple of drinks," she says.

"In a second."

He takes her in his arms and holds her tight. A huge, wobbling feeling of relief, of pain and love hauls through his body. It lasts only a second. Behind it a stubby awkwardness, a sense of dislocation and ill-formed plans scrapes by. She breaks away and wheels the boat into the channel and pushes the throttle forward. Before her is a gauge panel containing information Cot has no real understanding of. It reminds him of Jimmy's plane. He can pick out the speedometer. In a couple of minutes it's up to 40 knots. The big diesel engines stay quiet even at top speed. Marcella says they will run all day like that. She says the boat can go six hundred miles before the auxiliary tank cuts in.

"That ought to be enough," Cot says.

He goes forward to the open lounge and sits on a white cushioned bench. A feeling creeping like the wind—but not the wind that's blowing briskly, handling his face—presses in on him. It's like somebody's covering him with a pistol. He's suddenly rigid with fright. He leans back against the transom waiting for the feeling to pass. It won't—and then it begins to, slinks off in simpers and smirks. He's not getting anywhere. Not getting out. Cuba, shabby memorial isle, is in their sights. Banked like a green rug churned up against the Caribbean Sea. In this moment the whole island unaware, indifferent to them, each local *compañero* going about his business, each madonna, castaway, and fisherman raking together the necessary care and protection for another life in another day. Nobody knows they're coming. The sky is a rich turquoise blue peppered with tiny clouds like clean white dots. Beneath those dots in KW streets lie the sprawled and indelicate dead. Cops and gangsters. Maybe townspeople too. Little boys will finger stray bullet holes. Tonight a new misery, born in the tropics. He feels as if he's hanging from a wire suspended between enormous nullities. The best he can hope for is to be left hanging there for a while. The westering sun glances off the water in short sparkling ricochets. Chuck Burle, Spotty Suber, Ennis Placer: cohorts among the fallen. He saw them go down. And Jimmy Nightingale, too. And Jake Rouse and Carl Pickens, cops of Key West, and Joe Cosmopolis who played with him on the football team. The names like wounds he sucks with his tongue. The wind pushes him like a hand. He could fall over backwards easily enough. He could throw himself in the ocean, like some old Roman, Virgilian, from another time. But he won't. *A boy like you is going to pay for every breath he takes*—that's what his father told him. You're going to pay for it a thousand times if you don't change but you can't change and even those who change don't get any dispensation. Was that true? His life was just a string of wild guesses. The couch under him smells of plastic, and faintly, of vomit. Ordell bought the boat right off the showroom floor. He had to have it, had to, like it was a pair of new shoes, wear it home from the store. He'd driven the boat onto the reef at Key Largo. They had to pull it off with a bulldozer from shore. But the boat was okay. Ordell had made the marina at Garrison Bight by dark, parked it with all the lights on.

As they enter the Gulf Stream long, moiled lines of trash begin to show up. Plastic pails and melon rinds among long streaks of pale grease and cloudy tailings, wooden pallets, coconuts, and the busted housing of a cabin cruiser bobbing with one end tipped high like a possible refuge, slip by. Marcella has to slow down. They push against the big current, heading slightly east at first, not meaning to, but without realizing it steadily losing the track, correcting by feel, then over-correcting, until they're headed west of where they want to go. Marcella's no expert with the electronics either. She can't get the GPS to engage. A squall blows up out of a blue sky and in a moment drenches the boat. They have to run slowly for the rain that seems to pour out of huge reservoirs. The sea bucks like a horse, kicking up spray that whips off the wave tops. They're all at once climbing the backs of huge swells like lathered hills. The seas break over the bow and kick along the deck in foaming sheets. They can't see much. Marcella throttles down and runs slowly, climbing the swells as if they ride in one of those clanking funiculars that crawl up the side of mountains. The boat wallows and pitches, trying to slew sideways. They're both afraid of hitting something, some sea creature or chifforobe or drifting leftover from the remote and useless past. She's begun chanting, blurting snatches of old songs and prayers, gripping the wheel as she does so.

"I think we're backpedaling," he says. He's just come in from out in the bluster.

She leans over the console peering into what looks like nothing but spray. "Get wet?"

Water drips into his eyes. "Hope we don't get runned over."

She starts to say something but stops and to Cot it's as if her brain's been jerked up thrashing, her mind that is, and he sees her fighting, losing ground, hating the loss and holding on, her hair that has no gray in it matted against the side of her head, her long nose shiny and red, her hands gripping the wheel as if it's the rim of a chalice holding the one true elixir. He wants to move up behind her, to spell her, relieve the press and stall of whatever it is nagging through the storm, but he doesn't, knows she won't take it. The squall whines and squeals, emptying itself.

By the time the storm lets up they're rounding the western tip of the long, Lepidosaurian island and pressing on beyond, heading south. She realizes they've gone too far, or thinks she does. Dark's coming on. The squall has burned itself out, and now the ocean lies before them, slowly rising and falling in a long-distance breath, shining and white streaked. They've both been sick, Marcella more so.

"Let me take it," he says.

She bangs her palm against the wheel and bares her horsey teeth. "Take it how? Take it where?" She's near to cursing him, to flinging down responsibility like an offending appliance. "These fucking reefs run forever."

Los arricifes de coral, he says silently to himself, backing away, coming up close again.

"Fuck this," she screams and elbows him.

In her mind she shades him out like she would shade a puppy out of the sun with her hand. The world all around her is dotted now with shaded places. She hates herself for what she's done, but she doesn't want to stop doing it. Coverts and hideouts and caves hidden by bushes and forts set up in a world turning to wilderness—that was life, and you took it under your wing as best you could. She makes a noise like a cat would make denying rumors.

He wants to touch her but he knows not to. She leans against the wheel, turning it slightly, shading a little more to the east, maybe the southeast, heading into the dark out of which Judgement Day will come, the sun already climbing hand over hand through the big troughs and valleys of the wild Atlantic. She puts speed to the boat.

Now he can touch her.

He slips behind her and takes her shoulders in his hands. Her hands on the wheel are strong, blotched. There's nothing much he can say right now. They can smell the land, murky and feculent, a smell like rotting fruit—mangoes maybe—and trash fires. "You're tired," he says. The tension in her shoulders begins to give way under his fingers that dig gently in.

"You're the smart one," she says and angles herself away from him. He lifts his hands off her. "No," she says.

He can hardly tell what she means, everything between them is so spare, harsh, splintered.

He puts his hands on her again, with just two middle fingers pressing the long muscles in her back. He senses her giving in; senses the coarse, repellent grief, surrender of armies. He lets his hands rest lightly on her. They can go days sometimes without her allowing any touch. He'll say I thought I was the brutal one, and she'll only stare at him as if he's a ruiner of children and pets. He kisses her backbone, following the strung dice downward, touching just enough for the touches to be kisses. It's as if he's lifting tiny particles off her body. She says, "I can't see what's ahead of me."

He knows what she means and wishes she hadn't spoken.

"I never can."

"You don't have to."

He knows what she means there too. "It doesn't come as naturally as you might think."

"I don't think that. But you don't know."

"Know what?" The last time he asked *what?* she said he didn't know how hard it was to be a woman. That isn't the only thing, he told her.

"I don't know," she says now, which he understands to mean that she knows exactly. He winces, but so deeply inside that it doesn't show on the surface of his body.

"Everybody gets confused around here this time of night."

She snorts, bends her head toward the big wheel, turns quickly and kisses him on the lips. "I saw Muncie Baker holding up his hand that was covered with blood.

There was a look in Mrs. Tillman's face that I'd never seen anywhere—so much pain. And Estelle, the ranger at the fort?—she was lying on the ground holding her arms up."

"Everybody letting go."

"No, Cot, that wasn't it."

Unnerved, something come loose in his mind, he begins to wander around the boat. Three steps down into the big combo living room, kitchen and sleeping compartment. He fiddles with taps, turns on the water, washes his hands, pokes into the refrigerator, pulls out a bottle of seltzer and drinks from it. The refrigerator smells of turnips and faintly of rotten meat. A fold-down table releases rolled-up charts and the red plastic-bound ship's log.

He sits at the little fold-out seat and reads the log, Ordell's rushed and twitchy script:

"Hazards of hope and duplicity. Rained all day. No fish in the ocean, we ate cold hamburgers and sat in the stern bay arguing. She won't give in about anything that is important to me. She senses what matters most and takes that as her own and won't let me have a sip of it. She treats me like a burglar who's begging to be let off. I could throw her into the ocean and explain her away like indigestion. Christ. The ocean is so blue you'd think that was the only color God loved. I hate the fucking ocean. Here they come the big swells swollen like a sickness. I might kill her yet."

That's for January 18th, this year.
For January 2nd, Ordell wrote:

*"Her infidelity's like a goiter. You ignore it but really
you can't stop thinking about it. rain all day. the
Ocean's gray as ashes. Gulls followed us all the way
out crying like the betrayed. they know something we
don't admit to. She says she's giving up the old life, the
one she's stretched out like a series of bedsheets she tied
together to let herself down from a prison—that's the
way she talks—but I don't believe her. Near Doomsday
Shoal the water's clear as a bell a hundred feet down
to a sandy bottom. I would swim down to it and sit all
morning resting my nerves. Or maybe screaming."*

December 16th, off Big Elbow Light:

*"She dived in and swam a circle around the boat. We
were anchored over a coral shelf at the edge of a deep
drop-off into blue water. I called to her to get out but she
wouldn't. Then I saw a shark—maybe eight feet long
with a white-tipped dorsal—swimming around her. It
swam slowly at a distance. I started to call to her again,
but i didn't. I turned back to the book I was reading, a
biography of Disraeli—thinking I am the center of this
circle—thinking I am trapped like her. But it was a kind
of enticement—I knew I could break out. A little later I
heard her climbing the ladder. My heart was thumping. I
don't know why—or do—"*

December 2, Lat 23.15 Long 81.08:

*"All day rode the swells with the engine off. I felt what
it is to be flotsam, jetsam, rising and falling with the
tremendous weight of the Gulf stream under us. Once
I would of thought of this big river of water as infinitely
replenishing, as self-cleansing and pure but I can't believe
in such things anymore. You see the trashiness of the
ocean, the stains and grease patches riding on it. She
came topside and stood there yawning, so beautiful like
a lovely horse in the shade. I slapped her across the eyes
after she told me she was in love with"*

The bottom half of the page and all of the next one
back are torn out. He carefully closes the book and tucks
it under a small stack of books and folds up the desk. He
goes into the forward cabin, lies down but gets quickly
up. He starts back out into the big room but that feels too
proximate to her, to her kinetics. He can hear her cursing, shouting. There're no words in what she's saying,
and he tells himself it's this that keeps him away, repels
him. He lies down again. A panic catches him, but he
makes himself stay still. Abruptly his mother's presence
is all around him—and not only around: He's become
porous: she sluices in and out of him; maybe leaving a
residue, maybe not. For a time he has no memories of
her. He has—call them sparks, flashes of a drained, as-
cetic face, torn by wind; fingers touching chess pieces
in a room lit by candlelight; lips washed by a fat, gray

tongue. Warm spots and cold spots pulse in his chest. Not far behind his eyes a breeze shakes the red flowers of an achiote bush. A sense of give and take, like a philosophy, rises to power and ebbs. He smells roasting hamburgers, followed by an anguished feeling of emptiness. On the stinging surface of his cheek he feels his mother's ancient slap. Where she is can she still feel his? He's sure he believes in a continuing presence. A poke-around, nosy apparitional something, prodding and pausing to fiddle with useless matter, maybe caress it, trying to recall some stumped and useless business that no one else on Earth at this moment has in his mind. Many are thinking about her tonight, but day by day the number will diminish until no one is. They're thinking of others too this night. Funerals to come. Eventually each of us will lie in an unmarked grave. Spane said that, morbid fellow combining this with that to make a murder. What gives? Cot had quit the football team midseason of his senior year—he didn't know why. And then quit school just before the Christmas vacation—he didn't know why—and took the bus to Miami and got a room out at the beach for fifty dollars a week and sat on his little balcony lonely as a gull reading *Parsifal* and thinking of the bitterness in his soul. He shopped in a Cuban market on Washington and sat in the park eating a papaya with a plastic spoon. Marcella found him there. She brought him a Christmas present of a rolled-up Brueghel print, Isaac Babel's collected stories, and a plastic pack of jockey shorts. I got a mama for that last, he told her, and she said that woman doesn't want to speak to you. And she didn't. Not for years. But after a while things changed. Life was just long enough to wear most folks out. Marcella hadn't criticized him or asked him to come home. She lay on the bed naked, looking at him. I'll do anything you want, he said. But she said she didn't have a thing on her mind.

Tipped left, then left again, fumbling in the dark past Juventud, past Cantiles, Rosario, and Largo del Sur, left turn at the lights of Giron, up the Bahia des Cochinos onward to the *playa* where the invasion museum sports a Hawker Sea Fury loaded with rockets and on to the narrow strip of sand sloping down from the concrete trenches—unmanned now, going back to grass—where a hundred yards out they drop anchor, row the dinghy in to shore and sleep the sleep of the almost dead among the weeds beyond the tide line.

In the early morning two old men carrying a couple of small throw nets wake them. Cot speaks to the men in Spanish and for some reason shows them his Cuban passport, the one he first got years ago and renews through his father since, even though he can tell they aren't officials and don't ask to see it. He's jumpy and overfriendly and the men say OK, OK, and murmur, not to each other but to some secret listener in their hearts and Cot can see this, and he sees too the future dwindling ahead of him, flattening out like whirled-up dust settling from a passing car. He thinks maybe I'll shoot these guys but doesn't;

he goes on grinning, turning the pages of the passport, showing the stamps for Peru and Martinique and Belize and Trinidad where in Port of Spain in a gunfight in the middle of Constitution Street he took the lives of three Indian gangsters who had cheated Albertson on a rights question. The passport has a blue plastic cover and contains stamps of entry and exit. No current entry stamp, but he doesn't show the men that. One of them has a glossy gray beard. The other is slender with an old man's slenderness that doesn't look like good health. Cot asks what they are after. Bait, the bearded one says. *Anzuelo.* His eyes glisten with excitement.

"We're traveling," Cot says. Marcella, kneeling in the sand behind him hasn't spoken. The men wave discreetly at her, their old-man hands almost limp.

They follow the men up to the village that's a collection of small tin-roofed houses along a dusty coral street among breadfruit and mango trees and seems essential to something he's got no good idea of. Frayed tufts of banana trees stick out from behind the houses. There's a store with a screened front tacked on and in the yard under a big mamey tree benches where you could sleep away your life. He'd like to do that; he's always felt that way he thinks and knows this isn't true. They buy bread and Egyptian peanut butter and eat breakfast under the dark green leaves of the old tree, from time to time pointing out little features of life around them. An old woman smokes a huge cigar; a man with a cheek filled with something elastic, maybe bubblegum, maybe betelnut, chews steadily; a child holds up the hem of her frilly dress revealing frayed khaki shorts underneath.

Marcella looks up into the tree where on the nearest limb ants march in double rows and says "I want something to get a grip on me." She laughs. "That's not what I mean. I mean the other way."

"Maybe both at once." His mind skips, jumps along for a sec, then pauses and he thinks: *time to rest now*, but then it skips ahead again not really lighting on anything.

The store proprietor, a fat man in a glossy blue shirt, directs them to a man who drives them in his dog-nosed Ford pickup to Playa Giron where they catch the jitney to Havana. His father is out when they get to his apartment, but they sit in a little park on the other side of the street and wait for him. Some old men are repairing a small electric motor under the almond trees. The trees are in full white bloom. After a while his father comes down the street. He doesn't see them sitting, half slumbering, in the warm breeze under the trees. His father looks frail and Cot's heart goes out to him but he doesn't get up. He watches as his father walks carrying over his shoulder his patched guitar. At the door to the apartment building— three stories around a courtyard with galleries along all three floors—his father turns and looks at him. He has known he was there, Cot thinks. He gets up and the two men meet in the street that's streaked with tar patches and almost empty. He takes his father in his arms. He can feel the boniness and this alarms him, but he holds his father as tightly as he can allow himself. His father smells of bacon, old sweat, and alcohol. He kisses Cot's neck with dry, tender kisses. Then Marcella comes up, and his father kisses her too. They go together into the building and climb the stairs that are wet as if from a rain—from leaks, his father says.

On the steps to the third floor Cot stops his father with a hand on his arm. There are small scaly patches on the old man's brown skin. He intends right there in the empty midday stairwell to tell his father about his mother, but the words catch in his chest. His father smiles at him. His old hawk face is filled with a quiet, long-discredited happiness. His eyes glisten. "*Papi, un momento,*" Cot says. Marcella has gone on ahead and waits for them on the open gallery. A small breeze shuffles a few leaves in a nearby mango tree. The pale flowers stand like candelabras among the leaves that look to Cot like bunches of green knives. "*Mami . . . ,*" he says and stops. His father says nothing, only looks at him. Grief like a cold stoniness in his chest, like a command and punishment, dislodges. His father grasps his arm with the strong left hand that scribbles the stories of his *novelas gráficas* and pulls Cot to him. They embrace, his father crying. Cot smells again the dried sweat on the old man's body, the animal grease, and he thinks he can smell the tears, hot in his nostrils like the smell of heated iron. Marcella looks down at them from the gallery. In her eyes Cot sees the placement and character of his life—so it seems to him. The loose frills of an asparagus fern sway in a hanging pot above her. She looks sadder than he's ever known her to be.

9

Two days later on Ciudad San Antonio Street a man pops like a cork out of the flung-open doors in an ornate stone facade and hails him. It's Manual Cosa, one of Albertson's men from Miami. Cosa invites him into the bar he has just hurled himself out of. Cot's reluctant but he goes anyway. He carries snugly tucked-in one of the two pistols he's brought with him from the boat they abandoned in the Bay of Pigs. He sits with Cosa in a tall wooden booth opposite the bar while Cosa tells him men are on their way to Havana to kill him. He flexes his hands continuously as he speaks.

"Are you one of them?"

"You know that would never happen," Cosa says with a smile that reveals his bleached, worn-down teeth. He speaks as if they're close friends though they're not. "I am only here to see my mother, but I thought I would find you and warn you. I was lucky to glimpse you walking down the street. You got a limp now?"

"No. Who's coming?"

Cosa gives him two names that are not familiar to him. He makes a quick squinting or wincing movement as he says the names—Cantrell, Markus—as if trying to conceal something from himself.

Cot glances at the open door of the bar, at the oblong of pale yellow light that looks from where he sits like the clear light of destiny. He imagined that they would make a life now in Havana. That Marcella would come to love the city and want to stay. The government would never extradite a Cuban citizen to the States. He and Marcella would marry and she would be allowed to live and work here, maybe practice law. It could easily be worked out. His father has influence. They would walk in the evenings under the big poincianas in Adelia Park. They would sit on the long white benches and listen to the stories told by the old men gathered there. They would eat iced slices of mango from patched white napkins. They would lie in bed at night and talk of simple things, like farmers. Cuba was still an old country, still lingering in the olden times. Out in the ruralities life was hardly different from that of the ancient Roman countryside. His heart is beating hard. It's almost as if it isn't his heart. Even the smells, the raw coriander, the peppers—are different here. The scarred wooden table they sit at, the signs above the bar advertising Venezuelan beer, Caporals, *empanadas fritos*. He knows it's rigged. In his mind that is. An imaginary life he is always at least half living. Movement is the key to everything—Spane told him that once. It didn't matter. Along the edges of his life reality and fantasy wash up together and mingle. Through an open door in back he can see a brown and white goat tied by its neck to a stake. A little girl bends over it, cleaning it with a rag. She looks familiar, she could be his younger sister, sunk back into time and lost in the tides, marooned here in another life, another kick out of the infinite universes. *Each leaf, each pebble has a life of its own.* Who said that?

Cosa is talking of his mother—*his,* not Cot's.

"You know those lines in Virgil," Cot breaks in, "right at the end of the first book of *The Georgics* where after he's been talking for a few hundred lines about country weather and climate and the patterns of the stars he suddenly calls out to Caesar and says everything's gone to shit, that right and wrong are inverted and crimes and war are everywhere—how it's like in a chariot race where the horses get loose and you can't control the chariot—you know that part?"

"Sure, Cot, yeah."

Down the long brown room, rising like ghosts of the up-fumed dead, he sees shapes bent over the backs of the men sitting at the bar, of others hunched at tables counting days and coins and lost loves.

"I'm sorry," Cot says, "I didn't mean to interrupt you."

"That's okay."

"Come on. I'll go with you to see your mother."

"She's not at home right now," Cosa says drumming the table.

Cot sees the truth in the man's face; it stands out, distinct as an old tattoo.

"Well, let's walk over to her place. I'd like to see where she lives."

They head down a long sunny street, not ambling but not hurrying either. Two men in white *guayabera* shirts pass and one of them looks familiarly back at them, a nobody pretending to be somebody, or vice versa. Cosa directs Cot into a small, less sunny street. A few spindly pines sprout from shallow depressions along the urban sidewalk. At the corner a large mahogany tree fills a sunken median space. The trunk's painted white halfway up. Low, unpainted concrete buildings shrink back from crumbling pavement. Three boys in identical yellow nylon jackets move off the curb to let them pass. Doors like cabinet panels are recessed below balconies from which hang long haggard strands of *cameron de rosa*. They turn into another street not so nice. Fixed in an intersection is a small park with a large drooping banyan set among yellowed royal palms. Cot turns and sees that the two men in white shirts are following. Up ahead and in an undersweep down to a wide flat area are the tracks of the municipal train station. Lines of passenger cars rust in the hot sunlight. Beyond the little park a weary industrial landscape of low factory buildings and warehouses. The banyan has let down its dark strings and branchings like barriers before something darker. Off to the side in a narrow playground boys are playing basketball at a skirtless hoop. Shirts and skins.

"Humidity makes you slimy," Cot says as they enter the shade under the swamp-smelling banyan.

"What's that?" Cosa says, but Cot already has his gun out. Cosa doesn't have time to prepare himself before Cot shoots him in the head. The bullet balloons his cheeks as his big body caves in and falls. Cot dashes around the side of the banyan tree, moving cleanly and without obstruction. On the backside he ducks in among the long, down-dipped strands of the tree's branching. The two men following come running around the tree, bent at the waist, crouching as they come. Cot shoots them both as they run. One lunges forward as if he's trying to catch something in his arms and lands on his face in the dust. The other falls as if thumped suddenly from the vivid air and careers onto his side. They look dead enough to be dead. Cot's breath is tight, concealed, taking a break. He makes himself start breathing again, long stroking inpulls. He takes the pistols from the two assassins, takes quickly their sweated-on American dollars. The basketball players are out of sight around the other side of the tree. Ahead in the china-white sunlight, out where the wide, empty yards of the train station begin—Casablanca it's called—no one's about.

Cot moves around the side of the tree on feet that are almost weightless. He's thinking of the winter in KW when it got so cold they took the rugs up off the floors and used them for blankets. A rustling in the dark leaves is only rats. Cosa lies on his side with his arm under his head. Cot squats beside him, a man he shared a strawberry soda with once on a rainy street in Tampa. A man who, he knows, has no mother in Havana. With his knuckle he touches the skin on Cosa's forehead. It's still warm, like life. He rises and walks slowly down a packed earth path leading out of the little park. He feels as if he's drugged, or maybe—for the time being—undrugged. He can see into the spaces of the day. Locate the unburdened *jouissance*. A loose, wavering sensation places itself calmly into empty spaces in his mind. Every melting bonbon, discarded fingernail, has a life of its own, he's sure of it. Even the dead, clogged with blood. At a spigot he wets his handkerchief and bathes his face. The sky over the city is a clear, unobstructed blue, small handsome white clouds in the east. Havana skies aren't encumbered with pollutants. You can see the stars at night, some nights, if you step away from the lights. And even in the best neighborhoods there aren't too many streetlights, sometimes only fat Russian bulbs strung on poles, casting a palpable amber glow rounding off a plush darkness. Watching him, the basketball players stand on the court as he once stood in José Martí Park in KW with a basketball snugged against his hip watching Curtis Pell carve a diamond into his arm with a knife. He wishes he could go among them, ask them to let him play, but he knows this is impossible, and knows this thought or desire is only the wish for a wish.

On his way home—just before he boards a pedicab and rides rattling through city streets—limping gamely along, he comes on a parade moving down a wide avenue past big lemon trees. He starts to duck down another route, but then he makes himself stop to watch the defile go by. It's difficult to make himself to do this, like lifting a large stone or a car bumper or saying to someone you love that you know what's being concealed. He's sweating and feels light headed. Girls in stiff ruffled skirts and satin accordion bodices, men in one-piece satin suits—Cubans, Bolivians, Peruvians under their national flags, with balloon sleeves and tightly wrapped leggings with bells attached, Venezuelans, Santo Dominicans carrying picador hats, sovereign principalities of the Caribbean basin—dance by, often several dancers bouncing back and forth a step, advancing along the wide boulevard with its stained wooden doors and stained, unpainted stone facades holding steady, the dancers sweating in the hot spring sunshine of the tropics, one group after another, secernate only in the colors and ages of the participants—each group alive in its own world of particularities and energy—dancers whirling, grinning as they spin and bow, advancing behind pickup trucks carrying gigantic speakers blasting chant-like rhythms, islanders and Central Americans with Indian blood, skinny folk from coastal cities and capitals, farmers and fishermen—yipping and crying out, with their open hands dashing sweat off their foreheads. *They're going on without me*, he thinks—meaning the children, or everybody, or the world, meaning even those close to him, dancing away in brutal rhythms tamped down by worry and despair, by hope or fantastical leanings. He stands abruptly ashamed as a group of schoolgirls in orange-sherbet shorts and white tops with the words LIBERDAD Y UNIDAD emblazoned in glittery red sequins across their chests perform bows and striking leaps in front of him as if they recognize him from some vivid particolored other world. He tries to give them the benefit of his full-on blankness—or no, suddenly and without meaning to, his faked delight and complete understanding of and even love for what they are doing here on Earth—but it's like looking into glare. He reaches into his pocket for money to pay his way out of this, stops, slaps his bare arm as if for mosquitoes, and grins foolishly. Everyone in the crowd is engaged, delighted, filled with fresh life, or they're expertly faking it. He doesn't know what to do. He wants to turn away, wants to dive for cover behind a bush or maybe throw a bystander ahead of him as a shield or maybe he could pull his pistol or tear open his clothes but body and limbs are made of cement. Inside this casing he senses an eruption gathering itself. This has happened before. He's got to get out of there quick. But still he can't move. His face burns. His body is being sorcerised in some archaic transfiguration into ugly beastliness. The girls, grinning and jumping in the air, break away and thank God skip down the street. He's about to sob—sob and cry out—but he doesn't and as the bands and dancers pour in a tide past him he wonders why, the answer floating just ahead of him, blurred and wobbling, unreadable. But he's not really looking for an explanation. He sways, shivering, unable even to step back from the massive sunlight and clamor. A hugeness, an endlessness, seems to be located—*is locatable*, he thinks—in every part, in that girl's bulbous gold ring, in a sailor's glance, in a monkey-faced boy sucking a piece of ice and in all the clanging music in his head of change and uselessness and covert action and a capriole of the heart's make-believe, he's got it, or almost has, like a thousand times before, at the track, in Marcella's arms, in gunfire and expertise, always shifting as it comes, always beleaguered and estivating or leaping, dissolving into fumes and uncached hopelessness even as it gets here. Every sound, every look and concatenation, has a life of its own, he knows this for a fact, but what does it matter. It's impossible to bear. And then this knowledge or figment passes, and still he is standing on the street in a small crowd of spectators and the dancers are straggling by and a few are singing revolutionary songs that do not exactly fit the music the trucks are playing. He is who he has been, what; an approximation of it. He buys a guava ice and eats it, his teeth chattering, the red juice dripping from his fingers. He can't tell where it comes from—maybe from out of the swirl and gusting of life that just held him like a baby in its grip—but he knows, as if the facts have been scrawled in chalk on the street, what Marcella has done, and he knows what he will do. I've known right along, he thinks, and thinking this it seems true.

So he took a pedicab back to his father's apartment and waked Marcella who was sleeping on the narrow bed in the extra bedroom. Single drops of sweat had collected in the wells of her eyes. She came softly, supplely into his arms. He dabbed the sweat with the tail of his shirt. A quivering breeze picked solemnly at the thin curtains, pulling them out and letting them go. The curtains were blue and printed with ships in full yellow sail. "Are you happy to be here?" he said, half joking, half not.

She hesitated, a slice of sunlight catching in her eyelashes, and said narrowly, maybe joking, maybe not, "I love the antique dust." Her dark eyes were glossy, still hampered by sleep. She licked the skin under his ear. "All last year I thought I couldn't go on this way with you—or, no, I thought I could, but that it wasn't possible."

"It's never really been possible, has it? We've just gone on with it anyway."

"I don't think like that. Maybe now I do a little, but no—it's not a change, or even a resolution. Something's been cut away from me. I thought I was . . . I mean . . . everything became unfamiliar, even you. I moved away."

"Where to?"

"I don't mean really. In my mind. Now I'm back."

"It makes you sad."

"Yes it does."

With one long-fingered hand she pushed her black hair out of her eyes. Outside someone, a child, said, "I am the prince among wolves." (*Yo soy el principe entre los lobos.*) "I mean," she said, "that what *was* impossible, isn't. Now we can."

But won't, he thought.

She looked away from him. Her tongue licked along her full bottom lip. What she was concealing started a shuddering inside him, but he knew it didn't show.

"Have you seen Pop?"

"He said he was going over to Consuela's."

Consuela was the woman his father had been involved with all these years. He had once thought she was the reason his mother had left Havana for good, the reason his father, who trailed his mother to Key West, had returned to Cuba. He didn't think that now, or only that. His mother had been following some other circuit, following something like a principle that wasn't really a principle. Something more a feeling, or an index of a feeling, some understanding that the world was filled with sadness, say, that no one would miss out on sorrow—a drift, like a winter tide when the surges came in slow rising swells and, quietly, with great power, pulled what lay on the beaches out to sea. His own choosing of the life he led seemed like that, and in that way, seemed to him the ordinary progression, or restatement, of life, from parent to child, the passing on of response and call, the way his own dark brown eyes were his father's, his light curling hair his mother's. He knew there was more than that, but he thought that the *more* itself was part of a drift of possibility, of chance and a hard-minded preference.

She got up from the bed. She was wearing her yellow underwear. She had slept under a light cotton coverlet, yellow with red tea roses printed on it. He went out into the living room while she got dressed. On his father's slanted desk at the front windows were panels he was working on. *Fotonovelas*. That wasn't the word. They were graphic novels—comic books for adults, for middle-aged women mostly, these days, *gráficos*. In one panel a woman with full sculpted lips and beautiful eyes looked expectantly back at a man who was staring at her. "*Incluso riquezas—incluso el amor . . . no son suficientas para mi*," the man said. Even riches—even love . . . are not enough for me. What is? He thought he knew. Out in the street a pedicab passed carrying two tourists, a man and an enormously fat woman, in white clothes and identical straw hats. The man was trying to look through a pair of brass binoculars. Without returning to the bedroom Cot said, "Pack your bag."

Marcella came and stood in the doorway. She was a tall woman, heavier than the slender girl she had been. She leaned against the door frame, brushing her hair. Her eyes, on him from the first instant, seemed to come more sharply into focus. His cat was like that, he thought, when he returned from one of his trips—her eyes going wide for a second in a kind of simple amazement that it was him. It was a look they shared, he thought, he and the cat and Marcella. But now she frowned, grimaced, so that lines bunched between her heavy eyebrows; this was a look that was only hers. She pressed her finger hard against the side of her long nose, turning it. "Are *you* packed?"

"I'm going to hang around."

"Oh, Cot."

"You knew about CJ, didn't you?"

She glanced, once, lightly it seemed to him—in a single instant—out the wide front windows at palms and tamarind trees and hibiscus flowering, at the quiet street in the old part of the old city, at an old woman in a worn, ruffled yellow dress waving a folded umbrella as if conducting a slow, silent orchestra. "Yes," she said. "Afterwards."

"Did you know Ordell would kill Mama?"

"No. I never knew that." She clutched herself in her arms. "I didn't think it. I didn't dream it."

"Sometimes one thing leads to another."

"You don't always know."

"You get a feel for it."

"Still, you don't know."

He saw her then, marooned on an island in an island apartment in the shallow sea of the old Indian tribes—thinking: one of those old men down at Playa Giron was an Awarak, some few still around—marooned in the hemisphere, on the planet, in the whirling system of stars. And on and on. The air in the apartment smelled of his father's aftershave. An old Cuban, lime-smelling concoction. His father had tired of his mother, of her intensities, of her sure-footedness.

He took a step, reached for her, but she backed away.

"No," she said. "Don't save me." Her face had suddenly turned old, ancient, she had become an old woman tapping at plastic window blinds, straining to hear the steps of her dead ones.

"Is that why you came down here with me?"

"I don't know."

As he spoke, as he stood there with the sunlight from the open front window raining on him, burning his body, leaching his mind, he reconfirmed that there were facts he didn't want to know. She had called Spane in Miami. He didn't want to know that. She loved another man. She had already left him. He didn't want to know. He wanted simply to walk around these facts without even glancing at them. *Don't tell me.*

He said, "What did you plan to do?"

"Stay with you."

"No, you didn't."

"Oh yes. That's what I planned."

"In shabby, unfumigated Havana."

"Good times are coming again."

"We'll all get rich."

"That too."

"Do you have the emeralds?"

"No."

"Didn't Ordell find them?"

"No. That's why he went up to Lauderdale. Those head-knockers grabbed them."

"Spane'll be glad to hear that."

A cricket chirped somewhere—no, it was a gecko. They were all over down here in the houses, slim white lizards chirping their commentary from the ceilings.

"Cot."

She looked into his eyes. He could see the collapse, the caving in. But she didn't back away or turn, she didn't drop her gaze. He could feel her sinking her leads and grapples deeply into him, sense the following commandos of her power entering him. She could see all the way to the bottom; that was what he counted on her for.

"Why Spane?"

"I don't know."

He jerked his fist up: he could feel the power in his body, feel the arm raised strong as a derrick, lifting a hundred feet into the air, feel the great weight of the boom that strained his shoulder and his back, but he didn't let it loose. It was like putting the brakes on a planet. He twitched, shuddered.

She reeled away, as if blown loose, but this movement, the elaborate near fall, the catching of herself against the flowery arm of the couch, of her standing—looming, he thought—before the particularized, self-perfecting day outside, was all an act, a formal presentation. He wished he'd hit her, but it was already too late for that. The next instant crowded in, jamming signals, proposing new approaches and lies. *I got to get going.* Her face looked smaller and creased as if it was mummifying before his eyes. Her hair was dry, and he saw that it had a few long white strands mixed in with it.

"We're on the other side of the Gulf Stream," she said.

"Great Wall of the Americas." A twitching had begun in his left arm, a fresh compilation making itself known. "*Spane?*"

"Sure."

"*Si—claro.*" He knew it would get worse. But when it got worse there would be no shock. He was glad of that. "You call him Mikey?"

"Miguel."

"When should I expect him?"

"Tonight."

Her face was white, or no, white with tiny dark blotches fading into the hairline. She had always thought her hairline was too frizzy. White nappy, she called it. She had learned Cuban dances, Cuban songs she sang in grade school wearing a bright red bandana around her neck.

"Papi?"

"Oh, Cotland. He's at Consuela's. He doesn't know anything."

"That might not matter to Spane."

"It will. Don't worry."

"Don't tell me not to worry, please."

"All right."

"Where're you meeting him?"

"At the Ambos Mundos Hotel."

"That turista pile? Jesus. Is he staying there?"

"Yes—I don't know."

"Come on, Marcella."

"Cot, I. . . ." She started out of the room. A defiance, a hardness crackled in her body—he could see it—flared, and flickered out. She stopped. There was a gloss of sweat on her face. "I wish people had air-conditioning down here."

"It's all green in old Habana."

"I'm swimming in shame."

"Are you?"

"Sloshing."

"What was Ordell's cut?" Things had clarified, like ice cubes in a drained glass.

"On the emeralds?"

"Yes, May."

"Fifteen percent."

"That's all? Murders, mayhem, destruction of local families . . ."

"It's two million dollars, Cot."

"Well."

"He proposed a deal to get the gems, and Miguel agreed, after which Miguel told him he would kill him if he didn't get them back."

"He would. Yes."

"Ordell was terrified. He didn't know what to do."

"So he went and shot Mama."

"Yes. Because of that, and because he hates you, Cot."

"Did he think I had the stones?"

"He didn't know. He thought you would give up."

"I already did that—a long time ago."

"Ah, Cot."

"Stop saying my fucking name."

"All right."

He could see how tired she was. He could see how she had been carried far beyond what she could bear. These little islands, he thought, that we hold sacred and plan to flee to. That fade as we approach them.

"He was supposed to kill me."

"Yes. But you gave the gems to CJ."

"But I never told Mikey."

"_____"

He had told Marcella. "You're a real killer, baby."

"You sound like you always wanted to say that."

"Not to you."

A bird—he didn't know what kind—flew by outside with a quick sharp striking of wings.

"He told me he was going to take the emeralds from you."

"Ordell."

"He said you would trade them for your mother's house."

"I didn't need him."

"Yes, you did."

"_____"

"He could have held you up forever. He could have taken the house."

"I guess I missed something with you two."

"I guess."

"Well, tell me this." He stopped because he didn't know what to say next.

She didn't say anything.

He felt—somehow felt—that what they were saying had been said a million times before, as if the words had been scraped up from the grotty carpets of twenty-dollar bedrooms and second-run movie houses, and not even dusted off, not even looked at or sorted, used again. Old familiar scuds and wrake. The inside of his mouth felt dirty. His brain, his heart, all of it, felt dirty. He could see that whipped, shamed, scared she was still in a rage. He stepped toward her, the fingers of his right hand cupped as if holding an offering, of sweet loquats say. But she shrank from him—he saw it—and quickly, so quickly that he could tell himself, if he wanted to (he didn't want to, not yet), that she hadn't flinched, pulled herself into alignment, into the shape of one who was still in love with the one she hated; who thought she could pull it off.

He was going to touch her anyway. But then he didn't.

She smiled at him, a new, tremendously complicated, evasive smile, half-caste and localized. She would not even bow her head and say *You can do with me what you want*. She wouldn't, even now, allow anything like that. He had loved that she was such a strong-minded woman. Able to bear the consequences of what she had to do. He stared at her. He wanted to break her down and study her. Take her to the laboratory. She looked back at him from another world. The faint shuss and rattle of almond leaves came from outside. In this season, dry season, the wind would turn around sometimes. They weren't far enough south to wholly miss winter, if winter was strong enough. Even in Havana women walked around in January in old sequin-flecked sweaters, men in patched windbreakers. But it was spring. The plumeria flowers had crept back onto bony gray branches. The flamboyants bustled up their barrages.

"Come on," he said.

She preceded him into the kitchen where from under the sink he took a coil of laundry cord he found there and made her tie herself up with it. He completed the job, making the knots firm and the loops tight against her skin. She was hog-tied—that was the word. She believed him when he said he would kill her if she didn't do what he told her. He lifted her and carried her over his shoulder and lay her on the bed. He put a clean rag in her mouth and blindfolded her with a yellow bandana that still had the crease marks in it. You can still get away he thought of saying but he didn't. Then he left the house and took a cab the fifteen blocks to Consuela's apartment and sat in the living room with his father drinking a glass of *agua dulce* and listening to el Presidente's speech on the radio.

"Democracy," Consuela said from the living room, "like Christianity and Brotherhood, is not to be found among those who claim them. These great principles have flown to some other, undiscovered lands." In the back of her apartment came the sound of her finches, quarrelsome tiny birds expressing themselves constantly. From the bathroom window he could see down in the courtyard a couple of old women feeding chickens. One of the women wore a red bandana around her hair. His face in the mirror looked plasticized and faded. A parrot screeched from some hidden place. His face seemed to be the face of one who lacked governance. He got down on his knees and tried to pray, but he felt cumbersome and lonely there. He got up and looked out the window at two men who were setting up a card table in the backyard. The women were sitting in folding chairs under a senna tree talking. The men divided dominoes and began to play. It could go on and on like this, like it had in childhood where there was always another interesting development. If they asked at his trial he would say that was what it was like to work for Albertson, or had been. The parrot screeched again, its voice almost breaking into speech. It wouldn't know what it was saying, as he hadn't known when at six he shouted Cuban war cries taught him by Manuel Cordoba. He pressed his ear against the inside wall. "Rat-tat-tat," said Consuela, mimicking a machine gun in illustration of one of her martial points. She always talked of obedience. Of how one must submit to a greater power. He liked that. Someone—or something—you had to answer to. He bathed his hands in the sink, washing with Consuela's lemon-scented soap. Then he took a shower, supporting himself against the wall as the water ran over his head and back as he had seen a gangster do in a movie. The water was cool, refreshing. He dried off with one of Consuela's fluffy yellow towels. He sat on the side of the tub naked saying bits of *The Georgics* to himself. Virgil had been often at the beck and call of governance. He had lived under the ruthless, corporate hand of the Caesars. The pressure twisted things. He would read the Greeks next, Sophocles maybe. The sky was pouring through a soft funnel of cumulus. Birds like scraps of paper, of testament, blew by.

The old lady was insubstantially drunk, as was his father. Rafael had told him that he usually wound up—meagerly, faintly, superficially, as he put it—drunk, whenever he spent any time at Consuela's. "It worries me," he said, but Cot could tell it didn't worry him much. He was old now. Age was like a crust upon him, under which moved the muscularity and mind of a younger man. But this younger man was becoming more and more deeply trapped by the more and more impenetrable crust. His hands holding the glass were veiny, the long fingers more sinewy than ever. The hands still flexible and strong, able, like patched equipment, like everything down here, reworked and able, aged devices opening and closing like clockwork, fixing and holding.

Consuela, talking of liberty, served cut up bits of sausages and pickled palm hearts and stems of lemon grass or something like it slathered in hot sauce. Cot rubbed the hot sauce on his lips. It burned, and he started to sweat. His father looked at him and grinned. Cot tried to take his father's hands in his, but his father pulled away. "I don't want that *picadeni*," he said. He didn't like anything on his hands, not even the smell of soap. From the street came the cries of vendors and a man saying "I will propose a solution impossible to resist," and then someone blew a brief squealing blast on a horn.

As his father studied his face Cot tried to will a blankness into his eyes, as he had as a boy but was never able to; he wasn't able to now. Well, let the old man look. The smell of some complicated cooking came from the kitchen, coriander and cumin, hot pork. The walls were painted pale blue like the porch ceilings in Key West. What do you see, Papi? Ill-lit, banged-together excuses and windedness? His father studied his face without speaking. He had been a young man with promise—his father had—with genius, they said, capable of writing great novelistic works. But his father said that was only the dream of those who didn't really know him. He had wanted something besides the imperatives and gauges of any kind of genius and that something else he'd done. "I couldn't keep hold of your mother," he would say sometimes, but that was another matter. Yes, well, there was always another matter. Cot had wondered if he could convince his father to flee the approaching killers, but now, up close, inside the rasp and clutch of his father's dreaming, he realized he couldn't convince his father to flee anything. A searing pain flashed behind his eyes. He bent over his knees.

"Milk," his father said to Consuela. In a few minutes they would be marching around the room singing old mountain guerrilla songs. Consuela brought him a glass of chilled and diluted evaporated milk. He sipped it and put it down. The milk didn't touch the hollowness in him. Consuela was an anthropologist, of the ex variety, hagiographer of the old native tribes. In her youth she had taken Indian lovers, last of the Awarak-, of the Caribe-, of the fabled Siboney-style. She had borne at least three Indian children, maybe more, way back, but they had been lost to her, by way of disease and war and simple disappearance. Her life, she said, had become a happenstance, a drift through time. She talked like that.

"I got to be going," Cot said. He and his father lay on the thin couches in the big living room that had once been a ballroom in Consuela's family mansion, now cut up in slices into little apartments, except for this one. The finches cried out from the back. Consuela, half draped in filmy pastel scarves, floated around the room. "I got to go," Cot said. She looked at him as if she knew he believed everything she had ever told him. His father made his little patting, half-clapping motion, and rubbed his hands. He was a man who sought precious things. So he had said many times.

Cot's mind wandered, shying from talk, like a child's slipping away from the adult business. In Key West they had retrieved his mother from the deeps of her chipped porcelain tub that sat quietly unabashed on its four lion's paw feet. Word of this had crossed the Gulf Stream to get here. Word. Syllables memorized like a parrot's speech. Cries of finches, of street hawkers, of agents outside seedy nightclubs. A ditty sung to tourists. *Sunk*—retrieved, they said, expelled like a bite of bitter fruit or a fact declaimed in the street—his mother doting on her own death, the brilliant Key West day leaning down like an old man looking at a bright feather on the floor—word of it prattled, groaned out, lilted in caprice, tolled as fate, whispered in hotel coffee shops and government offices, slipped into el Presidente's liturgies: all falling short of the truth. Even the most alarming facts, the heartbreakers, in this case didn't eliminate confusion.

The pain sliced again, burning, in his mind. A heaviness in his body, clanking chains heaved through the hollowness. "It's got me cockeyed," he said out loud.

"No, no," Consuela said, misunderstanding, "you are welcome here."

He smiled at her. The cry of parakeets, a drumming sound from the street, "*Hola*," a voice sweetly said somewhere not far away; he heard a bus change gears, heard the cross cries of gulls, the voice of a man yelling that he could not be made to . . . to what? *But you don't understand*, someone was always saying, even here in the *Paradiso Comunal*. In Havana streets people moved without drawing attention to themselves, often silently, waited silently in lines for corn meal and tapioca starch. Pedicab operators leaned on their vehicles under the vast branches of laurel de India trees counting, dream cash.

"Well, it's okay," he said as if his father had asked him something. The old man didn't answer. We hardly recognize each other, he thought. It was as if they had become more and more distantly related. Eighteenth cousins by marriage and foster families, ghosts of an irresolvable past run through fingers grown crooked and stained with indigo.

"Come, boy," his father said. "I will walk with you, and then I will return here."

Cot wouldn't stop him. He would instead reach his hand out, no, he would take a step forward, his bare feet—Consuela allowed no shoes in her house—making the palm-straw rug crackle, and take his father in his arms. Maybe that would work. But it was like hugging a scarecrow. The finches, sealed in their rooms, groaned and prattled. Was he the only one who heard the birds?

His father's body rustled and settled in his arms. He saw the old man crouching in a doorway crying, saw his mother lying under the ground in the dark, no shoes on her feet. He could taste his father's breath. Sense the thoughts like pale divinations drifting out of darkness. The Quarterback, they called him at headquarters, the younger men mocking him as he walked down the long hall to Albertson's office.

His father began to cough, hacking hard, and then he whirled in a slowed-down motion and vomited on the carpet.

Consuela, without comment, cleaned the gray froth up with a rag and a bucket of fresh water.

His father sat huddled in a chair, his feet drawn up like a girl's.

"Papi," Cot said.

"It will pass," his father said.

"Something will," Consuela said, her voice raw and unappeased.

His father trembled. Or maybe he was only shifting his feet.

"I got to go," Cot said and leaned his head back and closed his eyes.

It was afterwards, at the track—how long ago? a week?—money gone, too much money to make up, owed to Camp Billings's bookies over on Calle Cinquo—or no, maybe it had been later, when he ran into Jack Bellieau, outside the little parlor attached to the rear of Sammy's Athletic Bar on Maxwell Ave., that he decided. Seeing

Jack had determined something—though he wasn't sure how, or what (maybe it was Jack's tentativeness, his step off the curb like a man not sure whether he was standing on a curb or a cliff, the uselessness of everything Jack was up to, his nutty familiarities and impiety, the tarnished silver ring Jack had tried to give him)—that settled something in him: he'd decided to get on the late bus to Key West. He was going to fix things for Mama.

Well, he'd done that.

"Let us now go," his father said getting up.

"You okay, Pop?"

Yes, yes, of course—bustling in his slow old man's way, retrieving his straw hat and putting it on his head, adjusting the angle. A certain reflexive jauntiness still available, even in a time of grief. This appealed to Cot. He slid his arm along his father's back. There were still strong muscles there, stretched and thin, worked out over a drawing board. "*Vendre a usted en la oscuridad de la noche*," said the beautiful Morena as she disappeared into the side of a comic book panel. *I will come to you in the dark of night.* The inevitability of fate—there was no other topic for the *novela gráfica*. The rest of us standing under the trees in the twilit dark waiting for our bus to freedom. He hoped his father would be able to work to the last. *Al igual que la muerte clap de dos manos frias. Death like the clap of two cold hands.*

They walked out together into the sunshine that was like a clear varnish on flowering bushes and trees, on the pavement crumbling before their eyes and on passersby hurrying toward their fates. His father resettled his hat—cattleman's hat—squarely on his head. His eyes had a dreamy look, but behind the dreaminess was a sternness that had frightened Cot as a boy. Now it touched him. These strong men who had left their strength somewhere behind them—he too was becoming one of them. Across the street a breeze filled the tops of coconut palms, shook them violently and let them go; the fronds hung stiffly as if the breeze had never been there.

"I love the softness of evenings in Havana," Rafael said maybe for the tenth time in his son's hearing, maybe the twentieth. He was arranging things, but his son couldn't really know that. You had to settle even the words you used, the thoughts that came as you walked each morning to see the ocean purling and stitching against the old seawall. The walk home from Consuela's was one he had taken many times. But rarely with his son. It was something new to settle in its place. A green ice truck passed. Two men clinging to the back were drenched with water from the melting ice. That too, and the parakeets flashing in their flock overhead, quarreling as they went. And the young women in their sporty hats, the little boy in a red shirt throwing a ball against the side of a building. There was a vastness you were part of, and it was necessary to arrange and codify and settle things with this vastness. But none of this could he say to his son. He listed slightly as he walked, and told himself this was because of the weightiness of his thoughts and let it go at that, but even so there was he knew a new voice calling to him from the dark, rising from among the others. He had been strong enough to hold these voices off or evade them or outwit them but his strength was failing. The women and men in his books were his charms and fetishes constructed and thrown out ahead of him like decoys for death to snap at. That was a way of looking at them. His guitar, his raffish clothes and hat, the routes he took on his walks, his solitude, were disguises, evasions, feints. His wife had known too much, saw too clearly. And now she called to him. He shuddered and his son put his arm around him, but this did not help and he shook off the touch. He was too scared to be touched. He saw terrible things coming through the dark. Her voice—her death—had tipped the dark toward him. He sensed it groaning and shifting, the huge movement of blankness as it began to slide. "*Te pido*," he whispered. I implore you.

Cot thought he himself was listing—staggering—loose and unhinged, but he wasn't. A breeze pushed solemnly through the heavy leaves of a nearby *guasima* tree, and it seemed as if it was pushing its way, lightly, through him too. *Then we just drop*—picking up a thought, interrupting himself, disagreeing with the shapes and forms of consideration that lay inside him like tiny scuttled vessels. Make a mistake—any mistake, press time too hard—and bang. Strange thoughts for a killer. He almost laughed. But he saw her, Marcella, lying on her side on the bed, trying to hold her head up like a fish sipping air. I have to go, he had said, terror buzzing like a hive inside him.

But I want—and stopped. *I want order and gainliness and a peacefulness without resolution and snappy parlance and kindness and hot home fries on a winter morning and to live quietly in the thoughts of a loved one and quickness and pleasure like a breeze moving in green leaves*—and on and on, he thought.

He groaned and he must have started to tip over because his father caught him in his still-firm grip, a grip that almost hurt. "You have to give things time to pass," he said. "That's what's difficult."

Who's got that kind of time, Papi?

He smiled at his father. The breeze rattled a red sign outside a barber shop as they passed through a small square behind one of the old municipal hospitals, used now for government offices. Office of Paper Bags and Bits of String. Office of Quirky Communiqués and Rambling Asides. A Cuban flag had been painted hanging from a third-story window. In the window a small boy waved. Cot waved back though he could tell the boy wasn't waving at them. His father smiled his halfhearted smile, the one he had started with after he and Ella broke up.

"Do you want to sit down?"

"Maybe a minute."

Cot raised his face to the washed blue sky. It was late, the ancient unremarkable dusk had come on. Thin clouds, that looked worn out, nearly erased, drifted north. All of this, every job, every kiss, aimed at an easement, that peculiarity in the universe that allowed a person to be released into time. He dropped to the green wooden bench—as if from a height, he thought catching himself on the scarred wood—as if fallen from the sky. His father eased down beside him, and they bumped shoulders, two large men, reeling from blows. Well, they were not the only ones. At Florio's coffee bar across the street, two men sat on stools before the outdoor window, their canes leaning beside them. The counterman, a fat man wearing a white brimless cap, served them tiny china cups of espresso. His father nodded to the men. One nodded back, a slim fellow in plain Russian glasses. "The world wakes and re-awakes," his father said, "but all remains the same."

Cot laughed. "You got to lay off all that philosophizing, Pop. It's going to make you dyspeptic."

His father reached in his pocket, brought out a few barky scrawls. "*Aguedita*," he said. "I abound in roots and curatives."

He held the gray curls out to him. Cot took one and chewed the hot, not bark but root wood. "This is exactly what I need. They say malaria's coming around again. Thanks, Papi."

Cot got up. They were only a block from the apartment. "I'll go on," he said.

"Wait."

The look in his father's eyes made him sit down again.

The old man leaned against him, a spare weight of familiarity and devotion, with his head against his shoulder. But this, apparently, was not quite enough. He slid down so his head was in Cot's lap. From there he looked up at his son, a look depleted and sorrowing, in it undarned tatters of feeling, of delays and embargoes of the spirit, parings and swollen knots, grimaces and old ransacked grievances, tears patched up and recycled, the remnants of love, nothing anyone could do anything about. Cot smoothed his father's forehead, his lank gray hair. His father closed his eyes. For ten minutes, maybe more, they remained there, Cot's broad hand just touching his father's head, holding the old man as he slept.

10

Carrying a bouquet of red bougainvillea sprigs Cot approaches the apartment through the park. He stays out of the front-window sight line. A small boy comes by, a boy in worn canvas shorts, snapping his fingers, and Cot offers him money—two American dollars to deliver and five on return—to get the flowers to the third floor, number 3-6, and give them to whoever answers the door. The boy, with a grin, takes off to do the job. Be sure to knock hard, Cot tells him as he goes. He eases off at an angle, crosses the street and stands in the shadow of a small up-rearing of areca palms, watching. He sees the boy knock and wait. No one comes to the door, no one cracks the pulled-down blinds. The boy looks around and knocks again, but no one comes. An old freezing sensation, herald of hardy and insistent matters, returns to his body. Sometimes it's like an illumination, this chill, cold light of a radiance that shows the future. The boy presses his ear against the green wooden door and listens, then lays the flowers against the sill and scampers away. Cot walks around into the out-of-sight-line part of the street, and as the boy exits the forecourt hails him. The boy's eyes glitter with excitement and he pants theatrically. Cot gives him his five dollars in singles, pressing them firmly into his hand.

The living room, that smells of plumeria blossoms, the kitchen, spare and dim, and the bedroom where he left her, are empty. She's gone, he thinks, but he knows she isn't. An immense tenderness that makes him move as if adrift in a dream overtakes him. There's not so much a blankness between him and what's coming as there is an eternity of never-was. He finds her in the bathroom. Spane—say maybe it's not Spane, say it's a henchman, but no matter, that man too would be Spane as a robber or a wandering sociopath would also be Spane, any scorpion or biting snake or malarial mosquito, Spane—had closed the door, or Cot would have smelled the blood. The killer dragged her in there and without bothering to untie her killed her with a knife. There's blood all over the white and green tile floor, blood on the old narrow metal bathtub, blood in the sink and on the white walls.

A rush of terror, call it that, unindemnified against the hollowing instant, tunnels right through him. He careens into the living room, slapping the air like a man slapping gnats, and can't find himself, can't get the layout, spills onto the couch, climbs as if the couch is tilted against a wall he has to get over, and falls back. He wants to stretch out, extend his body. Everywhere the air touches his skin burns like fire, but he's shivering. In an instant he's up, scrabbling at the front window to get out and catches it in his head that he has to stop. He freezes. Time bangs a hammer against a steel rail. No one outside. Probably Spane saw him come in. He's again the hunted one. "That's all right," he says. "That's okay," his throat dry and aching.

He checks the front door and limps back into the bathroom. Each step carries him deeper into a nausea. In the mirror his face is the face of a man raised from the grave, color, expression, even the features themselves, replaced by a mask of ignorance and dread. He looks like some ancient peasant, head lifted from a furrow. But this peasant is filled with a shame he's already trying to evade. "I didn't . . ." he says groping for exculpation, an exit. There is none.

His strength sloshed with deadness, he drops to his knees and can't for a while get up. Eventually he hoists himself to his feet and trying to pay attention to the ringing in his ears as if from there will issue another more benevolent and resurrecting order of being sits down on the curled rim of the tub and looks at her.

Marcella—ex-, former-Marcella—is half sprawled, half stuck between the toilet and the window from which in lazy swirls the insubstantial curtains lift and sink. The ropes haven't even been loosened.

Carefully, taking pains, he releases her. Crying softly, haphazardly, making little slippery sounds, blubbering, he lifts her and puts her body in the tub. She's only four, maybe five degrees cooler than living life but he can feel these degrees like arctic ice. Her face is unbloodied, clean; her lashes are like tiny black wings on her white cheeks. Years ago her mother visited a conjurer, an old lady on Angela Street in Key West, in an attempt to put a spell on him that would take him out of her life. No power can do that, he told her. Except this one, ay Cot.

He has to pause for breath, let his wind catch up. He backs into the hall, turns, cumbersome as a truck, and heads for the kitchen. The hall, the kitchen, every sight line recedes into an infinity of impossibility. Still, he gets there, stepping from fabrication to fabrication as if from stone to stone crossing a river. Carefully, almost fastidiously, every movement a screeching curse, he gets a mop, rags, scouring powder, and the galvanized tin bucket from under the sink, comes back and cleans the bathroom. He has to stop twice to retch into the sink; nothing rises. Special issue, he thinks, re this, but realizes even so he's coming back to himself. He's minutes, eons past her, active in the new version of the world. You get used to it, they say. Twenty years of Variety Work (as Albertson called it), and the business now finally here unraveled and played out. *You think so?* Well, time will tell.

He cleans her body last, saving as always, the best for the time when the other, less fine, is out of the way. Between faint ring lines on her neck are the wounds—stabs into the veins on either side—that Spane's knife made (he knows this knife with its deerbone handle and four-inch fluted blade); wounds no longer bleeding that Cot dabs at, two small slits that he covers with the tips of two fingers. At the edges of her smoke blue eyes a delicate spray of lines that you think you could brush away with a touch. Her face, rubbed each night with lotions and emollients, isn't tanned. Her lips are thin but soft; she has a way of blowing them slightly outward as she speaks that makes her, especially from the side, look like a child, farm child maybe, fisher child, island child with a soul unhampered by special pleading or rancor. He touches their surface, turning the upper back a little to reveal her teeth. The gloss of her spit is still on them; they look part of the living world. A cry of commingled happiness and grief stops before it reaches the surface. He falls over onto the floor. His face hits the tile, momentarily stunning him. He presses at the pain with two fingers, encouraging it, pushes himself up. "Don't worry," he says, "I'm not going anywhere," looking her in the face as he speaks, the words, he knows, a further desecration. He stands up, reaches for something, but forgets what it is before his hand is fully out. For a sec he doesn't know what to do. He's never before spoken to a corpse. He's not one of those—unlike Little Mizell and Sparks, Jimmy Canada—who likes to chat up the stiffs. He passes over the dead as you would pass over a silent unbrokered river on a bridge. He does not look again at his face in the mirror. Except for the first quick involuntary touch he does not tend to his own slightly bleeding cheek. He returns to his work, climbing back into the tub. He has already undressed her; already, using the harsh brown Russian soap, washed the blood out of her clothes, soaping white cotton blouse, loose green cotton karate pants, pale yellow bikini underwear in the sink, wringing them out and draping them over a cord his father hung across the window (all the blood wasn't out and for a moment he hesitated in a crushing dilemma, unable to go on, unable to begin again with the washing, stalled, the shame and sorrow burrowing like a sting into this moment he was afraid he wouldn't get out of, until, his body creaking underneath him, his hands began carefully, slowly, to wring the shirt). There's no hot water but the sun has warmed the pipes that run from a catchment on the roof, and he lets this sunwarmed water pour over her body, biting his lips as he does so. He knows she is changing in his hands into something else. Has changed. He tells himself he is changing too, right along with her, translating as he goes, learning the customs, edging deeper into her new country, but this isn't so. He thinks of spilled papaya seeds, black as a bird's eye, offered in her eight-year-old hand, of moments of half surprise in a cool winter's twilight, of night flooding over them from out of the big island trees. For her the nights, from now on, will all be the same. He lays his body on hers in the tub. As he does so a little more blood squeezes out of her cuts but he doesn't notice it. He kisses her deeply in her mouth and tastes with his tongue the exhumaceous silt, and lies there, ashamed and settling in, clutching her.

After a while he's able to get to his feet. He carries her into the bedroom and dresses her in fresh clothes and lays her on the bed. There're a thousand things in his head, but it's hard to pick the right one. His father will spend the night at Consuela's. He goes out to the kitchen and fixes himself a sandwich and sits eating it, the textureless Cuban bread, the peanut spread that's not really peanut butter, thin slices of a papaya he finds in the little fridge. The refrigerator shuts with a clamp. He eats and then sits at the table as the day draws closer around him, the twilight easing through its quelled and lingering performance, the night, adrift and not particular, freighting its featured quality silently in. Once, he gets up and goes into the bedroom and lies down beside her on the worn blue chenille spread. He's placed two small squares of adhesive tape over the cuts in her neck, and as he looks at these his body goes hollow. He retreats to the living room and sits on the couch, gets up, goes back into the bedroom, retrieves his copy of *The Georgics*, and returns to the couch. He can't read the book in the dark, but his finger finds his place marker, a two-dollar bill folded lengthwise on which he's written the words *I am gainfully employed*. One glance and the page, the bees, and the young bulls on round Etruscan hills, will come alive again, but he'll have to turn on the light. He's memorizing the poem as he goes along. He read passages to her, but she was not as taken with Virgil, or farming, as he was. "Plowboy," she called him. He leans back against the couch. The night is like a bad smell. Like a disease, a fever borne in the blood, a thickening surge sinking deeper into his body. He makes himself stay where he is until the sensation of this passes. He doesn't turn on the light.

The clock by the bed says three A.M. No way to tell how many shooters Spane has outside waiting for him. He pictures them tucked into notches, creases, folds in the landscape. Their Miami hotel rooms like so many silent shrines awaiting the little priests' return. He goes out to the kitchen, gathers paper scraps from the pile of old newspapers his father keeps under the counter, dumps the trash from the galvanized tin can into the sink, stuffs the papers in the can, and just after he sets the concoction on fire uses Marcella's mobile phone—battery almost gone—to call the fire department. *Huge fire on Calle Tremana, upstairs it looks like. ¡Ponte las pilas! ¡Ayúdame!* He goes out to the living room, opens the front door and sets the brightly burning papers in it. The papers burn swiftly and from a nook in the shadows he throws balled-up newspaper on the flames.

In five minutes the trucks are there. In six the firemen are running up the stairs. He has slid her body under the bed. The firemen burst in, carrying axes and long poles. Just before they get to the third-floor gallery he kicked the can across the threshold. The first fireman, a young man wearing a helmet painted white, seems surprised to see him.

"Anyone else in here?" he asks.

"*Solo estoy aquí.*" No one.

He has his father's drawings rolled up under his arm.

These he gives for safekeeping to the next-door neighbor, an old man with knobby bare legs under bush shorts. There are four or five trucks, old vehicles with large tires and rounded snouts. The street fills quickly with gawkers. Everyone has come out of their apartment. He's able to slip down the stairs and through the crowd into the park across the street and away in the wooly darkness of the false dawn.

He makes his way by cab, riding in the rear of an old humped Buick, his head leaned back on the cloth seat, his hand resting on the hinge of the roll-down window that's been repaired with screws slightly too small for it. Through streets that are as dark as if they're uninhabited, as if Havana is an old dream that played out and even the sleeper has gotten up and gone away. On Avenue Mareña amber lights run in strings, pole to pole, down to a lighted area. His heart seems to be pumping faint flares, gas rings, and tatters out of his body in lumpy effusions. He can feel Marcella moving around inside him, like an old woman in a deserted house, opening door after door. He grips the armrest, and it comes off in his hand. He tries to reattach it but can't. He starts to say something to the driver, but he can see by his eyes in the mirror that he's already caught the situation. *"Disculpeme,"* he says. He feels himself shaking, but when he looks down his long limber body he is as still as a wood carving. The driver's square dark head doesn't move either. Remnants of her—spirit, he would call it—cling to him like bits of life itself. A wild despairing notification, bill of sale, burns as it flies up through his mind. He presses his back against the seat, or thinks he does. He can smell the ten thousand bodies that have ridden in this cab, sense the dreams and hopes, the desolations carried like little knobby treasures. The sky above the city is spotted with brown summery clouds, large and stuffed. In the east the dawn pretends its time has come. *Not yet.* His thoughts—his knowledge, the facts poking from their covert—touch him lightly with acid fingers. He grips his left wrist. He's right-handed but his left wrist is larger than his right. Even in the smallest things there are misalignments.

A man, loose and muddled-looking, shouts from the sidewalk, a heavyset American in a madras jacket, swaying on the corner before a shop that sells Iron Curtain watches. Cot nods at him. The man grins hugely as if they are friends in on a secret. Cot signals to him, stops the cab, and calls him over. The man, who seems to be drunk but maybe isn't, moving abruptly, comes to him. He carries a narrow-brimmed straw hat in his hand. "You got a sec, man?" The man goggles him. "I need your help."

The man throws a look skyward, stands as if transfixed, as if pondering the depths of space, opens the door and splashes down. "Lost?" He has a scruff of white beard and his eyes are mistrustful "Where you going?"

"To the Ambos down there"—indicating with his head: *we all know it.*

The man chuckles in a superior, nonthreatening way.

"I'm staying at the old International. A queer spot I'll tell you that."

"What once was, eh?"

"You said it, buddy. I tell you. I came here as a little boy with my parents, and it made Las Vegas look like a methodist church camp. Where we going?" His voice is strong, undrunk.

"The hotel."

Obispo is blocked off for tourists, so the cab turns away from the waterfront onto Soledad Marcos. Down the block the pink hotel gleams like a salmon cake. The man looks sleepy. Cot puts his hand on his shoulder. "Still a ways to go," he says. He has the driver turn down Mercaderes and stop. "What is it, brother?" the man says. An oddness about him, about his manner that under other circumstances would make Cot wary.

"I need you to carry a message for me."

"Spy business?"

"Somewhat."

"I wouldn't think there'd be any secrets in this place any government would need to know."

"There're enough secrets between this cab and that hotel door . . ." He lets it go. He's been a loosener of secret material, pry bar. "Go to the desk and leave a message for Mr. Miguel Spano. Ask them to call him."

"Miguel Spano. Okay."

The man starts out the door.

"Wait," Cot said. "The message."

"Yeah. What is it?"

Cot knows this is a bad idea—this courier. "Just say Plaza de Armas."

The man repeats the park's name slowly, working the syllables with his tongue. Cot offers him a twenty-dollar bill, but the man looks insulted. "Okay," Cot says.

"Plaza de Armas, Miguel Spano," the man says, his eyes narrowing as he speaks, as if the words are the unpalatable answer to a question he's already grown tired of asking himself

"Thanks mucho," Cot says.

A couple of gold-spangled jackets pass, murmuring. "Drunken ladies," a voice says. Gulls, up late, cry, wheeling below bottom-lit clouds. Essences, Cot thinks: we get distilled. The man, thick and square, gets out of the cab, heads for the door, his shoulders thrown back. Cot watches him enter the hotel. Ernest Hemingway stayed in room 511, a room that looks west along Mercaderes Street, over the old red-tiled roofs toward the cathedral and the waterfront; you can peep in through a roped-off door. The hotel claims Hemingway wrote *For Whom the Bell Tolls* in that room. Even hotel managers are living in a dream, Cot thinks. He's sweating in the humid air. An early morning rain is on its way. With two fingers he presses hard at the center of his forehead. Something, a complexity, her face, expressing her arrival in another zone, the dusk light falling on his hands through the bathroom window, some half-bit encyclical is trying to come through. *Spirit is the continual motion toward freedom from nature.* Who said that? Virgil, pulling a fast one?

Maybe Jackie. Or his mother as she walked with him under the *canafistula* trees to Fausto's for groceries. We're all on our way, at all times traveling, she would say sometimes. Marcella picked it up. I'm on my way, she said.

The man, who he noticed looks vaguely Hemingwayesque, exits the brass hotel doors and walks toward the cab. "I got him," he says as he comes up. He opens the door and slides in. "Yeah," he says his head tilting to the side so Cot can see a sharp, burning scar on his neck. "I called him up and gave him the info on the phone."

"That was good. Here's the twenty—"

He withdraws his hand as he says the words, remembering the man's pique at being offered money. The man grimaces. "I told you . . ."

"Yeah, okay. I'm sorry. But thank you."

Cot waits for him to get out of the cab, but he doesn't. His belly protrudes above his white slacks like a shiftless tendency. "Thank you," Cot says again.

"De nada," the man says. "You sure you don't . . . ?" he lets the question hang in the cool damp air.

"I'm sure. Sorry." He doesn't know what the man's talking about. Some mystery of his own.

Cot waits another moment. He might have to make the man get out, but he doesn't want to do that. The man turns his head, squinting back the way he's come. The sidewalk is empty. "I like that place," he says.

"Listen," Cot says. "I need to be on my own here."

"Actually you look as if you need company."

"I'm serious."

The driver turns in his seat, a shock of heavy black hair falling over his forehead as he does so. "*¿Problemas aquí?*"

"It's okay," Cot says. When this is over he will carry Marcella's body from his father's house, dig a grave in the park across the street, and bury it, and then he'll return to the house where he'll crawl into his father's bed and curl up close to him. This thought swings slowly like a torn paper lantern above a darkened doorway. "What's your name?" he says to his accompanist who has not moved to exit the cab.

"Stubbs. James L. Stubbs, from Fort Wayne."

"Mr. Stubbs. I need this cab to myself now."

"What you need is somebody to set you straight. I know some things."

"You a thinker? Fort Wayne mastermind?"

The driver watches them through his rearview mirror that has a St. Christopher medal and what looks like a tiny head carved into an avocado seed attached to a string hanging from it. Cot grabs a clawful of the man's stomach flesh.

"Awf." The man swings an elbow, catching Cot in the temple. Cot lurches to the side, his head, just at the back corner of his skull, hitting the door frame. For a moment he doesn't know where he is, or who. Then he's back. The man is grinning at him, a narrow, non-Hemingwayesque grin. One front tooth laps slightly over the other. "Easy on the bad manners," he says.

Cot reaches for his pistol behind his back, but the man

hits him again before he can get his hand on it, knocking him hard against the door.

Cot feels as if he was shaking his head, but he in fact isn't moving. He seems—no, the cab, seems to be moving. But it too is standing in the same place, just down the block from the entrance of the Ambos Mundos, out of the door of which Spane, following a couple of the Miami boys has just stepped.

Cot pushes forward in the seat and tries to open his door.

"Hey," his companion says, "I was just saying—"

"Sorry . . . ," he's having trouble working the door.

"You owe me fifteen dollars," the driver says in English. "That door doesn't open from the inside."

"I was just saying," the big man says, "I'm Jimmy Stubbs, Detective Sergeant, Fort Wayne, Indiana, police force."

"You propositioned me," Cot says sounding foolish to himself. His mouth feels cottony and only half his.

Another couple of Miami guys, Squinky Dukes and Nolan Sanderson, come out of the hotel after Spane, who is standing next to a large planter filled with a trimmed ficus bush. How did he get all these guys into Cuba? "I got to go."

He reaches for his money clip, but the detective catches his wrist.

"I could call the cops," Cot says.

"Who they gon believe—me or you?"

"I'm a Cuban citizen."

"You're a Miami lowlife is what you are."

"Miami?"

"I could see it a mile away."

"Wizard."

Cot stares into the man's large, sea-blue eyes. Does he know him? Or is he only some mustered bad angel from his dreams? Maybe a local finger man. "*Lo siento, verijas*," Cot says.

Stubbs pops him again. "Cunt, ay? Now take that wad out of your pocket—take it slowly—and pay this good man."

"Listen. I have to go. It's essential. I have to meet somebody."

"One of your lowlife friends, I reckon. You squirts are still trying to get back in here, aren't you?"

"We're a new crowd." He's the one tired and drunk, not this man.

"Nothing you do's new, bucko."

Cot has out the silver clip Marcella gave him, and it lies like a thin small fish in his lap. He needs to retrieve the bills. He hasn't changed any money. He works a twenty free, the paper sliding greasily under his thumb, and hands it to the driver. "Keep it," he says.

"You're five short," the driver says in a sour voice.

"*Pescador mosca*," Cot says, his eyes narrowing. "Okay." He hands the man another five.

"Now you let us out," the detective says to the driver in Spanish. "I'll walk with you down to that plaza," he says to Cot.

"That's not a good idea."

"Oh? I need backup?"

"I'm meeting my girlfriend."

"Miguel Spano?"

"That's not her name."

Stubbs motions to the driver, unnecessarily, since the cabbie is already out and opening the door. As Cot moves to the door Stubbs grabs him by the belt in back, finds the pistol, and shoves him out. He makes him stand on the sidewalk while he frisks him, the familiar indignity. He finds the other pistol in his sock that is strapped down with a green rubber band. "Mr. Smarty," the detective says in an affected, childish voice.

"You'll be surprised how little you get out of this," Cot says. The plates of his skull hurt where the man hit him.

Spane and his men have already disappeared up Obispo, headed toward the park. He shivers. The cop strikes him between the shoulder blades with the butt of his own pistol. "You're wearing out your welcome," Cot says staggering. He looks back at the cop who is jamming the pistol under his flimsy, color-spattered jacket. In the window of the cab he catches his own face: face of an alien, a stranger—and not just that, sees the heap uprisen, as if a small section of sidewalk, or the earth underneath it, had wrinkled up. "Just a drift of atoms, bud," he says to the cop.

"You're about to slow down to dead," the cop says.

Cot straightens up. For a second he forgot she was

gone. He is blinded suddenly by the knowledge of everything about her he had never touched. His mouth tastes
bitter. A passing woman pats her hair with careful fingers
as if there's a secret hidden there and nods forlornly at the
man she's with. The night is cool and has a sour sea smell.
A boat whistle gives two short blasts from the canal, out-
let to the sea and the Gulf Stream. Cot thinks he's going
to vomit, but he doesn't. Time is loose and wallowing,
fading slowly in and out. *There are no other people like you*,
she said, as if this was a great thing. *You're wrong about that*,
he said, hopefully.

He begins to walk toward Obispo Street. The cop follows, speaking as he comes, telling Cot in a low, dispas-
sionate voice how he's a nobody, a nothing, a puss blister
popped in the womb, only a stinking puddle people have
to walk around so as not to get the slop on their shoes, a
useless, puerile, rotten—

"I already been over that," Cot says. "Get to the good
part." He flicks one of the trade glances at the cop, the
one that says: *I got you memorized*.

The cop catches the look and tries to fling it back
but can't quite. This one's on me, Cot thinks, checking off the fear rat-slipping in the man's eyes, feeling a
loose ID with him, both of them out way too far. "Slow
down," Stubbs growls, but Cot keeps moving, not fast
but steadily.

The other side of the street is lit up past the old *palacio*
all the way to the park. The lights seem to beat on the
mottled, scaled, high blank sides. *It's beautiful, just beauti-*

ful. The speckled walls like a fossil lizard skin weathering into a monument—everything taking one step back, he thinks, bust-ups becoming embraces, all that, and the rest slipping sideways into extravaganzas nobody plans. *As you were, friends, now and forever.* In CJ's tomb he could smell what it was to be dead.

The cop trudges beside him, breathing hard. "This's going to be bad, huh?"

Cot ignores him.

Ahead the tables and chairs of a couple of fair weather restaurants are piled against the front of the buildings across the street from the park. Long loops of wire hold the furniture in place. Tall royal palms stick up from among the big *varia* trees bordering the park. The men ahead, far enough ahead to be at a distance that separates wondering from surety, come back into view—only for a moment—as they lope across the wide street and go in under the trees. Cot knows them all. Considine. Mizel. Erlanger. One—is it Nolan, dumb as spit?—has looked back just now, but he appears not to have recognized them among the drifting tourists in the resiny lights by the wall of a palace, and Cot knows this couldn't be.

With the cop following he crosses the street, passing before the verandah of the *palacio*, where Batista and Grau and Machado and the other *capricios* dwindling into a murmurous past sipped champagne with gangsters, his forebears, where the Maximum Leader in his days of triumph ripped phones out of the walls, set fire to the beds, and careened hooting among the gilded furniture.

A dog barks from some place far ahead, on the other side of the park, beyond trouble, a small inquiry, apologetic and erasable. A ship's horn. His grandpa, whom he never knew, maybe his ship. Motion, any motion, is a slip to freedom. *Is that it?*

He stops at the corner, waits, takes a step, presses back among stacked and shackled café furniture. Here's the hard part, one of the hard parts. He intended to be the one already in the park. Now he'll be the one the others got a look at. Step by step through the slop to this place. The cop comes up behind him. "Yeah, yeah," he's saying into his phone, "the corner of Obispo—no, right at the park." He speaks in Spanish, a brusque and colloquial, Mexican-sounding Spanish. Life shakes you until you're rattled and look for reasons. But there's only the motion. Is that it? *Fretful you*, she said. *No more than's necessary*, he answered.

Stubbs snaps the phone shut and snugs up close. Cot can smell his sweat mixed with . . . the smell of apples, is it? He turns away, a variance, like a house among palms, rising inside him, takes a step back, and vomits against the wall. A thin effluvium, brown against the pale wall, trickles to the sidewalk. *You eat me from the inside*, she said. *Lentamente*, he said. The cop puts his hand on Cot's back. The hand feels as wide as a plate, as heavy as a plate filled with rocks; it seems to press him down so he has to square his legs to stay on his feet. Nausea lashes him, but he holds on, to balance, to what he thinks of now as purpose (and calculation and faith and resolution and possibility squeezed like a rock squeezed into diamond), to the unbuckling march, that is, to the next moment. *Naturalia non sunt turpia*, Virgil said, or something close to it: Nothing dirty in nature. *But spirit moves anyway to a better neighborhood.*

He straightens up. "Let's go."

Stubbs lifts his hand, but it's only to get a grip on Cot's shirt. He holds him from behind, pressed in close. "You getting too old for hoodlum work, fella." Cot can smell the man's breath, a mix of alcohol and wintergreen. Fort Wayne is a farm town, right? He hooks the cop's leg with his, kicks forward, and smashes him to the pavement. He whirls as Stubbs falls and catches the pistol—his own Beretta—before the cop can fire it and tears it from his hand. The cop cries out, or tries to, but Cot stomps him in the face, stomps him again, and feels the cop's teeth break and his skull give under his heel. He takes the man's little pistol from his jacket pocket and works it under his waistband in front. The cop moans, and Cot stomps him again. "Country boy," he whispers.

He eases left, runs along the front of the restaurant, and slants across the street past shuttered bookstalls and into the park under dense, fragrant shade. The air is cool, lighter as if he's crossed a border into another, less solid country. There are amber pole lights at intervals along paved pathways, but off the center lines among gushed patches of areca palms and big roble trees just coming into bloom the park is dark. Cot angles left, away from the spot where Spane and the others have entered. He stops under a large trimmed schefflera bush and waits. He can't hear anyone. He thinks he sees movement up ahead, a pale patch disappearing around the side of a small square concrete monument. A breeze edges without a sound through the top of a large tamarind tree. A voice—off to the side, not nearby—says "You got him?" It's Nolan's voice. "Fuck, shut—" Squinky's voice—and a gust of damp breeze cancels the rest. Cot's waiting for the one he senses, just up ahead behind a bank of bushes, to let himself be known. Long nights in bushes he remembers, hunters outside some ugly house in the Grove or by a sidewalk in a rundown district, once lost among viney pines on an estate up in Delray Beach, waiting for a betrayer to show himself at his bedroom window in a house dark as a tomb. An emptiness, the loneliness of unoccupied space . . . and there he is.

Cot runs low along a large shambled hedge, steps around behind the slim shapes of a couple of tall cypresses and shoots Bobby Noticia—crouching, looking the other way—straight in the face. Bobby, a short, fleshy man with hairy forearms he likes to keep exposed, staggers back with a look of bland and untroubled surprise and collapses into a small gray-leafed bush. Cot is on him quick; he snatches his pistol from his hand, flings it away. A shot whips by his face, and Cot cries out and leaps in a lunging fall behind a small flowering hibiscus. The sound of the shot's not muffled by a silencer. Cot thinks it came from Squinky's 9mm Glock. They couldn't have brought guns into Havana could they? Maybe they came by boat. Spane too is a Cuban citizen, a spy if the truth were known, a shambling, avuncular presence at Miami anti-Castro rallies, son of a cofounder of the old *Movimiento de 26 de Julio* standing with his hands clasped before him under the painted loggias of the brotherhood as they buried another of the old-timers. Maybe he receives dispensations thereby.

A rustle in bushes across from a small grassy patch— Cot lies with his pistol tucked under him, the barrel pointing toward the bushes. His eyes in the amber radiance cast by a small pole light look closed, his body still, not breathing, but he's watching Squinky and Nolan advance, each from a different part of the bushes. Just as Squinky steps free of foliage Cot lifts slightly and fires, catching him with a single bullet in the forehead. Squinky's eyes jam up into his head, and his mouth twists as if he's saying bitter words, and he pitches face-first onto the grass. Nolan's flat expressionless face meanwhile doesn't even wince, but his hand is slow. He gets off a wild shot that kicks up soil in front of his own feet, and Cot shoots him in the body twice, low and then high in the chest. Nolan staggers, takes a couple of mincing steps, falls to his knees, and slumps back on his ass leaning forward; he's dead, sitting there.

Cot's already on his feet running, dodging between trees. He notices a large gray cloud high up, moving stately as a frigate. The moon hasn't come out yet. A single star, frayed and delicate, hangs near the front edge of the cloud. Thoughts of a mangled reclamation whip by in a flash as he cuts between bushes, veering across trails, past a small tree in full pale bloom that seems suddenly catastrophic, leaps a patch of pavement, and enters an area where clumped low succulents are arrayed around a little fountain water trickles out of. Over from the way he's come, catty-corner, he sees movement. He fires instinctively. Someone, some American, cries out. Cot runs at an angle toward the voice, keeping bushes between him and the place the cry came from. He stops under a small shrub that smells of iodine. He can see a man crumpled on the ground. It's Archie Erlanger, old friend he used to go bowling with when they were younger, bowling, like in-line skating, like dynamiting fish, a fad that passed through the troop without leaving any mark. "Archie boy," he whispers, "sorry."

"Cot, I didn't mean. . . ."

Cot shoots him again, and he's silent.

He turns to go, to slip between two bushes shaped like Christmas trees, but a shot he doesn't hear just grazes his temple. A burning streak of pain, amplifying in deepening shades of red as it goes, sprays in his brain, and he hits the ground, out, gone.

He comes to with Spane squatting over him. Spane's smell—of ginger and cigar smoke—envelopes him like a cloak. Spane has his knife out, and he's cutting Cot's left shoe off his foot, his half-boot. Cot can hear the leather parting and it feels like his own skin cut into, and this makes him want to shriek but he doesn't. He can see the meager and breeze-shivered top of the big ceiba tree that every Cuban schoolchild is told is the tree under which the country was founded; he knows this tree. Cuba another memorial gift to the West from Indians no longer on the scene. Spane is speaking to him, but Cot can't understand what he's saying. "You murdering freak," Cot says.

"That who that was?"

He can hear him now.

Spane is saying something, speaking earnestly, his head bowed over his cutting that has almost reached flesh. "*Mutilado*," Cot whispers and the knife stops and Spane lets his breath whistle out between his teeth. "You would know," he says. His wide face, leaning over him, sags away from the bones as he speaks, giving him larger jowls, making his sharp dark eyes smaller. Spane is trying to explain something to him. Cot sees that, some figment or false aspiration, some moral certitude or reckoning come on like a philosophical principle, like the notion of spirit *contra natura*, or love eternal, even for killers, that you can lean over and sample from the freshly crumpled body of your enemy, some joke and crazy way of looking at things that they all have going for them, dumb villains, careening around the neighborhoods, crouching over the fallen, whispering clichés to the dying. It's the energy that makes killers do that, you can't keep it quiet—

"It doesn't matter," he says.

Spane sticks the tip of the blade in Cot's cheek. Cot flinches away, he can't help it. The stab hot like a bee sting, jabbing into Ordell's fork marks. Spane sits back on his heels. There's the sound of voices on the other side of the park. Automobile lights in a street that's been closed to traffic for years. Shouts. It isn't hard to tell what's coming.

"I think they want to speak to you," Cot says.

"No trouble from those *cuntalingos*," Spane says. He looks scared, and feverish, and dislocated in some essential part. "How you feeling?"

"_____"

"Yeah, well, okay, I'm so sad about it." Spane taps himself in the temple with the blunt side of the knife blade. "I'm sad about your girlfriend actually. *Our* girlfriend. I'm not sad about her husband, that DA asshole. I did you a favor on that one. *He* won't be missed."

"Not now," Cot says. Even in this faded light he can tell Spane is shook. Maybe looking over the edge into the other world, the one just like this one except you aren't in it yet. "I'm coming," the dying say as if they know. His head hurts. But he doesn't say anything. Spane is still talking, expelling words in a rushed, whispery but clear voice and preachy manner, an eagerness that's not really believable. The knife flashes in the amber light, but it doesn't touch him again. Spane's smile—Cot can see it—looks slightly puzzled.

"My foot," Cot says faking agony and reaching.

"Yeah. I'm sad about that too," Spane says looking at the work boot cut almost fully away in an open gap over his pale sock, "I know I was after something—I am, man, after something—those gems—" but Cot is after something too, and he finds Bert's little gun snug against his belly, snatches it out, and before Spane can react, presses it against the man's temple and fires. Spane's eyeballs go instantly black, his mouth rubbery. He falls over in the grass.

Cot kicks at his fat body and springs up and runs fast away from the sound of the voices speaking their charged and eloquent Spanish, the cut boot slipping on his foot as he runs, slowing him a little, but not enough for anybody to catch him.

He crosses town into an older, darker part where the streets are wet from a rain he hasn't noticed and parts of buildings project out over the street like displaced ornamentation, follies and extrusions darker than the buildings themselves. The sky is a bland and murky strip rivering above his head. A man comes up to him, a small person in a shirt that is vaguely yellow in his mind, and tells him he will show him the way to go. He leads Cot by the hand into an even darker street where from open windows women moan in a language never heard before in the world. Cot has to stop and fix his boot, and the man waits for him softly panting. When he stands up the man takes his hand again and leads him to a large stone building on the corner of a street that is still running quietly with nightlife. At the curb men stand before barrows that smell of burning charcoal and fried meat. Cot can see the fires like red bedding in the barrows. The men wear hats with the brims turned down. In the building is an upstairs Peruvian restaurant, and the man leads Cot to the door and stops. He won't go in. Cot understands that he wants his tip. Cot gives him five dollars in American money and climbs the stairs to the second floor, enters and takes a seat by the window. Down in the street men speak to one another in depressed and wheedling voices. A small Peruvian woman wearing a dark red apron comes up to him and asks briskly what he wants to eat. Cot orders the *aji de gallina* and drinks an Inca Kola as he waits. He doesn't want to think about anything, and this is surprisingly easy. He asks the waitress for some tape, and the woman brings a roll of black duct tape to him. He uses this to close up his boot. The air in the restaurant seems foggy and charged as if it's hooked to a mild electrical current. The woman brings the chicken stew, and Cot eats it rapidly. He has never been so hungry. He thinks: I will stay here in Cuba, maybe buy a little house down in Playa Mayabeque where Daddy used to take us on the bus to go swimming. But the thought of it, the thought of his mother running on the beach in her white shorts and shirt makes a pain start up. Maybe the mountains, he thinks, over in the Sierra Maestra, up where the air is cool. The restaurant is nearly empty. Only an old man smoking a pipe at a table in the corner, a Chinese couple eating slowly from a huge pile of *jalea* fat pink shrimps poke out of. Cot drinks a cup of coffee and scratches from his pocket the Cuban pesos he took off the dresser at his father's place. On a radio on the counter they are

talking about him, and talking about the body the firemen discovered under his father's bed. The mention of
her stabs through him, and he can feel the strings and
mucks of his insides tearing and he wants this to go on,
obliterative and sullen, the stupid aliveness that he will
now sink back into, and he starts—or maybe does only
slightly—to rear up like a horse startled, some fresh snake
moving across his feet, rises and steps back. He's glad his
father didn't have to be the one who found her, a favor
in the *desastre*. As he lays down bills he smiles at the man
behind the cash register, takes a toothpick from the little
clear plastic turnstile on the counter and digs between his
teeth for remnants.

Outside the restaurant the night is darker than before.
Maybe there's been a power failure. The red coals in
the barrows gleam like the familiar vestiture of a ritual
common and immutable. He starts down the street and
soon loses his way. Huge, pale, finned automobiles like
the strung-together catch of some mordant, vanquished
magnifico, are parked end to end along the curbs. They're
dusty as deserted furniture he runs his hand over. Shop
windows are ghostly and contain behind their streaked
picture glass items hulking and shrouded. The buildings
rise into a gloom of starless night. As through a big *júcaro*
tree a breeze checks and comes on, sidles left, and drops to
the ground, something—a figure, tangle of life—seems
to rush from his body and dissolve in the dark. He stands
looking after it as if he is looking at something pulpy and

real, but there's nothing. A moment later a light goes on behind shutters off a balcony. A woman's voice, small and harassed, begins to sing, a song in English that is almost but not quite familiar to him. He stands in the street listening and shivering. The singer goes abruptly silent, and the light is switched off. He smells jasmine just as the feel of some being—shady and imprecise—flows past him. *I know you*, he says, but nothing answers, nothing stops.

Through blank streets he walks steadily. The windows of the tall stone houses are shuttered. He turns up one street then another, making his way in the general direction of his father's house. But he knows his father won't be home. He enters a bar, orders a beer, and sits drinking it at the long mahogany *contador* that curves away into haze. Men with huge, baggy lips enthuse in long disquisitions concerning stinginess and failure. Streaks of faint light run like patterning along the upper part of the walls without showing any radiance. A man bumps against him and apologizes profusely and insincerely. A pummeling, weighty sadness overtakes him and almost drags him off the stool. Maybe I shouldn't resist *anything*, he says to himself, but he tries to keep his place and does. The man wanders off, waving at him over his back like an actor in a movie. A woman in a filmy dress edges into the scene and makes short and pithy remarks concerning his manhood, but he ignores her. She hits him hard in the side. He gets up and feeling the night pressing about him, feeling as if the air itself is sooty with darkness, he speaks to the woman, calling her Louisa, as if this is her name. At the sound of the name she instantly becomes meek and sidles away, abashed, as if he has gotten it right.

On Marcella's phone he calls his father, but an unfamiliar voice says *hola.* "*¿Por que no se ven?*" the voice says. Why don't you come in? "After a while," Cot whispers, and closes the phone. *Al ratito.* He asks the bartender for tape to repair his shoe that has opened up again, and the bartender hands him from under the bar a roll of bright yellow carpenter's tape. He tapes his shoe, studies it, and then tapes the other, uncut shoe, as well, gives the tape back, thanks the bartender who nods his head in royal dispensation, and leaves the bar.

It's as if molecules are slaking off him. He's leaving a trail. Okay by me, he thinks holding himself tightly upright. But something's loosening, something's already worked itself loose. At the corner of San Juan de Dios and Las Comidas he sees, as if established by the darkness itself, a man standing just outside the even deeper darkness of a tree's shadow. It's his father. Cot knows he has been waiting for him. His father is carrying his patched guitar slung over his shoulder. Cot's heart races. He experiences a rush of happiness. It's raining a little, hardly more than a mist. His father smiles as he approaches. The city around him is still dark, swept over by a blackening hand. He embraces his father, and his body feels strong, muscular like that of a young man. His father's face is unwrinkled, the face of a man in the fullness of his strength. They walk together down the street that is as dark as a cave, so dark that he can't make out his father walking beside him. He takes his father's hand. After a while they reach a small park and enter and walk among the trees. The park smells sweetly of *cassia nodosa* flowers. They sit down on a bench they've groped their way to. Cot's afraid, punished by the dark, as if by a confinement that might be endless. His father says something that Cot can't make out. Cot wants to ask him what happened with the police, but he can't find the words. He wants to ask him what will come next, wants to tell him how much he loves him, wants to ask his forgiveness—or no, not forgiveness, he wants to admit everything, enter a plea of guilty, in shame and obedience, in fealty, like a man stepping from the ocean after a long swim, exhausted and relieved, utter the simple facts—forgiveness can take care of itself—but he doesn't. His father rubs his arms, making a soft chafing sound, almost like the sound of an animal rustling in leaves. Cot can hear this, but he can't see it. Then he doesn't hear his father anymore. He waits, but there's nothing, and he knows his father has left him, and he knows what this means. The air is cooler, almost cold. He senses the ocean nearby. The Gulf Stream that swings in close to Havana as Havana reaches out to it. The sky is clearing, cleansed, faintly bright, host, clouds, the whole frolic and piquancy spread out above the city. What a miracle! It's as if he can smell the stars, inaccessible to him.

From among the dark trees the regulators of his fate advance, precise as dancers, toward him.

Acknowledgments

The prologue appeared in *Ploughshares*. Thanks to the editors.

BOOKS BY CHARLIE SMITH

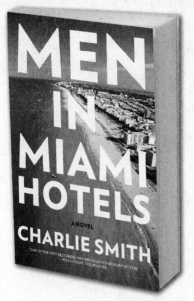

MEN IN MIAMI HOTELS
A Novel

Available in Paperback and eBook

The story of Cot Sims, a Miami gangster who returns to Key West aiming to—among other things—save his mother from homelessness after a recent hurricane. For love, for cash, and for the hell of it, he snatches a trove of emeralds that his boss, the relentlessly vicious Albertson, keeps hidden on a small island. And then trouble, coiling around him for years like a snake, bites.

THREE DELAYS
A Novel

Available in Paperback and eBook

"*Three Delays* is so stunningly composed, so wildly, implausibly, excessively written, that it makes the entire shelf of novels from the last generation superfluous....
This book consists almost entirely of the incantatory, rebel-angel prose that has made Charlie Smith a consummate outsider, and also one of the very best prose writers in contemporary letters."
— Rick Moody, *The Believer*

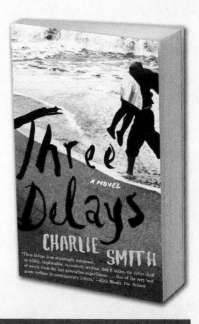